The Viking Hoard

Art Theft Mystery
Book 3

Bea Green

ROUGH
EDGES
PRESS

In memory of Sarah Jordan

The Viking Hoard

"Gold is little comfort for the kinsman dead."

—*Örvar Odd's Saga, C.11*: Viking Proverb

Prologue

Simon liked the silence under the surface of the sea. Only the sound of his apparatus interrupted the peace as he swam across the seabed, hunting for scallops. Sometimes, if he was lucky, he would catch the clicks and whistles of a nearby dolphin pod.

Dolphins liked to feed on herring, especially during the winter months, and the waters near Lewis and Harris were teeming with the fish.

Many years ago, Simon's great grandfather, Rory Buchanon, sold cured herring to merchants travelling down from the Baltic States. In the end, though, his thriving business had dwindled to nothing in the run up to the Russian revolution. Politics, as often happens, had ruined the livelihood of an ordinary fisherman.

Since then the Buchanons' financial affairs had fallen on yet harder times and Simon hadn't managed to buck the trend, either.

At present, the restaurant he'd started from his bungalow in Drinishader was running at a loss. There were many reasons for this. The perfectionism of his wife, who would only use the finest and freshest of ingredients in her cooking. The décor of the dining area, which could have done with a makeover. And the weather was a big problem. The Hebridean winter was too bleak for tourists to consider a visit, and even when there were tourists around, few fancied driving to Drinishader for their meal.

Other businesses on the island found a way around the miserable winter months. Some of the art and photography galleries on Harris, for example, shut their doors for a good chunk of the winter, but continued to sell their work online.

Moving methodically through the clear water, Simon thought about the bitter argument he'd had earlier on that morning with his wife, Janey. One of the many arguments they'd had over the last six months.

He grimaced to himself.

In many ways, their argument that morning had felt like the final nail in the coffin of their marriage. She'd had enough of living on a shoestring budget, just making ends meet, but it was clear to him that she was done with him, too.

He hovered above the bottom for a moment, eyes vigilant, as he spotted a familiar shape beneath him.

Reaching out, he snatched a king scallop from its sandy shelter.

Lying buried beneath the sand, there had only been a faint outline indicating where it was.

Shoving the shell into the black net bag, he turned to find some more.

As he scooped up several more scallops in quick succession, his bag getting heavier as he did so, he felt the anger and hurt towards his wife ebb away. Truth was, the sea had always been his therapist, his spiritual healer, his escape from the anxieties of life above water.

While he swam the sunlight reflected off the pristine white sand below, tracing intricate patterns on the dunes built up by the ocean's incessant currents.

On the edge of the North Atlantic, the unspoilt beauty of the Hebridean waters had to be seen to be believed. Every shade of blue and more besides shone luminescent on their shores. Teal, turquoise, navy, sapphire, aquamarine, azure, cerulean. No artist's palette could ever do it justice.

The Hebridean coast was to Simon, and many others, a piece of heaven on earth.

And there was Janey, nagging and pressurising him to leave this magnificent ocean to take up a job at the Isle of Harris Distillery. Based in Tarbert, the job would restrict him to a desk and four walls for most of the week, while Janey continued to run their ailing restaurant.

A family friend, well-meaning enough, had set up the job offer for Simon, not understanding that the Buchanons in Harris were reared with the ocean and the land, both of which were as much a part of them as breathing was.

Simon knew, beyond a shadow of a doubt, that if he accepted the job his spirit would be snuffed out like a flame on a guttered candle.

Somehow, he had to find a way to mend the black hole in their finances without giving up everything that made his life worth living.

He drifted up towards the air above him, his bag now full of king scallops.

Surprisingly fast swimmers, a few scallops had

managed to escape his clutches, propelling themselves across the sand at speed. He'd let them go. After all, they were desperately seeking their freedom, much like he was.

He broke through the surface, scattering droplets of water like confetti as he shook his head.

A seagull was hovering above him, head bent down, curious about his movements.

Pulling out his mouthpiece, Simon began to swim towards the shore, tugging his bag of scallops with him.

A chill wind was blowing on his face and he felt grateful for his dry suit, insulating him from the worst of the ocean's freezing temperatures.

Ahead of him, parked up on a grassy slope, was his bright-red van. Apart from his children and dog, the van was his pride and joy.

His young Border Collie, Bandit, would be waiting for him inside of it, impatient to be let loose among the white wisps of cotton grass.

Walking onto the beach, Simon felt his breathing shorten as his dry suit cooled down and the wind buffeted him.

There wasn't a soul to be seen, despite the fact it was early April and the sun was out.

Dangling his flippers in one hand, he stopped for a moment to unhook the bag of scallops from his belt.

With sand sticking to his diving shoes, he walked briskly up to his van, the scallop shells knocking against each other in the bag.

As soon as Simon opened the van's door, Bandit leapt out, brushing rudely past him.

Without stopping to acknowledge his owner's presence, Bandit ran away as fast as he could, his tail wagging ferociously. Never the most obedient of dogs, Bandit didn't want Simon calling him back before he'd had a chance to explore.

Stopping a safe distance from Simon, Bandit sniffed at an interesting patch of grass and then raised a leg.

Simon dumped his tank beside the van and placed his bag of scallops on the van floor.

He unzipped and then pulled off his dry suit, the rubber peeling away from his body like a crust, leaving his skin bright pink underneath.

For a few seconds, Simon stood stark naked beside the van, the breeze caressing him with icy pinpricks.

When he couldn't stand the cold any longer, he grabbed his clothes and started to get dressed.

Although he was chilled, he took his time dressing because he loved the feel and smell of clean, dry clothes after a scuba dive.

The small pleasures in life, he thought to himself, as he pulled a fleece jumper over his head.

Once he'd got himself dressed, Simon picked up his Thermos and a tennis ball that had seen better days, and followed Bandit to the edge of the beach.

He sat down among the clumps of cotton grass, their white heads nodding in the wind, and poured himself a coffee.

Bandit was busy. He was digging away at a rabbit hole on the side of a grass-covered mound.

That should keep him entertained, thought Simon, savouring the rich tang of coffee in his mouth. He was glad he wasn't obliged to throw the ball because it was a game that Bandit never tired of playing.

He turned and watched as the waves curled onto

the beach, tinting the white sand a shade of ochre and leaving a trail of bubbling foam behind.

The tide was starting to come in, which meant it was getting late.

It would soon be time to go.

He wondered if he should stop by their local corner shop on the way home and buy Janey some chocolates to soften her up, but with the mood she was in these days, she was quite capable of griping at him for having spent the money.

Sighing, he finished off his coffee and stood up.

He looked at Bandit and saw he was carrying a long and very dirty bone in his mouth.

"Bandit!" he beckoned.

Bandit, rebellious as ever, stayed where he was, his trophy dangling from his mouth.

What the hell was the bone, wondered Simon, looking at it.

It looked big enough to be a cow's bone. Possibly the femur.

"You're a disgusting dog, Bandit, you know that?"

Bandit wagged his tail.

Exasperated, he called for Bandit again, trying to inject some sternness into his voice this time.

Bandit turned a deaf ear and Simon lost his temper.

For Pete's sake, if it hadn't been bad enough quarrelling with his wife, he thought, he was now going to fall out with his dog too.

He marched across to where Bandit had positioned himself, only to have Bandit run away to the water's edge, bone in tow.

Simon's shoulders drooped with weariness

Damn it.

He didn't have the mental energy to play a game of cat and mouse with Bandit. He turned instead to look at the rabbit hole, with the pile of fresh earth scattered about its entrance.

Bandit must have been a hound in a former life, Simon decided. One of these days, he was going to come to grief and get trapped inside one of his digs. Serve the bloody dog right, too.

Bending down to peer inside rabbit hole, he caught sight of something at the edge, glinting in the sunlight.

He picked up the object, which was surprisingly heavy.

Bit by bit, he scraped the earth off it.

It was a kind of collar necklace, he surmised, studying the object curiously.

He felt his heart beat faster with excitement.

The necklace appeared to be made of two intertwined pieces of gold, with a lizard's or dragon's head attached to each end. Beautifully depicted, the heads had miniature scales carved into them and four intact eyes, made of blood-red stones, sparkled up at him in the morning sun.

Stunned, Simon stared once more at the rabbit hole.

What the hell had Bandit uncovered with his digging?

1

Mike

An orange fedora followed the crowd heading from Ladbroke Grove Tube station to Chepstow Villas, the area dedicated to the antiques section of Portobello Road Market.

Portobello Road Market in Notting Hill, London, was considered the world's largest antiques market, with over a thousand dealers selling their wares.

Taking its name over 300 years ago from nearby Porto Bello Farm, the antiques market attracted wealthy buyers, as well as the tourist and the curious bystander.

The name of Porto Bello Farm supposedly originated from the British capture of the town of Porto Bello, in Panama. The town Porto Bello was taken from the Spanish back in 1739 and the English landowner must have named his farm Porto Bello in an orgy of nationalistic fervour. The origins of Portobello Road Market, however, didn't match the modern-day reality of a market whose atmosphere was both vibrant and multicultural.

Matching the festive atmosphere with its garish-ness, the bright-orange fedora weaved its way through the pedestrians crowding the street.

The fedora belonged to a portly man, who was also wearing a khaki blazer and shirt, dark-blue jeans, and a pair of aviator shades.

The man came to a stop at a stall selling antique jewellery and began to study the glass display cases.

Each jewellery case was fixed to the table with metal chain and a padlock.

For several minutes the owner of the stall was occu-pied serving his customers, but when he finally turned to approach the man in the orange fedora, he looked startled.

"Blimey, Mike. What on earth have you got on today? You should be down at Portobello Green, getting some tips for dressing."

Mike smiled, unoffended.

"Nice to meet you, too, Farshid. Well, what you have you got for me?"

Farshid looked put out.

He glanced around, then leaned forward, both hands on the table.

"It's too busy right now to talk. You were supposed to be here at nine," he said crossly.

"Not on a Saturday, mate. You've had me out on a wild goose chase before, Farshid, remember? You know what they say, once bitten, twice shy. In any case, I'm not losing my beauty sleep for a man who sells stolen jewellery."

Farshid flinched.

"Keep your voice down or you'll regret it," he hissed, in a low voice.

Mike looked at him.

"Is that a threat?" he asked, calmly.

"No, no, of course it isn't," answered Farshid, flustered now.

A middle-aged couple stopped at the stall and began to look at the jewellery.

"Look, I can't talk now. I've got customers," insisted Farshid. "my nephew's arriving at three this afternoon to take over. Why don't you meet me in Holland Park at four-thirty? At the Kyoto Garden pond?"

Mike hesitated for a moment, weighing things up in his mind.

Farshid seemed earnest enough, he thought.

"This is important, Mike. You won't be disappointed."

"Okey-dokey. Don't let me down this time, Farshid."

With that, Mike tilted his fedora, and then disappeared into the throng once more, his hat weaving and bobbing its way towards the food stands, the smell of which had been wafting in the air and enticing him during his brief chat with Farshid.

After eating a kebab and browsing a few stalls, Mike made his way to the Kyoto Garden with no real expectation that Farshid would turn up.

He had sensed, though, during their short conversation that Farshid was scared of something, and that had to be a first. It took a lot for a man who routinely bought stolen items from drug addicts, professional thieves, and gangland bosses to be frightened.

And whatever it was that was bothering him, it was not something Farshid had dealt with before. Of that, Mike was certain.

Farshid didn't like walking on the side of the angels. He was happy lurking in the mud with the other slime-balls in his trade. Like many others, Farshid knew that he'd be handsomely compensated by Mike for any art theft information he could divulge, but he hadn't availed himself of the opportunity in the six years Mike had known him.

Hoping Farshid wasn't playing any tricks on him, Mike walked up to an empty bench positioned close to the waterfall at Kyoto Garden.

He sat down, startling the peacock that was perched on the back of the bench.

Hopping onto the ground, the peacock rustled its feathers in disapproval and walked off.

Mike finished the remains of his take-away coffee and then tossed it into the bin next to him.

He pulled his hat low over his eyes, crossed his arms, and gazed down at his loafers with an impassive face.

There were worse places to wait for someone, he decided.

If only it were Meg Ryan turning up to see him, instead of a man with a greasy mullet and his neck, wrist, and fingers covered in chunky gold jewellery.

He sighed to himself.

Even though it was late afternoon, the park was busy.

A boy screamed as his dad chased him across the grass.

An elderly couple, holding hands, walked past, politely wishing Mike a good afternoon.

To the left of him, a woman, surrounded by carrier

bags, was tossing bits of bread to the Koi fish in the pond.

The bench shook as someone sat down.

He turned and saw Farshid was seated at the other end of the bench, his legs crossed and his left hand gripping the arm rest as though it pained him to be there.

Dressed all in black, with a trimmed beard, Farshid looked just like a character from the film *Men in Black*. Only the heavy, gold jewellery he wore let him down in that respect.

"Didn't think you were going to make it," commented Mike.

"Yes, I know, but this time things are different," explained Farshid, staring straight ahead at the pond.

Mike noticed Farshid had a carryall beside him. A positive sign.

"So, you're worried," said Mike, stating the obvious.

"Yeah. I don't like the seller. It's one of your lot."

"Really? Gone over to the dark side, has he?"

"I'm deadly serious, Mike. I haven't dealt with a cop before and I don't intend to, either. Risky. And the goods are too hot to handle. This isn't going to end well."

"Do you have a name?"

Farshid smiled.

"Nope. The go-between called the cop Radge at one point. Apparently, up there in Scotland, that means someone who is aggressive, or difficult. I've come across a few of those in my time."

"So where do I come in?" asked Mike.

Farshid turned sideways and stared intently at Mike, his black eyes glinting.

"Someone's found treasure. Real treasure, man. And they aren't declaring it to the state. They're trying to flog it on the sly. Two pieces have already been sold. I was offered all three pieces at the start, but I wouldn't touch them with a bargepole. Don't have the dosh for them anyway."

"Three pieces?"

Farshid snorted impatiently.

"There's more I've been told. There always is. But you can't sell everything at once."

"What kind of treasure are we talking about?"

Instead of answering, Farshid bent down and unzipped his holdall.

He pulled out an A4 envelope and passed it to Mike.

"Those were sent to me by my contact."

Mike opened it and eased out a wad of photos, which he placed on the bench between them.

The topmost photo alone was enough to make him catch his breath.

It was a photo of a torc; two thick pieces of gold twisted round each other with what looked to be a dragon head at each end.

He picked up the photo and studied it closely.

Lifting another three photos, he saw they were all close-ups of the same thing.

He then glanced through the rest, noting that two of the other objects were a silver cup, with runes engraved on the side of it, and a small gold pin in the shape of a cat, with a coloured stone for its body.

"Viking or Anglo-Saxon?" he hazarded.

"Viking by the looks of it. Discovered on one of the

Scottish islands up north apparently. Similar place to where they found the Lewis Chessmen."

Mike rubbed his chin as he studied the photos.

"How do you know any of these are genuine items, Farshid?"

"Because the seller is also using as proof a Two Emperor coin for any buyers."

Mike whistled.

A Two Emperor coin was rare, depicting the Anglo-Saxon King Alfred the Great and Ceolwulf II. A single one was valued at a hundred thousand pounds.

"Interesting. You say two pieces have sold already?"

"Yes. Sold in Birmingham. To Mariella Giuseppi."

Mike whistled softly to himself.

"Mariella Giuseppi? The Midas Touch jewellery designer?"

"Yes."

"This isn't the first time I've crossed paths with her. She's a real pain in the ass."

Farshid shrugged his shoulders.

"Stuff's still up there in the Jewellery Quarter for now, I think, but it won't be long before they'll try to move it."

Farshid sat up and looked at Mike.

"Look, mate, there's more where this came from. So I've been told, anyway. You have to do something about it. This cop's trying to get the stuff sold on the sly, but it's going to blow up in his face sooner or later. He's not doing a good job of keeping it quiet."

Farshid sniffed.

"He's a total amateur and doesn't have a clue about how to do these things. If he's not careful he'll find himself in a tight corner. It won't just be the Met that wants to get its hands on him, there'll be others, too. Loads of them, in fact, and what's more, they won't be too nice about it. I'm worried that if things get really messy it could drive some of us out of the business."

Mike nodded.

"Can I keep the photos?"

"Yeah, sure. I don't need them. I'm washing my hands of the whole thing."

Mike gathered up the photos and slipped them back into the envelope.

Farshid stood up and looked down at him.

"You owe me one, Mike."

Mike nodded again.

"Yeah, I do for once. I won't forget."

"Make sure you don't. There'll come a day when I'll need you to keep the cops off my back."

"I hope not for your sake, Farshid. But I'll put in a good word for you, should the need arise."

Satisfied, Farshid bent his head and walked off, his DMs crunching on the pebbles edging the pond.

Mike stayed where he was for a while longer, watching two old men across the water race remote-control boats. The scene was taking him back to his own childhood, when his father would take him to the local duck pond to float a wooden yacht they'd constructed together.

Mike had in fact squirrelled away enough to buy himself a yacht for his retirement. These days he never had the time to take sailing lessons, but when it was the right time to sell off his business, he was planning to take a year out gaining sailing proficiency in Cornwall. Then he was going to set off across the Atlantic on his boat.

He had too many enemies in the UK now. Private investigators like himself had a short shelf life. The job was addictive, but the key to a healthy retirement was knowing when to step down from it.

His time was going to be up soon. He could feel it in his bones.

2

Richard

Richard was lying on a beach with Eilidh, dozing gently.

Waves were lapping at the sand two metres away.

A beach seller was spoiling the idyllic scene by shouting for customers as he walked past, dragging his freezer box of cold drinks behind him.

Richard wished he'd shut up and go away.

The man, dressed in a stripy shirt and shorts, called out again, loudly, right next to his ear.

"Oh, bugger off, man," moaned Richard.

Then he felt himself getting shaken and woke up.

He was lying in bed, his hand resting protectively over Eilidh's prominent belly.

She was pulling on his shoulder.

"Richard, your mobile phone keeps going off. It must be important. Hadn't you better answer it?"

"Yep," he replied, sitting upright and blinking as he tried to shift his sleepiness.

Eilidh giggled.

She pointed to his bedside table, where his phone was vibrating, its screen lit up.

Richard swung his legs off the bed and picked it up. "Hello?"

"Ah, at last," said a familiar voice.

Richard looked at his watch. It was five o'clock.

"Mike, what the hell? It's five o'clock in the morning!"

"I know, I know, I'm sorry, mate. I've been tied up for most of the night with other work and I thought I'd better get in touch sooner rather than later. Is Eilidh well?"

"Yes. Yes, she is thanks," mumbled Richard, struggling to cope with polite chit-chat that early in the morning.

He rubbed his eyes.

"Good, good. Listen, I've been told there's undeclared treasure been found up north."

"Rumour or fact, Mike? We get these kinds of calls quite a lot, you know."

"Fact. I've done my own bit of digging around on this. Rest assured, it's true. The treasure was found on the island of Lewis and Harris. A Scottish island. My source is solid."

"OK. Have the police up there been informed?"

"No, that's your job, Richard. You're going to have to proceed with caution, though. One of the cops is bent. He's the one flogging the stuff on the black market and I'm sure he's not going to be happy if you make an appearance. I'd get Lionel to speak to the area command in the Highlands and Islands division. Get you in that way. You'd better act fast because three pieces have been sold already.

I've got the photos and I'll have copies couriered to you. I'm heading up to Birmingham. Two of the pieces sold are being held there, probably waiting for the highest bidder."

"What era are we talking Mike?"

"Viking."

"If the pieces haven't been carbon dated, there's no proof they're original."

"It's the real deal, Richard. The woman who's bought the two pieces works in the Jewellery Quarter in Birmingham. They know their stuff."

Richard didn't say anything. The situation didn't sound good.

"Richard?"

"Yeah?"

"The cop is nicknamed Radge. Might be helpful or not."

"It's a little unusual for a police officer to have the time to find buried treasure, Mike. I wonder if there's someone else involved."

"Probably. I wouldn't be surprised if someone took the treasure to this policeman and was told to keep quiet about it."

"Yes, greed does it for them every time."

"Well, it's the way of the world, my friend. I'll keep in touch."

"Great, thanks Mike."

With the call ended, Richard sank back down onto the pillows and stared up at the ceiling.

"What was all that about?" asked Eilidh, facing him with her head leaning on her bent arm.

"Treasure," said Richard.

"Oh, goody."

Richard smiled.

Six months pregnant and Eilidh still hadn't lost her zeal for art theft cases. He had no idea where she found the energy.

Speaking of energy, he thought, *I need some coffee.*

He looked across at Eilidh.

These days Eilidh was trying to stay off the caffeine and it was proving an ordeal for her will power.

"I'll bring you up some breakfast, Eilidh, and then I'll get going."

She grinned at him, sensing his coffee craving.

"Enjoy your coffee," she called out cheekily as he headed for the bedroom door.

In the end, once he'd downed his caffeine for the day, it didn't take him long to get organised.

Running a stone-cold shower had helped him to waken up, too.

Letting the icy rivulets of water run down his scalp, he felt his brain reenergising. He washed himself down with shower gel, letting the potent grapefruit scent stimulate his senses while he thought back to Mike's call.

Was the treasure part of a Viking hoard or was it a Viking burial chamber?

He decided it was more likely to be a hoard than a burial chamber.

Finding any Viking treasure was always incredibly exciting, but from an archaeological point of view where the treasure came from could reveal many unknown secrets from the past.

Treasure could be buried as a hoard, left in the ground to be collected later, like the Galloway Hoard, which was found with a metal detector in 2014 in Dumfries and Galloway, Scotland. Back in Viking days, burying treasure was one of the safest things you could do to protect your investment, similar to hiding a stash in a safe or the bank nowadays.

The Galloway Hoard was a treasure store supposedly kept by three Viking men, but why they never returned for it was a mystery that would never be solved. The hoard had been constructed with a decoy layer, and below this layer the more valuable items had been buried.

Apart from a hoard, a treasure find might consist of a burial chamber, with the treasure and artefacts left to usher the deceased into the afterlife in good style, just as the ancient Egyptians had done. Though the Vikings, of course, had very different gods and beliefs to the Egyptians.

In Britain, the Anglo-Saxon burial chambers found at the famous Sutton Hoo dig were a good example of this. In the central chamber of a ship, beautiful artefacts were left behind as part of a burial ritual. It was generally assumed that only the very wealthy or powerful in society received such grandiose funerals.

To date, Richard didn't know of any major Viking ship or chamber burial in Britain. Ones of minor importance had been discovered in the UK, but not of the stature of the ones found on the continent. Many amazing artefacts had been recovered from Viking burials across Scandinavia and near the Danish/German border.

Maybe the constant friction between the Anglo-Saxons and the Vikings in England, or the Vikings against the Picts and Scots in Scotland, made prestigious Viking burial chambers less viable in Britain as a whole.

After all, Vikings had a nasty habit of raiding and

ransacking villages and churches in Britain for their wealth, while also abducting thousands of men, women, and children to sell on as slaves. The local population was bound to feel hostile towards them, even as occupiers. In view of this, Richard was of the opinion that Vikings were unlikely to mourn their chieftains with grand ship burials or chambers on Britain's land, but he was no expert on Viking history.

There was evidence, though, that in places like the Isle of Lewis and Harris, Vikings had settled and integrated with the local population. The Isle of Lewis and Harris was also a convenient harbour and important trading post on the Vikings' passage to Ireland, so a high-profile, wealthy Viking burial chamber was a distinct possibility there.

Richard stepped out of the shower, quickly dried himself with a towel, and then walked through to the bedroom to put on his clothes.

Eilidh was nibbling at her toast and showing no signs of wanting to get out of bed.

Once he was dressed, Richard bent over and gave her a kiss on the forehead.

"See you in the office?" he asked.

Eilidh nodded as she drank her orange juice and caught up on the messages left on her phone.

Leaving Eilidh to sort herself out before she made it in to work, Richard let himself out of their flat in Drayton Gardens, South Kensington, and made his way down the street.

The May sun was shining bright and the trees were in full bloom. No wonder he'd been dreaming of a summer holiday that morning.

He made his way to Gloucester Road Station and

took the Tube to Westminster, taking his suit jacket off in the heat of the underground. There was a silver lining to Covid, he thought, because with so many people working from home these days the underground trains weren't running at full capacity like they used to.

He arrived at the office before eight.

He found an A4 envelope sitting on his desk, his name scrawled across it in Mike's distinctive handwriting.

There was no doubt in Richard's mind that Mike's handwriting would've gone down a treat in the sixteenth century. With its swirling letters, it was, to all intents and purposes, indecipherable. The real conundrum was where Mike had been taught to write because his handwriting looked like the product of a Shakespearean calligraphy school. It was just as well Mike employed a competent secretary to help him with his correspondence, Richard thought.

Mike had his own contacts at New Scotland Yard, but delivering a letter so soon after their conversation was fast, even for him, and demonstrated the level of concern Mike had about the artefacts.

Richard picked the envelope up, slit it open with his letter opener, and watched a number of photographs slide onto his desk top.

Richard sifted through the photos, studying the torc, the cup, and the pin.

He logged onto his computer and did a search on the island of Lewis and Harris.

Off the north-west tip of Scotland, it was the largest island in the Outer Hebrides. Known for its beautiful scenery and beaches, many of the place names on the island were Norse and dated from a time when Norway had owned the islands.

The National Museum of Scotland had a notable collection of Viking artefacts discovered on the island, the most famous of which were the Lewis Chessmen.

The Lewis Chessmen were chess pieces carved out of walrus ivory and dated from around the twelfth century. It was a period in history when the Vikings were beginning to get converted to Christianity, hence the bishop pieces in the collection.

Found buried in a sandbank in 1831, eighty-two of the Lewis Chessmen pieces were now owned by the British Museum in London, with the remaining eleven residing in the National Museum of Scotland.

A few pieces were in private hands; in 2019 one Lewis Chessman, bought for £5, sold for more than £700,000 at Sotheby's.

Feeling excited for the first time, Richard decided to look at transport to the island.

The quickest way to reach the Isle of Lewis and Harris was to catch a flight from London to Edinburgh, and then fly onwards to Stornoway Airport in Lewis.

Richard scratched his head.

Somehow, he needed to get Lionel on board with the case.

He was hopeful of securing Lionel's cooperation. Normally, anyone who discovered treasure in Scotland had to declare it to the Treasure Trove Unit, who would then arrange for a council archaeologist to provide excavation assistance.

Nothing had been declared to the Treasure Trove Unit, and because the treasure looked to be important in terms of Scotland's heritage, it was going to be a priority to chase down the rogue sellers before the treasure vanished completely.

He looked at his watch.

Lionel would probably be ensconced in his office, catching up on his emails. Perfect time to catch him.

Without further ado, Richard took the lift up to the sixth floor and walked across to Lionel's office.

The door was shut, but despite this Richard could see the light was on inside.

He knocked tentatively on the door, wondering what kind of a mood Lionel would be in. It was anyone's guess because of Lionel's famously mercurial temperament. Usually, he could be counted on being in good form after the Grand National horse race, but the race only happened once a year.

"Come in!" shouted Lionel, in what was clearly intended to be a sing-song voice but sounded more like that of a caged tiger.

For some reason, lines from Mary Howitt's poem, *The Spider and the Fly*, popped into Richard's head.

> "Will you walk into my parlour?" said
>   the Spider to the Fly,
> "Tis the prettiest little parlour that ever
>   you did spy."

A vision of Lionel as a bloated black spider came into Richard's mind and made him smile.

He opened the door and walked in, surprised to hear Lionel sounding so cheerful first thing in the morning.

Lionel was leaning back on his chair, browsing on his mobile phone, with his ankles crossed on the desk.

"Dick! How are you doing?" asked Lionel, looking relaxed.

Richard gaped at him, unable to fathom what had put him such a good mood.

"Good, thanks. And you, sir?"

"Not bad at all. I've discovered today I've only got 503 days left until my retirement. Imagine that! 503 days! And it's going by fast, too."

"Yes, I'm sure it is, sir."

"Take a seat," offered Lionel, removing his feet from the desk.

Richard sat down, clutching the A4 envelope Mike had left him.

Lionel put his phone down and started tidying up the loose papers on his desk.

"What's up?" he asked, as he began to place the papers onto his letter tray.

"Real treasure, this time, sir. I've got it on good authority that Viking treasure has been found on an island off the north of Scotland, and it hasn't been declared to the authorities."

Lionel looked across at him, interest sparking from his eyes.

"Treasure? What are we talking about here? Coins?"

Richard emptied the envelope and laid out the photos in front of Lionel.

"No coins so far. At least as far as we know. A gold torc, a silver cup, and a gold pin have been shown around on the black market. Two of the items have been sold to someone in Birmingham, apparently. Mike Telford's heading up there as we speak. Rumour has it there's more of the treasure still left on the island of

Lewis and Harris. And what's worse, it seems there's a bent cop trying to flog the stuff. Not very discreetly, it would appear."

"The island of Lewis and Harris? Are we talking about two islands here, or just the one?" asked Lionel, confused.

"It's unusual. It's one island. The top half is called Lewis and the bottom half Harris."

Lionel exhaled, his nostrils flaring.

"Good grief! This is huge. Should we be alerting the Scottish Anti-Corruption Unit to this?"

"I think it's too early for that. We've no idea who's selling the stuff and I don't think Mike's contacts will tell him who it is. We don't want the cop going quiet, having already sold three priceless items."

"Fair enough," agreed Lionel. "How do we know they're not fakes?"

"They've not been verified, but Mike's contacts work in the jewellery trade and they know their stuff."

Lionel pulled on his ear: a nervous tic of his that always signalled his agitation.

"Not sure the police in Scotland will welcome interference from your unit, Dick."

"As the UK's Art and Antiquities Unit we do have some remit in terms of the treasure, though. I'll need you to soften the powers that be, so we can head up there and investigate without too much acrimony. Given it seems one of their own has been corrupted, they might consider our unit's involvement useful at this stage. They'll want the treasure recovered just as much as we do. It'll be a coup for the National Museum of Scotland, to say the least."

Richard decided to hedge his bets. Nothing ventured, nothing gained.

"I also wonder, given what we know, if they would share with us a profile of the police working on the island," he added, hopefully.

Lionel made a face.

"Doubtful, but not impossible. I'll do my best."

"Thanks Lionel."

Richard was about to stand up, when Lionel raised a hand.

"Hold on a minute, Dick. It's a good job you've dropped by because there are some important departmental changes coming up soon. I wanted to run them by you, even though it's early days."

This can't be good, thought Richard, as he watched Lionel pull a box of staples from a drawer and start to refill his stapler.

Lionel was buying some time for himself, which wasn't like him, because he normally went straight for the jugular on difficult topics.

"You know how keen the government are on private–public partnerships," began Lionel, after a minute, not looking Richard in the eye. "Goes on in healthcare, transport, etcetera, etcetera. This happens even with our British consulates nowadays, would you believe?"

He paused.

Sensing Lionel was needing encouragement to continue, Richard nodded.

"Well, the government have been looking at the allocation of resources to New Scotland Yard and they've taken an interest in your unit. They're now tentatively considering opening up the Art and Antiquities Unit to a private–public partnership, and in the fullness of time, aiming for perhaps fifteen percent of the operating budget to be funded privately from independent donors and trusts."

Richard stared at Lionel in disbelief.

"Yes, you see, the government feels that the country's heritage will be an attractive proposition for investment. I'm sure many organisations would be willing to donate to such a worthy cause," continued Lionel, somewhat hastily. "But anyway, the long and short of the matter is, we've been asked to scope it out."

Richard cleared his throat.

"Scope it out?"

Lionel winced, which didn't reassure Richard one little bit.

"Yes, I'm afraid I'm needing you to come up with some kind of a fundraising plan within the next six to nine months," answered Lionel.

"Ah, I see."

"We've helped out a lot of institutions and individuals in our time. I'm sure they'll do their bit," added Lionel, trying to be optimistic.

Richard remained silent.

Lionel started tapping his pen on the table.

"I know this is going to place a burden on your already stretched department, Dick. I'm afraid, though, this time it's out of my hands. Today's hot topic is the deficit. We all have to do our bit. If you need anyone from any of the other units to lend a helping hand, just ask. I can put you in touch with ministers who have worked on private–public partnerships before. You're not on your own in this."

Richard swallowed.

He felt very much alone. Overlooked, in fact. Nobody had given him a chance to defend his unit's funding.

In any case, why was his department chosen for a cut in funding? Maybe his department would attract contributions from rich and wealthy owners of priceless works of art, but it was a long shot, in his opinion. Some of the wealthiest people were also the tightest when it came to giving.

Then there was his time. How much of his time was going to have to be expended on this self-funding project?

He was going to end up like a desperate salesman, touting for custom. For sure he'd have to wheel Eilidh out, to do the sweet-talking. She'd be brilliant at it, he thought, but she was a valuable officer in her own right. Persuading organisations to contribute financially to their department would be a waste of her time and skills, too.

He sighed.

"OK, sir. I'll see what I can do," he said, glumly.

"That's the spirit! It'll all work out just fine. You might even get to the stage where you can expand the department," enthused Lionel.

Richard wished he could believe him.

But he didn't.

3

Richard

For the next few days, Richard completely forgot about the treasure and focussed on his other duties.

There was nothing he could do to speed up police bureaucracy in regard to his being given the go ahead by the Scottish authorities to head north in search of missing treasure. Knowing Lionel, he'd be working flat out to get permission granted. Any case which was likely to give kudos to their department always had his full attention.

The treasure, though, soon made its presence felt again.

At eleven o'clock one morning, Richard received a text from Eilidh, requesting his presence at New Scotland Yard.

By then, he was in the middle of a meeting at the Royal Academy in Piccadilly. The team at the Academy were discussing weaknesses in their security and the areas they needed to improve on in order to better protect their paintings.

They were jittery because four anonymous letters

had been sent to the Academy, threatening to destroy a painting in the building unless it was removed from public view.

The painting in question was *The Cat's Paw*, by Edwin Landseer.

The controversial painting portrayed a French fable, illustrating a story in which a monkey persuades a cat to retrieve roasting chestnuts from a fire and the cat harms itself in the process.

Both the painting and the fable were attempting to depict an aspect of human behaviour: one where people are duped into carrying out actions detrimental to themselves. Richard thought that in today's world, the fable could apply to scams like romance fraud, where lonely women are persuaded to send their life savings to a fraudster.

It was clear the painting's real meaning hadn't registered with the anonymous letter writer, and even if it had, Richard didn't think it would've made any difference because he was sure they were dealing with a fanatic. In truth, Richard suspected that the letters had been written by an animal rights activist because there were many people who disapproved of the cat's suffering in the painting.

He had nothing to base his theory on except his gut instinct because the author of the letters had carefully avoided leaving any clue that might reveal their identity.

Written threats weren't taken lightly by the Royal Academy. After all, in 1914 their portrait of Henry James, by John Singer Sargent, had been defaced by a suffragette called Mary Wood.

Mary Wood had attacked the painting three times with a meat cleaver.

Privately, Richard thought a Stanley knife would have suited a suffragette better than a meat cleaver. A meat cleaver seemed too domesticated, somehow, for a die-hard feminist.

No one seemed to know whether Mary was venting her disapproval for the way Henry James had portrayed the women's movement in his novel *The Bostonians* or whether it was just a general protest at the lack of political representation for women. Either way, the valuable painting had been left badly damaged.

Art was supposed to provoke a reaction from the public, Richard mused, while listening with half an ear to the Royal Academy's staff voicing their concerns. Trouble was, sometimes the emotions art provoked were quite extreme, and more and more these days, people seemed to be unable to control their feelings.

Eilidh's text had summoned him to the office for twelve o'clock, but Richard was supposed to have been back at his desk a good half hour ago, and true to form he was running late.

He wound up the meeting at the Royal Academy as quickly as he could. Packing up his briefcase, he promised them he'd send in an official report with detailed suggestions for improvement within the next couple of weeks.

Once outside the Academy, he strode along Piccadilly Road, weaving his way through slower pedestrians in front of him as he made his way to Green Park Underground Station.

He reached his platform, and despite the crowds, leapt onto the first available train. As a result of this, he travelled uncomfortably, his back pressed against the door, surrounded by people. It was the beginning of the lunchtime rush hour and the carriage was busy with commuters. Tourism in London was picking up with the warmer weather, too, which didn't help matters.

Leaving the train a few minutes later at Westminster Station, he ran the short distance to New Scotland Yard.

When he walked into the interview room Eilidh had pre-booked for them, he found a tired-looking lady, who he guessed was in her mid-thirties, seated on one side of the table.

Dressed in a pair of faded jeans and a zip-up hoodie, she was holding a mug of coffee between her hands.

"I'm sorry to call you in, Richard, but I felt this was important," said Eilidh, looking relieved to see him.

Trying to smarten himself up, Richard patted down his hair and straightened his tie.

"Of course. No problem," said Richard, smiling down at her as if he'd just casually strolled into the room and not run full pelt into New Scotland Yard from the Tube station.

He took a seat next to Eilidh and glanced with interest at the woman across the table. Eilidh always had a good reason for summoning him to a meeting and his curiosity was tickled.

"This is Janey Buchanon," announced Eilidh. "Janey, this is Chief Inspector Richard Langley of the Art and Antiquities Unit."

"Nice to meet you, Janey," said Richard, smiling at her.

Janey didn't smile or speak.

Instead, she gazed down at her mug of coffee.

Richard studied her for a moment.

She was pale, with dark shadows under her eyes and brown roots showing through her bleached-blonde hair

She looked washed out, exhausted, he thought. Like a person who'd reached a mental state that was beyond using social niceties.

"Janey's the wife of Simon Buchanon. She says he found some buried treasure on the island of Lewis and Harris," explained Eilidh.

Janey still didn't respond.

"Perhaps you could fill me in on the background to this, Eilidh?" suggested Richard, as the silence in the room dragged on.

Janey was clearly in a fragile state and living under a great deal of strain. He was sure he'd have plenty of questions to ask her later, but in the meantime, it would be good to give the poor woman a break.

Eilidh nodded.

"Well, as I said, Janey's husband, Simon, was the one who found the treasure trove in Harris. He took three pieces of treasure and one of the coins to the police station in Tarbert, to ask them about it. He was told to leave the items in their custody, which he did. Not long afterwards, his body was found floating near..."

Eilidh looked down at her notes.

"Taransay," interjected Janey, with a soft Scottish accent.

Her facial expression was calm and determined.

Not a woman to lose her head, even under pressure, concluded Richard.

"Taransay," repeated Eilidh. "On the Harris coast-line. He'd been scuba diving. The verdict from the post-mortem was accidental death by drowning, due to insufficient gas in his tank."

Janey nodded.

"Janey's adamant her husband was an experienced scuba diver and would never make the mistake of going out to sea without enough air in his tank. She suspects someone on Harris wants the treasure for themselves and events that have happened subsequently have confirmed her belief. That's it, in a nutshell."

There was another silence in the room as Richard digested this information.

Janey was now looking distressed and anxious, as though she feared she would be disbelieved. Which wasn't surprising given it was quite a tale and the accusations were momentous.

"Janey, you're a long way from Harris. What are you doing here in London?" asked Richard, puzzled by her presence in New Scotland Yard.

Janey bit her lip.

"I decided to leave Harris for a while. I don't feel safe there anymore and I've got the kids to think about. We're staying with my sister and brother-in-law in Essex, but we can't live there long-term. I need to get this mess sorted out and get home again."

Richard leaned forward, placing his elbows on the table and, out of habit, ran his fingers through his hair. Too late, he remembered his earlier efforts to tidy himself up, although he didn't think Janey would care in the slightest about his appearance, professional or not.

"What exactly happened to make you feel unsafe?" asked Richard, thinking she must be exaggerating.

"It's been a build-up of stuff."

Looking down at her mug, Janey fell silent.

Richard and Eilidh didn't say anything and waited for her to say her piece.

"You know, they never found Bandit, our dog," said Janey at last, her voice breaking. "I don't know what happened to him. I'm kind of imagining the worst. He was with Simon the day he went missing. He needed a lot of exercise so Simon took him out when he could. But the day they found Simon, no one saw the dog, and no one's seen him since, either."

Janey released her mug of coffee and pulled the cuffs of her top over her wrists.

"There's something really evil that's got into our island," whispered Janey, startling Richard and Eilidh as she leaned forward and looked them in the eye. "I'm telling you, there's weird stuff going on up there... horrible things. You'll struggle to believe it but I've felt it and seen it for myself."

Richard and Eilidh nodded, humouring her.

Janey read the doubt in their faces and smiled sadly.

"You see? You already think I'm mad."

"Janey, it's not our place to pass judgement on what you tell us," said Eilidh, trying to reassure her. "We're under obligation to take what you have to say to us seriously, and we will."

Janey shrugged.

Richard could now see Janey was doubting the truth of Eilidh's statement. Given the general public's lack of faith in the police, her doubts didn't surprise him in the slightest.

"Why don't you start from the beginning and tell us the facts that have led you to this conclusion?" suggested Richard.

Janey crossed her arms, her face thoughtful.

In the silence of the room, Richard became aware of the wall clock ticking away, reminding him time didn't stand still.

What's more, he was needing the toilet.

He smiled at Janey, trying to hide his impatience.

Janey's face visibly relaxed.

"A week after Simon's death, our house got broken into," said Janey at long last. "They must have been watching it because we were only out for a couple of hours that day. The whole place was trashed. Every drawer had been searched. Even the freezer drawers, would you believe? Not what I needed, with Simon dead."

A tear made its way down Janey's cheek and she brushed it away impatiently.

Janey had a fair amount of grit in her, decided Richard. She was on edge, definitely, but she was not mentally incapacitated or ill. She still had clarity of thought.

"Then, a few days after the funeral, I was invited to the police station for an interview," continued Janey. "A couple of police officers were there and they said that there were rumours my husband had found some treasure on Harris. Did I know anything about this treasure? I told them the truth. I said it seemed he had indeed found treasure. He had brought three pieces back to the house and shown them to me. I then suggested he take them up to the police station."

Richard groaned. The thought of the treasure site getting dug up and messed with was more than he could bear.

Janey looked at him in surprise.

"Sorry. Carry on," he said.

"I told them Simon had taken three pieces into the police station and I told them I didn't know where the rest of it was. Which was the gospel truth."

"You didn't know where the rest of it was?" repeated Richard, sceptical.

"No, honest to God, I've no idea what Simon did with it," answered Janey, looking at him straight in the eye. "Simon was buzzing the day he found the treasure. I was the one who urged him to go to the police station. I wish I hadn't now."

Janey bit her lip, holding back the tears.

"Anyway," she said, getting a grip of her emotions. "Simon said he was going to take a few items to show the police, but he was going to keep the rest back until he was put in touch with someone who was an expert in these matters. He said he knew somewhere safe for it, but it was better for me not to know. I think he had a premonition, even back then, that I might get into trouble because of it."

Janey looked up at them.

"Simon thought the police would direct him to some specialist in this kind of thing, but whoever he spoke to told him to leave the items in their custody and they would make sure someone appropriate looked at them."

"And did they?" prompted Richard.

"That's the weird thing," said Janey. "When they interviewed me, they told me no treasure had been left with them. Ever."

The quiet in the room was uncomfortable.

Eilidh and Richard glanced at each other.

"Do you have the name of the police officer your husband spoke to?" asked Richard, finally.

"No. Don't you think I would have told them that Simon left the treasure with them? I have no name. Nothing. My husband was never the greatest communicator," she said, with some bitterness in her voice. "And, of course, I'd no idea the trouble it was going to bring us back then, otherwise I would have demanded he tell me."

"Someone's taken a big risk," mused Eilidh. "After all, I imagine on an island with a tiny population, everyone knows each other."

"Yes, that's true," agreed Janey. "That's why I felt I had to leave. I felt threatened up there. I'm telling you, I wouldn't be surprised if they've dug up my garden by now, looking for the rest of the treasure while I've been away."

Richard pulled a notebook and pen from his brief-case's side pocket.

"Do you have the names of the two officers who interviewed you?"

Janey nodded.

"Constable Will McLeod and Sergeant Rory Petrie."

"Is there anything else that made you feel unsafe? Unsafe enough for you to come down here and stay with your sister, Janey?" asked Richard, thinking it

would take a lot to intimidate the woman sitting in front
of him.

"Yes, but I doubt anyone else would take it seriously. A couple of weeks after the funeral, I started
finding things on my kitchen doorstep. Every morning,
after I got back from the school run, I found a dead creature on the doorstep."

Janey paused for a minute, pulling herself together.

"First it was a decapitated fish, then it was a seagull
with a wire tied around its neck. I've had a dead vole, a
harrier, a woodpigeon, a rabbit with its legs broken. I
reported this to the police but they told me it was most
probably "gifts" from my cat. I knew our cat Leo
wouldn't go anywhere near a seagull, harrier, or rabbit.
My cat was a right softie and far too lazy. Besides, he
had a bell on his collar. Any creature would hear him a
mile off."

"A school-kid prank?" suggested Eilidh.

Janey smiled at her, but it was a bitter smile, not one
filled with warmth.

"You'd think so, wouldn't you? Except a few days
later, it was my cat, Leo, that was laid out on my
doorstep. Without his head."

Janey took her phone out of her bag, scrolled for a
bit, and then held her phone up to show them a photo
of a black and white cat, lying on the ground, covered in
blood. The head was missing.

Richard frowned.

"Did you go back to the police?"

"No," said Janey, slowly. "I decided that was a bad
idea. I wouldn't trust them an inch. Everything went
wrong after Simon went to them. I wish I hadn't told
him to do that. I didn't feel safe staying on the island.

Someone on the island knows there's more treasure around and I was going to be a target as long as I stayed there."

"It's hard to know what they were hoping to achieve by leaving a trail of dead creatures at your home," said Richard, voicing his confusion.

The whole scenario, in fact, puzzled him.

"I think they're trying to scare me off," insisted Janey. "Someone at the police station knows there's more of the treasure around. They know Simon might've told me who he spoke to at the police station."

Richard nodded.

"Just to be a hundred-percent clear, you think someone in the police force on Harris is corrupt?" he asked, looking at her.

"Yes," said Janey, bluntly. "But I'm on a losing streak, aren't I? I don't know who took the treasure from Simon at the police station the day he went in. I don't have any proof Simon was killed. I don't know who's been messing with my head at my home. Nobody's going to believe me and I don't blame them. Nobody in their right mind is going to believe allegations from a woman who's just lost her husband. They'll just say I've lost the plot with grief."

"It should be easy enough to find out who was on duty when Simon went in with the treasure," remarked Eilidh.

"But he could've gone in any time that week," said Janey, fretful. "I don't know exactly when he went."

Richard and Eilidh looked at her.

"I told you he didn't communicate much," she insisted.

Watching the disbelief on their faces, she blushed.

"To be honest, we weren't getting on at all well back then. We had big issues in our marriage. And I was busy. Spring is the start of business picking up at our restaurant," she added. "Whenever I asked him about it, he just bit my head off. There was no way of reasoning with him."

"Would his friends have a better idea of when he went in?" suggested Eilidh.

"Maybe," agreed Janey.

She shrugged.

"He had a few friends. Not many though. He was a loner, really."

"Well," said Richard, rubbing his hair thoughtfully. "It might surprise you to know that I've been informed, by a contact of mine, about a possible treasure find on Harris. We do look into these things as the Art and Antiquities Unit and we work UK wide. As soon as we get clearance, we're hopefully going to be heading up there to investigate."

He looked at Janey.

"It could be helpful to have you there, Janey, as you knew Simon best. You'd be best placed to know what areas he tended to frequent, what people he was close to on the island, and who he might have spoken to about the treasure."

Janey nodded in agreement.

"I can go back home to Harris for a couple of weeks, that's not a problem, but I'll be going without the kids. They won't mind. They're attending the local school at the moment, and they're having a great time playing with their cousins."

Janey paused for a moment.

"You're welcome to stay with me when you go up

there. I'd feel safer having someone else in the house, to be honest with you," she admitted.

"We'll definitely consider your kind offer," Richard assured her, remembering his chat with Lionel about cutting costs and raising funding for their department.

Unfortunately, he knew fine and well they wouldn't be able to take up Janey's offer of hospitality, but he understood her fears, rational or not, and wasn't underestimating what it would cost her to return to Harris.

Richard passed his notebook and pen to Janey.

"If you can write down your contact details for us, Janey, we'll be in touch to let you know when we'll be arriving on the island."

She scribbled down her details and then looked up, smiling wryly at them.

"You're going to have to watch your backs when you're in Harris. Someone up there has gone completely loopy. Whoever killed my husband, burgled my home, and left little 'gifts' for me isn't going to be a safe person to be around."

"We might have to take our chances," acknowledged Richard, wondering just how dangerous a police officer from a small island community like Harris could be.

Janey had a valid point, though. He wasn't used to the rough and tumble of police work, unlike many of his colleagues at New Scotland Yard.

He was certain there would be streetwise members of the Homicide Unit who could probably outmatch any islander police officer, in both aggression and craftiness. Not that he was suggesting he'd ever want to put it to the test. The police officers working in the Homicide teams seemed hard enough to rein in as it was, according to his contacts in the department, and would need little encouragement to take things too far.

However, there was one thing he was sure of. He'd have done a better job at flogging the torc and engraved cup on the black market than the rogue police officer had. The police officer had made a complete shambles of the sale. The fact that news of the island treasure had filtered all the way down to London and New Scotland Yard was a prime example of their carelessness. Obviously, a beginner at the game of fencing stolen goods, the bent cop hadn't managed to keep the sale of the torc and the cup secret, which meant that the ripples from the illicit sale would be widening ever outwards, and no doubt would soon be attracting a lot of unsavoury characters to the island.

Richard wasn't too worried about this.

Whoever might be trying to get their hands on the rest of the treasure had probably never dealt with the likes of Mike Telford before. Now that Mike had committed himself to chasing after the treasure, Richard felt it was doubtful a corrupt copper would be able to outwit him and gain the upper hand.

Mike, who was used to dealing with all kinds of lawbreakers during his eventful career as a private detective, could have taken a doctorate on the criminal mind and passed it with flying colours. Mainly because most of the time he thought like one himself.

Richard was sure Mike would pop up on the Scottish island in the near future.

Much to Richard's envy, Mike had significant financial backers and, in turn, a wide remit in his investigations. As a result of this, he could pick and choose the cases he worked on. He was supported in his work by a number of international governments, as well as several well-known and wealthy art enthusiasts and collectors.

The same kind of people Lionel was expecting Richard to approach, cap in hand, to raise funds for their own department.

Mike also worked hand-in-glove with several museums and a couple of high-profile auction houses. Items from a Viking treasure hoard would be just up their street, in the unlikely event that the Scottish government didn't consider them a national treasure that should be kept secure in Scotland's own prestigious museums.

Richard felt the call of nature.

"Eilidh, can I leave you to finish up? I need to dash," he said, in an urgent voice.

She nodded, looking surprised.

Without waiting for further encouragement, Richard raced out of the interview room to find the nearest toilet.

4

Mike

Mike took a bite out of his sausage roll and stared at the skyline.

There were cranes everywhere.

Birmingham was a city that was always changing, reinventing itself, and he couldn't keep up with its new architecture.

In front of him, three modern tower blocks were clustered together.

An ugly square building, which looked to Mike like a Kipling's French Fancy cake, was tucked in behind them.

When Mike had stood on same spot, two years ago, none of them had been built.

He averted his eyes and looked down at the canal.

At least the canal, winding its way through the city, remained unchanged.

A colourful barge drifted past, its paint peeling off.

The canal reminded Mike of a bygone era in Birmingham.

Meanwhile, these days, Birmingham's disused

factories, some dating from the time of the Industrial Revolution, were slowly getting converted into upmarket residential properties.

In their wake, coffee shops, restaurants, and bars had blossomed.

As long as they didn't erase the history out of Birmingham, Mike didn't mind. And boy, did Birmingham have a lot of history. There was evidence of human activity there dating back to 8000 BC.

The area Mike knew best, though, was the Jewellery Quarter, which had evolved over the space of two hundred years. Nowadays, it was estimated that up to forty percent of the UK's jewellery production came from there.

Trade in the Jewellery Quarter was much less than in the past, due to lack of demand and foreign competition, but Mike felt it needed to be preserved. The demise of the jewellery business in Birmingham would in his opinion be a tragedy, and what's more would also have a knock-on effect on the number of tourists visiting the area.

Mike was also worried the rich toffs would price out the people who lived and worked in the Jewellery Quarter, taking away its unique identity. He had good reason to think this would happen, because the Jewellery Quarter was considered a trendy place to live these days.

It had become even more fashionable after famous street artist Banksy painted a reindeer mural on Vyse Street.

The mural was of two reindeer painted onto a brick wall, right next to a bench. It reminded the onlooker of Santa's sleigh. No one really knew what the meaning behind the Banksy mural was but that didn't matter.

A video posted online by Banksy showed a rough sleeper lying on the bench, while the reindeer appeared to spirit him up to the night sky.

The *Birmingham Mail* had proudly reported Banksy's social media post:

> *"God bless Birmingham. In the 20 minutes we filmed Ryan on this bench, passersby gave him a hot drink, two chocolate bars, and a lighter-without him ever asking for anything."*

Another edition of the newspaper declared that the Vyse Street mural was attracting people from London to Dubai.

Mike felt this statement was dubious. Why would someone travel to Birmingham when they could visit Paris or Rome?

While the three hundred acres or so of the Jewellery Quarter had become the focus of business improvement initiatives by local government, there were teething problems because some of the property developers had complained about the noise coming from some of the factories in the area. The factories, though, had been there long before the property developers came along.

However, according to local shop owners, a truce had been reached between both sides, with some streets designated good for residential development and others earmarked for business premises.

Several workshops were still owned by the city council, so newbie jewellery designers, just out of college, were able to rent units at an affordable rate. So far, thankfully, the property developers hadn't managed to get their grubby hands on the cheap studio space. Not for want of trying, Mike suspected.

In general, local residents seemed content with the way things were going, which was just as well, thought Mike. There had been ethnic riots between communities in Birmingham before and sometimes it felt like it wouldn't take much to light the fuse again.

Using his hand, Mike brushed bits of the sausage roll's pastry off his jumper.

He picked up his Coke can from the ground, drank the dregs, and then tossed it into a nearby bin.

Scowling for a last time at the tower blocks on the other side of the canal, he started to make his way to Hylton Street.

He was in no rush to get to his destination, so he stopped for a moment in front of St Paul's Church, appreciating a small slice of greenery in such a built-up city.

St Paul's was another part of the city that remained unchanged, just like the canals. Birmingham's early merchants and manufacturers had attended the church, although no doubt the congregation was very different now.

Walking on, Mike passed through the familiar red brick buildings of the Jewellery Quarter and dozens of its retail units.

He came to a stop, ten minutes later, in front of a three-storey building on Hylton Street.

A brass plaque next to the entrance had *"The Midas Touch Workshop"* engraved on it.

Mike pushed open the door and walked into a tiled hallway.

On one side, behind the desk, was a uniformed man.

Mike studied him with interest.

The man was not a typical building attendant. For a start, he had a scar that stretched from his eyebrow down to his chin. He looked, in fact, like an Italian bruiser.

"Hello, may I help you?" asked the attendant, looking up.

"Yes, I was wanting to speak with Mariella Giuseppi."

"I'm afraid she's busy all afternoon and asked not to be disturbed."

"Could you at least try to ask her? Tell her it's Mike Telford. She knows who I am, and I've come a long way to see her."

The attendant thought about this.

"OK," he said, reluctantly.

He lifted a receiver and put a call through.

"Mariella, there's a Mike Telford down here, wanting to speak with you."

There was a long pause and then Mike could catch the Mariella's voice on the other side, talking volubly in Italian.

"*Sì, OK*," said the attendant, at last.

He put the phone down and looked at Mike with respect.

"You been in some kind of a relationship with her?" he asked.

"Sort of. Why?"

"She said that you can fuck off. You're banned from the building and if you resist, I'm to shoot you. Sorry."

Mike glanced at the attendant's jacket and saw there was indeed a suspicious bulge on the left-hand side. Guns were banned and illegal in the UK, but Mike wasn't prepared to question the security guard about this. That was going to be more trouble than it was worth.

He shrugged.

"You win some, you lose some," he said. "Someday someone should tell Mariella that it's *'better to have loved and lost than never to have loved at all'*."

With that parting shot, Mike walked out.

Instead of heading back the way he came, he reached the side of the building and made his way down the alleyway to the wasteland behind it.

Standing to one side, so he couldn't be spotted from one of the windows, he scrutinised the layout of the building.

There was a fire escape at the back, as you'd expect in a building where soldering and welding took place on a daily basis.

The third floor had the lights on.

Mike decided to chance it.

He climbed the rusty stairs until he reached the third floor and then peered through the window next to fire escape door.

It was a dirty window and Mike moved his head from side to side as he tried to get a look inside.

Before Mike had decided what his next move should be, he caught sight of a missile flying straight at him and ducked to one side.

Accompanied by the sound of breaking glass, a

hammer whirled through the window and then disappeared into the greenery below.

A curvaceous lady with a mass of blonde curls stuck her head out of the smashed window.

"*Sei uno stronzo!* Nico told you to fuck off. Why can't you take no for an answer?"

"Please, Mariella, I need to speak with you," pleaded Mike, raising his hands placatingly.

"No."

"It's important."

Mike bent down again as Mariella threw a pair of pliers at him.

This time, the tool caught the edge of his neck and nicked it.

"Ow! Shit!" yelled Mike, holding onto his neck. "You crazy woman, you'll be done for assault!"

"Ha! I know what you want, you dirty old man. And you're not getting it. End of story."

Mike looked down at the blood on his fingertips.

"Well, I'm happy to give up on getting laid, if that's what you mean."

"Bastard!"

An inkpot was hurled at him, but Mike managed to bat it away with his arm.

"Mariella, I have two buyers interested."

"I don't care."

"It would be an easy sale," Mike said, cajolingly.

"I told you, I don't care," repeated Mariella.

Mike quickly moved to the side as a mug went flying past his head.

He wondered how many other weapons Mariella had to hand. At this rate, it could turn out to be a long afternoon.

"The British Museum's interested," he said, as a last resort.

A speculative look came into Mariella's eyes.

"Oh, really?" she said, leaning close.

Mike relaxed as he saw her folded arms.

"Yes."

"Won't be good enough, I'm afraid. Can't compete with an offer from a Chinese billionaire."

"Come on, Mariella. Be realistic. I'm not the only one who knows you have them. They'll be others following soon enough. You need to get the stuff moved or you'll be in deep shit. Quick and easy, that's what I'm offering you."

"No, thank you! I've already had that from you. Quick and easy! Ha! Hell will freeze over before I give anything to you."

Mike rolled his eyes.

"For fuck's sake, Mariella. I'm not talking about our love life."

"Love life? Ha!"

Mariella reached out of the window with a metal ruler and tried to swat Mike's head with it.

Mike seized her wrist and held it in a firm grasp as Mariella tried to pull back.

"Let me go, you piece of filth!"

"Enough," said Mike, sternly. "Will you at least listen to what I have to offer?"

Mariella looked at him, her eyes suddenly swimming in tears.

She shook her head.

"I've already told you. I don't want anything to do with you."

Mike cursed himself for getting romantically

involved with Mariella in the first place. He really should've known better. In his line of work, you couldn't afford to mix business with pleasure. And what's more, *Hell hath no fury like a woman scorned,* he thought. He had to find out the genius who came up with that line.

He took a deep breath.

"Look, I'm sorry I left as I did two years ago. I really am sorry. But that was two years ago, Mariella. Can't you let it go?"

Mariella shook her head.

Mike looked at her.

"Please don't tell me you took the artefacts to get back at me."

Mariella started laughing.

"Oh, for goodness sake, Mike! I knew you had a big ego but this is the limit. The absolute limit! I've been working as a fence for longer than I've known you. Much longer, in fact."

"Well, if that's the case, you'll also know it won't be long before you're in danger."

"I know that, bright spark. The goods are leaving here soon."

Mariella tugged her arm free and glared at Mike.

"You need to go now."

"At least tell me who you're using as a courier."

"Nope, sorry."

Mariella moved away from the window and left the room.

Mike sighed.

It looked as though he'd come to the end of the road.

However, he wasn't one to give up easily, even when dealing with a feisty maniac like Mariella.

He had one advantage over her. His training enabled him to keep a cool head, unlike Mariella, who was as hot-blooded as they came. He knew Mariella pretty well and his gut instinct was telling him that she would probably keep the valuable artefacts close by her, at all times. Unless she was handing them over to a courier at the workshop that very day, there was a good chance she'd be carrying both items home with her.

It was also Thursday, and knowing Mariella she probably had plans to go out to a bar or a restaurant after work. Possibly with her Italian bodyguard in tow.

Mike made his way down the fire escape, walked up the road until he was out of sight, and then made a call.

Satisfied with the outcome of his call, he bought a newspaper, and made his way to The Hive Café and Bakery on Vittoria Street.

The Hive Café and Bakery was a community café, based in a large industrial building, and it helped young people with learning difficulties gain baking and cookery skills.

Having ordered a huge slice of chocolate cake and a mocha, Mike settled in for the afternoon.

He ordered refills until the café began to shut at quarter to five, at which point, after checking his mobile for messages, he made his way to the Lasan Indian Restaurant near St. Paul's Square.

He knew Mariella wouldn't go near an Indian restaurant, so he would be safe there.

He started the evening by ordering three starters, one after the other, spaced out. He resisted ordering a beer, aware that he had to keep his wits about him.

At six thirty precisely, a text came through from his contact: *Target left premises.*

By the time the next text came, Mike had eaten his way through onion bhajis with cucumber raita, vegetable pakoras, chatpati chaat, and several papadums.

It was now seven thirty and Mike was getting impatient.

He picked up the phone and read: *Target settled in Cucina Rustica. Can't get near the bag. Between her feet.*

Mike texted: *Don't worry. She likes her drink. Give it time.*

His mobile replied: *Good job it's your dosh.*

Mike sighed.

He texted: *Out of interest, who's she with?*

A grey-haired dude.

Romantic?

WTF? Could be. She's well tarted up.

OK.

Mike caught the eye of the waiter and asked for the menu. It was going to be a long night.

He also made a mental note to buy some Gaviscon Double Action from a late-night pharmacy at the earliest available opportunity. His stomach wasn't as strong as it used to be.

Halfway through his chicken korma, another text came in: *Definitely romantic* ♥

Mike wished the text didn't bother him as much as it did.

He started browsing Sky News.

At nine thirty, the waiter was standing by Mike's table with the bill.

"Anything else, sir?"

"No, thank you. I might finish up with a drink at the bar."

The waiter brightened up.

"Of course, sir. Anil will get you sorted."

Mike got up and made his way to the bar, wondering what alcoholic drink would put to rest the enormous meal he'd consumed. An Irish coffee, maybe?

Another text pinged on his phone.

Gone to The Jewellers Arms. She's trolleyed.

Hopeful, thought Mike.

If they didn't get the bag off her tonight, they might still get a chance to search her flat. Always assuming she went home with her Romeo boy, of course.

Twenty-five minutes later, he got the text he was waiting for.

Got the bag! She was busy gassing to a woman in the ladies. Big mistake. See you in 5.

Mike left his barely begun Irish coffee and made his way to their agreed rendezvous.

5

Eilidh

Eilidh stood at the front of the house, shoulders back, and let out a long sigh.

It was peaceful.

In front of her, the seawater rippled to the hazy horizon.

Rocks beneath her tumbled down to the water's edge, covered in barnacles and seaweed.

Above them, green reeds swayed in the breeze.

Further up the slope, where Eilidh was standing, irises were growing against the garden fence, tangled up among bright wildflowers.

A burn murmured next to the house, tumbling down the mossy slope, onto the rocks, then into the sea.

It was quiet, so blissfully quiet, thought Eilidh.

She felt renewed.

The same, sadly, couldn't be said of Richard, who was sitting at the picnic table, book in hand.

Even on such a lovely day, Richard was thinking about work.

He was busy reading a book called *The Golden*

Treasure of the Entente Cordiale. A book designed to be a real treasure hunt map.

Eilidh knew Richard wasn't interested in the book for its own sake. He was thinking of his department's future monetary woes. Ever since his chat with Lionel, the stress of raising money for his department was always at the back of his mind.

The Golden Treasure of the Entente Cordiale was part history book, part encrypted treasure map, and she knew Richard was hoping that if he cracked the nine puzzles in the book he'd be able to claim the £650,000 golden casket.

Michel Becker, an artist, had bought up the golden casket. Eilidh often wondered how such an important relic had come up for auction. Now it had ended up as part of an extraordinary national treasure hunt.

The casket had been gifted to France by Britain ahead of the signing of the Entente Cordiale, an agreement which attempted to end centuries of antagonism between the two countries. The Entente Cordiale was signed in April 1904, finally establishing a diplomatic understanding between Britain and France.

Given the all-time low of diplomatic relations between Britain and France these days, Richard was sure Michel Becker had created the treasure hunt as a publicity stunt because he wanted to remind people of a time when relations were actually good between the two countries.

Richard's interest in the casket, though, was more mercenary than sentimental or historical.

His latest effort at bridging part of his department's funding gap smacked of desperation to Eilidh, but she wasn't going to add to his woes by saying so. He'd come to his senses soon enough.

Eilidh noticed Richard had a deep frown on his face as he read the book.

He turned a page, lost in his own world.

Watching him, Eilidh hoped he was going to cope with the challenge of living with a baby and becoming a father.

She rubbed her bump.

It would probably be enough to make him lose the plot completely, like many new dads before him.

She sighed and looked out to sea again.

Eilidh didn't regret coming up to Harris. Stubborn to a fault, she had insisted on accompanying Richard.

Who wouldn't want to be on the trail of what could turn out to be one of the most significant treasure finds in the UK?

She felt no guilt about twisting his arm about it because she'd already made herself useful.

For a start, Richard was notoriously disorganised, often finding himself making bookings at the last minute and ending up with a second-rate choice of accommodation. Thanks to Eilidh's diligent research, they were now based in a lovely cottage, ten minutes by car outside Tarbert, and close to Scalpay.

A perfect, out-of-the-way location for their investigation, while at the same time enabling them to enjoy some of the awesome Harris scenery.

Eilidh looked at her watch.

She was dressed in her pyjamas and they were leaving soon for the police station in Tarbert, the same police station that Simon Buchanon had supposedly gone to with his three pieces of treasure.

She went into the house and put some warm clothes on. She was thankful that they were there in the month of May, because even in late spring the breeze in Harris was bitingly cold.

"Eilidh, are you ready?" she could hear Richard calling from the door.

"Yes, ready as I'll ever be," she said, smiling at him as she walked out.

Richard shut the door and locked up.

In a place like Harris, locking up felt like an unnecessary precaution. Harris, compared to London, felt safe and otherworldly, detached from the moral vacuum that the rest of humankind lived in.

This impression was further confirmed when they parked outside the police station.

They both stared at the tiny building in disbelief.

A wooden fence surrounded the garden in front of the police station.

The building itself looked no different to any of the other houses in the town. One storey, with a slate-tiled roof and roughcast, white-painted walls.

What's more, it was dwarfed by the coastguard building next door.

Only a small blue sign on the fence stating 'Tarbert Police Station' indicated that they were in the right spot.

"Is that it?" asked Eilidh, incredulous.

"Seems to be," replied Richard, equally baffled

They got out of the car and walked up to the station, feeling as though they were doing a home visit.

Richard rang the doorbell.

The door opened straight away and a broad man in police uniform stood at the entrance.

He had a jovial face, a shock of black hair, and caterpillar eyebrows.

"Hullo! Richard Langley, is it?"

Richard nodded with a smile.

"Wylcome! I'm Rory Petrie. Wha micht ye be?" asked Rory, peering at Eilidh.

"Detective Inspector Eilidh Simmons," said Eilidh, with a broad smile.

"Bonny as a picture," said Rory, admiringly. "Come in 'n git a cuppa. Ye tak' milk?"

"Yes, please," said Eilidh, smothering a smile at the blank expression on Richard's face.

Richard and Eilidh followed Rory, who led them to a room at the back of the premises.

Did this room double up as an interrogation room, Eilidh wondered as she walked in.

There was a wooden table and six chairs in the middle of the room. A bookcase, with some dog-eared paperback books in it, was against one wall.

Richard sat down on a chair at the table, but Eilidh stayed standing as she walked around the room, studying the information posters on the wall.

"Ah wull gang fetch Will 'n git th' brew," said Rory, disappearing off.

"Did you get that?" Richard asked Eilidh.

"Yeah, sure," said Eilidh. "He's going to fetch Will and get us a cup of tea. You're going to have to get with the lingo up here, Richard, or you'll be in trouble."

Richard nodded.

"Just as well you came with me."

"You're a very, very lucky man," said Eilidh, putting on a seductive voice.

Richard grinned at her.

"Don't I know it," he agreed.

Five minutes later, Rory appeared at the door carrying three mugs in his large hands.

Following behind him was a slender man, a good bit older than Rory, with a freckled face and a receding hairline.

"This is Will," announced Rory, passing round the tea

"Good morning," said Will, stretching a hand to Richard and Eilidh.

"Morning," said Richard.

Once Will and Rory were seated, Richard took out his notebook.

"May I ask how many of you work here?"

"Sure. Thir's us twa o'coorse. Then thir's John Duncan. He's th' detective inspector, based oan th' mainland."

"CID only turn up when there's a major problem up here, which isn't very often," explained Will. "Aleksy Nowak works here, too. He's a constable."

Rory nodded.

"He's Polish."

"And then there's Hamish Bennett. He's a sergeant. They're both on nightshift this week. The other sergeant is Tracey Donegan. We have four other constables, Stu Hall, Fiona Mitchell, Matthew McCloud, and Lewis Burns."

"Am I right in saying it was you two who interviewed Janey Buchanon?" asked Richard.

"Aye, poor wifie. She teuk her husband's death ill, so she did," said Rory.

"Yes, as you'd expect," agreed Richard. "However, she's adamant her husband came to the police station with the three pieces of treasure he'd found. Nobody seems to know what happened to them. Would you be able to tell me who was at the station on that day?"

Rory and Will looked at each other, uneasy.

"Please don't worry," added Richard, somewhat hastily. "I should reassure you both that we're here with the blessing of the Assistant Chief Constable of the Highlands and Islands Division, Sophie McLeod. We're not looking to create any problems. It's just that as a department we have to look into these things."

"Feel free to check with Sophie McLeod, if you wish to," interjected Eilidh, impatient with the sluggish pace of their meeting. "I'm sure she'll have spoken to John Duncan about us."

"Na tis a'richt," said Rory, after Will nodded at him. "Ah will gang check oor records 'n see if ah kin fin' oot whin he came in."

He left the room.

Will frowned.

"Are we being investigated?" he asked, in a quiet voice.

"Not at all. My remit is the treasure, that's all. I manage the Art and Antiquities Unit in London. I don't deal with any other unit unless it's necessary."

Will nodded, looking relieved.

"I remember Janey insisting that her husband left the treasure here," he said. "Nuts, poor woman. For a start, there's usually more than one person here at the station."

"What made you interview her about the treasure then?" asked Eilidh.

"We received three anonymous calls stating that Simon Buchanon had found some Viking treasure. We have to look into the calls, of course, just in case. This time it seems people were bluffing. People get bored on an island as quiet as this one. Easy for them to cry wolf over the stupidest things."

Richard looked at him curiously.

"You've heard nothing about the treasure since then?"

"Nope. Gone completely quiet on that front. It's a real shame Janey felt she had to leave the island with her children. My kids miss them at school, but I understand she needed to get away. She was breaking her back running that restaurant, too. It was hard graft, so it was."

Rory came back into the room, carrying a small piece of paper.

"'Ere we gang. Simon signed in on the twelfth of April. Fiona and Stu were oan th' premises that day. Och, 'n Anne, th' receptionist, tae."

"Brilliant. Thank you, Rory," said Richard gratefully as he tucked the piece of paper into his notebook. "We would, of course, like to have a chat with them when they can spare the time."

Will nodded.

"That'll not be a problem. Where are you staying?"

"We're staying near Urgha. At the Tystie Cottage," said Eilidh, thinking how Norse "Urgha" sounded.

Both men nodded.

"Juist gies yer mobile numbers and we'll git in titch," said Rory.

"Great," said Richard, scribbling down Eilidh's and his mobile numbers.

He ripped the page off the notebook and handed it over to Will, who'd held out his hand for it.

"Good," said Will, smiling. "Thanks for dropping by. I'm sorry we don't have much information to give you on the treasure. I hope it doesn't all turn out to be a wild goose chase for you."

It was crystal clear to Eilidh and Richard that both Will and Rory hoped their visit to Harris would turn out to be a waste of time.

Eilidh didn't blame them for this attitude.

Harris was such a peaceful, sleepy place. The pace of life there was slow and she didn't think anyone was prepared, least of all the police, for the turbulence that would follow the discovery of an important treasure trove on the island. One that might be of international significance, what's more.

The only ones who'd be rubbing their hands with glee would be the tourist operators on the island.

After they'd bid Will and Rory a cheery goodbye, Eilidh and Richard decided to stop at the Herringbone Café, which was located near the public car park

They placed their order at the counter and then went to sit outside in the small courtyard, enjoying the sunshine.

The courtyard was empty, with most people preferring to sit inside the coffee shop where there was a fire burning.

Even so, Eilidh could see a few faces peering at them through the café windows.

She guessed the tourist season hadn't kicked in properly yet, and they were both the new kids on the block. At least, that's what it felt like.

"Why am I suddenly feeling guilty?" mused Eilidh, turning her head to look at the harbour. "As though we're on holiday, when in fact this could end up being a murder investigation."

"Enjoy the sun while it lasts," said Richard, smiling at her affectionately. "I don't think the weather's going to hold out for long."

Eilidh nodded and tilted her head back to catch the sun's rays.

Richard reached across and caressed her hand under the table, sending little pinpricks of desire up her arm.

She opened her eyes, leant towards him and kissed him full on the lips, relishing his embarrassment as she did so.

Richard didn't do public displays of affection, but unfortunately for him Eilidh couldn't care less who saw them. Life was too short, in her opinion.

She wondered for a moment what the café's customers were thinking and then shrugged the thought away.

After a moment or two, she pulled away and smiled at him.

Richard shook his head in amused disapproval.

"You never change."

"No," she admitted, smiling.

"Andrew!" hollered a man on other side of the street, bending his head back to look at a window on the second floor of the house in front of them.

The sash window opened and a teenage boy popped his head out.

"Whit's it, da?"

"Th' ferry's arriving soon. Git yer arse doon 'ere."

The boy rolled his eyes and slammed shut the window.

Eilidh looked across at Richard, who was now studying his phone, his glasses halfway down his nose.

His tawny locks were curled at the base of his neck, his fringe covering his eyebrows, giving the impression Richard was a human sheepdog. She was going to have to drag him to a hairdresser's here or he'd end up with a mullet by the time they returned to London.

She thought about their relationship and felt some sympathy for Richard. The poor guy had no idea what was in store for him in the longer term. She was always going to be trying to fix his dishevelled appearance, even if it was a losing battle. She also knew she was never going to grow tired of teasing him with her public displays of affection. It was just too easy to wind up someone as sensitive and introverted as he was.

Leaving him to catch up on his emails and recover from her kiss, she undid the buttons on her cardigan. Stretched tight over her ever-growing belly, it was now causing her some discomfort whenever she sat down.

She sighed.

She was reliving all the awkwardness of her teenage years with her changing shape and she wasn't convinced her body would ever go back to what it was.

The health service ought to do a better job at preparing and supporting pregnant women, preparing them for the loss of their bodies during pregnancy and afterwards, she thought to herself. Especially when the statistics were so high for post-natal depression.

She looked up and watched as the waitress brought across their drinks and the two pieces of shortbread they'd ordered. Eilidh felt as though she could eat five of them. She was also adjusting to having food cravings every minute of the day.

"Ye 'ere oan holiday?" asked the waitress, with interest, as she plonked the drinks and shortbread on the table.

"No," said Eilidh, smiling. "Work, unfortunately."

"That's a pity. Thir's bonnie beaches round about."

"So I've heard," agreed Eilidh. "I'm sure we'll get a chance to take a look at some point."

"Mak' sure ye dae. It wull be worth yer while," said the waitress, nodding. "Anythin' else fur ye?"

"No, this is perfect, thank you," said Eilidh, getting an enticing waft of her decaf latte.

The waitress nodded and walked off to serve some other customers.

Eilidh giggled.

"Now we're really going to have to explore these lovely beaches. It's becoming more and more like a holiday."

"We'll fit them in," said Richard, sipping his Americano, which was piping hot, just as he liked it.

"Have you got any ideas while we wait for the others to contact us?"

Richard made a face.

"No, not really. Nothing above board, that is. I'm strongly tempted to ask a pal in the Fraud Squad to run background checks on the three who were on duty the day Simon rolled up. There's always a chance that whoever took the artefacts was needing the cash."

"Or they were just plain greedy," said Eilidh, ever the cynic. "I'd hold off if I were you. Doing a background check on another police officer is a risky strategy. It could come back to bite you."

Richard raised his eyebrows in surprise at her.

"I know, I know", said Eilidh, raising her hands.

"It's not like me to follow the rules and be cautious when hunting for these things. Must be the pregnancy. It's making me hyper-careful."

"It sure is," agreed Richard, recalling the many times when Eilidh had been more reckless.

Eilidh took a bite out of her shortbread as she thought about the case.

"At the back of my mind, I've my doubts about this 'dodgy' police officer," she said, at last. "We're basing our entire case on what Janey and Mike Telford have told us."

Richard said nothing.

She knew what he was thinking. Janey might be an unknown entity but Mike Telford was always on the money.

"I mean, Janey could have disposed of the treasure herself. Saying Simon left it at the police station could be a red herring," she insisted.

Richard shook his head.

"Mike's contacts said it was a police officer who got in touch with them. They always check these things out because they don't ever want to get caught by an under-cover sting. The fence was either brave, or else a complete gambler, to go ahead and buy items of such rarity and value off a police officer. Full of pitfalls. A corrupt police officer's going to be conspicuous and there's no anonymity. They're not going to be able to change their identity and go underground when things get difficult, which sooner or later they always do. The fence has to wonder too what'll happen if the police officer decides to confess at some point."

"The whole thing seems so improbable."

"It does, but finding treasure's improbable, too, and

yet it happens, more often than you'd think. Especially now that metal detecting in the UK has taken off and become a national craze. And throughout history bizarre things have been done for the sake of treasure..." Richard took a sip of his coffee. "I'm debating whether we should ask Janey to take us to where Simon went scuba diving. She said he found the treasure on one of his scallop hunts."

Eilidh wrinkled her nose.

"Not sure that's going to be worthwhile. We've only got limited time, and in any case, he's supposedly moved the treasure from there, hasn't he?"

Richard put his mug down and groaned.

"I know. I'm still struggling to come to terms with the fact he moved the treasure from its location. Total madness. Quite aside from the treasure, the site itself could have revealed new, exciting historical facts. It's quite possible the treasure was part of a Viking burial chamber. Any archaeologist worth their salt would be utterly horrified by what he did."

Eilidh nodded.

"Yep. Regardless of whoever sold the treasure on the black market, Simon Buchanon doesn't come out of this squeaky clean, either. I think we should waste no time in meeting with the people he knows on the island, especially his close friends and family. He might have said something to one of them about it."

"We need to call Janey and make up a list of potential interviewees," agreed Richard. "We should try and find out more about the man himself, too. The answers to this riddle all lie with him. We're not going to find where Simon hid the treasure unless we can get inside his head."

Some customers came out into the courtyard and the tables started filling up.

Richard leaned back on his chair and relaxed. There was no point carrying on their conversation with eavesdroppers close at hand.

Taking advantage of this, Eilidh pointed to his shortbread.

"Are you wanting that?"

Richard laughed.

"Take it. I can order another one."

Eilidh felt like she'd won the lottery.

She pulled the plate towards her and set to.

6

Richard

Richard was standing outside the Time or Tide pub, waiting for the others to turn up.

The building was made of grey stone, wood and thatch, blending in with the dull colour of the sea in front of it.

Richard estimated that, at a conservative guess, the house was maybe forty metres long. Its shape looked exactly like a Viking longhouse, except for the chimneys at both ends, puffing out clouds of dark smoke.

Five seagulls were perched on the roof, twisting their heads backwards and forwards as they watched the people below. Their presence probably had something to do with the aroma of fish and chips emanating from the pub door.

The smell of fish and chips was melding with that of burning peat from the chimney. It was so pungent that Richard had a feeling he was going to have to put his clothes in the washing machine as soon as he got back home.

He became nostalgic for a moment, remembering

his student days and the times he'd washed his clothes after carefree drinking sprees in smoky London pubs.

Smoking in pubs was banned now, of course. These days the die-hard addicts smoked outside the pubs he used to frequent in London, often dressed in skimpy clothes even in the coldest of weather conditions.

The indoor smoking ban wasn't affecting business in Harris. A steady stream of pubgoers had been entering Time or Tide while he waited outside, many of them staring at him with interest as they walked past.

Several wished Richard a good evening, much to his surprise. As a born and bred Londoner, he wasn't used to being greeted in a friendly manner by strangers. In London such a greeting would make you check you still had your wallet on you.

His first impression of the pub's clientele was good. Most seemed to know each other and all ages were gathered there. As yet, he hadn't spotted any potential troublemakers, which was just as well, because he hadn't been at all keen on the location for the forthcoming meeting.

It was out of his comfort zone to deal with work matters inside a pub. No doubt Mike Telford would feel right at home conducting business there. However, Richard did not think a pub was an appropriate place to try and have a serious conversation about Simon Buchanon and the missing treasure. The police officers he was meeting, though, had insisted on welcoming him in true "Harris" fashion, which of course meant alcohol.

If the mountain won't come to Muhammad, then Muhammad must go to the mountain, Eilidh had said sternly to Richard, keen for him to go along with it.

Eilidh, as always, wanted things to move on swiftly,

but Richard sensed that in Harris nothing happened at a fast speed and he was beginning to very much doubt their investigation would.

While he was at the pub, Eilidh was going to wait at their house for Janey, who was dropping by to help her make up a comprehensive list of Simon's friends and family.

Eilidh was also hoping to persuade Janey to introduce them to some of Simon's close acquaintances. Within a small island community, they both felt that the best way of gaining a measure of trust with potential witnesses was to be introduced by someone known to them.

"Ye'r th' Sassenach, aren't ye?" asked a deep voice, behind him.

Richard turned around and found himself looking down at an old man with a walking stick.

The man had an unkempt look about him, like a mothballed jumper that had been left in the cupboard for too long, but his black eyes were bright and intelligent.

"Sasse–what?" asked Richard, confused.

The man spat on the ground, only just missing Richard's shoes.

"Ne'er mynd, laddie. Ye'll fin oot soon enough whit that means. We've tae mony o' ye sassenach comin' tae bide 'ere. We fought a lot o' wars tae keep ye fowk oot o' Scootlund."

Richard looked at him in amusement.

"Well, I can assure you, I won't be staying here long-term."

"Guid," said the old man, nodding his approval.

He turned and walked to the pub.

Richard didn't dare go and open the door for him. Somehow, he didn't think the gesture would be welcome.

"Richard! Sorry we're late! Long day at the office," shouted a woman from a distance.

Richard turned to look up the hill.

His welcome party had arrived at last.

Tall, blonde, and broad-shouldered, the lady at the front of the group was dressed in a pair of sports leggings and a sweatshirt.

She strode confidently down the hill, swinging her arms.

Her actions had an almost military air to them, thought Richard, as he watched her cross the tarmac to where he was standing.

Walking behind her was a man with a shaved head and a middle-aged woman in a red suit.

Fiona Mitchell was the blonde woman, he guessed. The bloke was Stuart Hall and the smart, middle-aged lady in red had to be Anne Gibson, the receptionist.

"Nice to meet you at last, Richard. We were told you were coming up to see us a good few days ago," said Fiona when she reached him.

"Yes, these things always take longer than you'd think," admitted Richard, nodding his head.

She offered him a hand.

As he shook it, he noticed the veins on the back of her hands bulged outwards.

Her handshake was firm and strong, crushing his fingers in its grip.

Maybe she did some heavy-duty workouts at the gym, he thought, wincing. Not that he was an expert on any kind of exercise. Far from it.

He noticed Fiona had a tattoo of the Argentinian revolutionary Che Guevara on her right wrist.

He resisted a smile. He couldn't imagine anything more alien to Che Guevara than the sleepy Scottish island they were on.

"He was a freedom fighter," explained Fiona, seeing him do a double-take at her tattoo. "Something that I'm all in favour of. Anyway, let me introduce you to Stu Hall."

He turned and shook hands with Stu, who was standing awkwardly beside him.

"Good to meet you," Richard said, with a smile.

In faded jeans, a grey hoodie, and a puffer jacket, Stu looked young. Almost a teenager, in fact.

"And you must be Anne Gibson, the day-time receptionist?" asked Richard, turning to the woman in the red suit.

"That's right, sir," said Anne, not volunteering a handshake, but smiling warmly at him instead. "Always there between nine and five-thirty."

"Have any of the regulars introduced themselves?" Fiona asked Richard.

Richard shook his head.

"No, but some of them did say hello."

Fiona laughed.

"They don't bite, I promise. I'm making them sound like candidates for the dragon's den, aren't I? They're not such a bad bunch, when you get to know them. Have you seen the inside of the pub yet, Richard? It's quite different."

"No, I'm afraid I haven't ventured in yet."

"Quite right to wait," affirmed Stu, with a grin. "They're a nosy bunch. You wouldn't have had a minute's peace if you'd been sat in there on your own."

"Well, let's not waste any more time chuntering out here. Let's get in there. We deserve a drink after working overtime today," said Fiona, striding to the door.

She held the door open for them and they trooped in.

Unsure what to expect after Fiona's cryptic comments on the pub, Richard realised "quite different" was an understatement.

He struggled to find words to describe the interior

Macabre? Eerie? Sickening?

Harris was turning out to be full of surprises.

The inside of Time or Tide looked like it was celebrating the Day of the Dead. Except they weren't in Mexico, only on a small island off the north coast of Scotland.

The first thing to grab his attention on entering were the animal skulls. Hanging on each wall, their empty eye sockets gazed out at the pub goers. At a glance, there appeared to be at least twenty of them.

What the hell were they? Sheep? Goat? Deer?

Richard had no idea.

Despite the skulls, the pub's interior was stylish and modern, with oak floors and the walls painted a rich burgundy.

Grey tartan curl-around sofas were placed next to the tables.

Sheepskin rugs lay in front of the fireplaces at each end of the building, and above each of them was hanging a stag's head with magnificent antlers.

The stag heads at least had glass eyes, which was an

improvement on the black eye sockets belonging to the other skulls.

Real or fake, though, the stag heads weren't to his taste. He wasn't at all keen on stuffed animals and would never have chosen to have them displayed in his own house.

Looking at the stuffed stag heads, he was reminded of two stags they had spotted near their cottage the previous evening, their mouths full of grass and their antlers looking like oversized reef coral.

Eilidh had stopped the car next to them, wound down her window, and taken a photo.

The stags had stared back at them, their shining black eyes unblinking, their jaws chewing away at the grass.

They had locked eyes for at least a minute.

Then, with an unspoken signal between them, both stags decided to turn around and walk off.

It was a magical moment for Eilidh.

As soon as they were back in the cottage, she started downloading a photo of the stags to her Facebook page.

Richard sighed.

He wondered if the deer would be standing back at the same spot that very evening.

Taking his eyes off the wall, Richard followed the others to a table at the far corner of the room and sat down.

He glanced down at the glass table in front of him and had another shock.

Under the glass top, the table pedestal was made entirely of bones.

The bones were glued together, one on top of the other.

He bent down to take a closer look.

"They're real," said Stu, watching him with some amusement. "The owner has a dark sense of humour. As you can imagine, these bones became a talking point when the pub first opened."

Richard nodded, speechless. He'd never come across anything like it before.

"Well, my shout. Richard, what would you like?" asked Fiona, standing up to get the first round.

Richard smiled.

"A Coke would be fine, thanks. Not from the tap, though."

"A Coke?" repeated Stu, in horror. "Come on, man, you can do better than that. You're in the land of gin and whisky."

"A Coke's fine by me," insisted Richard, smiling politely.

Stu looked in bemusement at Fiona, who shrugged, as though implying Richard was something of an alien species and best to leave him be.

She took the other orders and made her way to the bar.

Stu turned to Richard.

"You don't drink?"

"I do drink, but it's not something I like to do when I'm away on police business," replied Richard, aware he was coming across as standoffish and uptight. He hoped it wasn't a bad omen for the evening.

"But why? It's only us here tonight."

"Oh, Stu, leave him be!" remonstrated Anne, looking cross. "He can do as he likes, for Pete's sake."

But Stu wasn't willing to be silenced.

"I don't get why you won't have a dram with us," he

said, persistent. "No need to be a party pooper here. We're all colleagues."

He's like a dog with a bone, thought Richard.

Bones were becoming a recurring theme.

He fixed a smile to his face.

"Two reasons. I've got the car with me today and I need to drive home afterwards. I also want to remember all the information you can give me about the case, too."

Silence greeted his words.

"Well, I guess that makes sense then," said Stu at last, looking uncomfortable.

Richard wondered what Stu's people skills were like. Judging by his behaviour so far, he couldn't see him providing adequate support to any victim of crime. He seemed to have a sensitivity chip missing. Did that make Stu a thief, or a possible killer? He doubted it. He seemed too immature, for a start.

Disguising his somewhat uncharitable thoughts about him, Richard leaned back and put his hands behind his head.

"So, Stuart, Friday, April the twelfth. We were told you were on duty on the twelfth of April, when Simon turned up at the police station?" he asked, wanting to get to the heart of the matter before Stu's goodwill vanished completely.

Stu shook his head.

"I didn't see Simon when he came into the police station that Friday, no. I remember that day. Not likely to forget it, either. It was a bloody nightmare in the morning. A farmer rang up complaining his sheepdog had gone AWOL, scaring his cattle off their pasture. The bloody cows ended up blocking the road to Roghadal."

Stu huffed.

"Stupid animals. Between us we managed to move them on, but it took the better part of the morning."

He made a face.

"You've no idea what it was like, Richard. There I was getting shouted at by the car drivers and the farmer, and all I was trying to do was get the cows off the flipping road. Felt like telling the whole lot of them to F-off... I was this close to walking away," he said, motioning with his thumb and forefinger. "Anyway, one of the car drivers came out to help and between the three of us we managed to clear the road."

Richard nodded.

"Sounds pretty grim. But what about the afternoon? Did you get some time back at the station?" asked Richard.

"Nope, I was out a good bit of the afternoon, too. Fiona had had a rough time of it the day before with a domestic abuse case, so I volunteered to go out again. The ferry had arrived with a passenger who was plastered. He was causing the other drivers a lot of hassle as they were trying to disembark, so we got him banged up until he sobered up. Job done. There's never any point trying to reason with them, when they're that far gone."

"True," agreed Richard, remembering the times his father, who was a heavy drinker, had staggered around at a wedding or a party, resistant to any attempts to make him sit down and oblivious to the attention he was attracting.

"I saw Simon come in on the twelfth of April," chipped in Anne, who'd been listening to their conversation with interest. "He didn't want to tell me what the problem was. First he asked for Will, but he was on leave that day. Then he asked for Fiona, so I went and fetched her."

"Did you notice if he was carrying anything with him?" asked Richard.

Anne frowned, trying to remember.

"No, not that I noticed."

Richard said nothing, disappointed.

"Well, he was carrying his rucksack on his back, but he always did that," said Anne, after a moment. "That's nothing new."

"True," said Stu, agreeing with her. "Simon always carried a rucksack. It must've stank, mind you. If he wasn't carting around scallops and food in it, he was carrying toys for that dog of his. Nuts about his dog, he was. Spoilt the dog rotten."

Richard nodded.

"Enough of the interrogation. Where's Fiona?" asked Stu, peeved. "I'm needing a drink."

He stood up and looked over at the bar.

Richard followed his gaze.

A tight crowd had gathered at the bar, wanting their drinks. Catching Covid obviously wasn't a concern for those using the establishment.

Given the weirdness of the rest of the décor, Richard studied the bar with interest.

From time to time, the crowd parted, moving aside to let someone walk off with their tray of drinks.

The small glimpses Richard had of the bar reminded him of a Bosch painting. Definitely a Bosch painting depicting eternal damnation, he decided.

Bones belonging to animal legs (or so he hoped) were lined up vertically across the front of the bar.

In the centre of this gruesome collection of legs was a skull that looked ominously human.

Having reached the front of the bar, it seemed Fiona was getting served her drinks at last.

"Do you know the pub owner?" Richard asked.

Both of them nodded.

"Everyone knows everybody," said Stu. "It's a small population."

"Where on earth did he get his obsession with bones?"

Anne grinned.

"You'll get used to it. Some folk don't like it. Strangely, most of them are churchgoers. I thought they were supposed to be into life after death and all that. To be honest, I don't even notice the bones anymore."

"The thing is, you never forget this place after you've been to it," said Stu. "And that's always good for business. You'd be surprised to see how busy this pub is during the tourist season. The tourists absolutely love it. When they drink in here they're constantly taking selfies."

"The man who owns this place also owns the butcher's shop on Main Street," added Anne. "I reckon that's where he got the bones from."

Fiona was making her way towards them, carrying a tray of drinks.

"Don't say anything negative about the pub to Fiona," said Stu, quickly. "Her and David, the pub owner, have a thing going. Friends with benefits, I think you'd call it."

Richard nodded.

"Here we go, folks," said Fiona, placing the tray on the table and handing out the drinks.

Both she and Stu were drinking lager, but Anne had opted for a glass of red wine.

Catching sight of Anne swirling the wine in her glass, Richard began to feel nauseous. Surrounded by bones, skulls, and the two stag heads, the red wine was reminding him of blood. Especially so after she'd told him about the butcher's shop.

Fiona passed Richard his Coke and sat down.

"Richard's been asking about Simon's visit to the station on the twelfth of April," said Stu, after he'd taken the froth off his beer and heaved a sigh of satisfaction. "Turns out, you're the only one who met with him that day."

Looking at Richard, Fiona nodded.

"Yep. I met with him that day."

"What did he want to talk about?" asked Richard, curious.

"My, aren't we getting serious all of a sudden," commented Fiona in a flippant voice as she put down her glass.

She tapped her forehead with her finger.

"Not sure now. The weather, maybe?"

Richard frowned. Was she playing games with him?

Fiona laughed at the expression on his face.

"Sorry. Only kidding, Richard. Simon had a valid complaint that day. He wanted to report a suspected arson attempt on Scalpay. He thought he knew who it was, too, and wanted me to warn the teenager off. The boy's been causing a lot of bother." She shrugged. "So, I did that for him. It was no problem, really."

She took a few more sips of her drink.

"Major crime's very rare on these islands," she explained. "Main reason being that you can't get vehi-

cles or livestock off the island without taking the ferry.
Easy to hunt people down if you need to. But we've
recently had a spate of wildfires, and we suspect most of
them are started deliberately. There's no major damage
been done as yet. The weather's too foul half the time
for that, but it will become a problem come the summer.
If it continues. I'm hoping a few warnings will do the
job of preventing any problems."

"And Simon made no mention of treasure that
day?" asked Richard, trying to steer the conversation
back to the subject that interested him the most.

Fiona shook her head.

"Hell, no. I wouldn't have kept quiet about that, for
goodness sake. Treasure on Harris? That would've been
huge! I don't understand why Janey keeps harping on
about treasure. I've never put her down as someone
who's unhinged. I mean, I know she lost her husband,
but still."

She made a face.

"I reckon there were issues between the pair of
them and Simon told her some porkies about finding
treasure to keep her quiet. They had financial problems,
I believe, and their relationship was really quite tense.
We were called out to their house about two and a half
months ago, because the neighbours up the road heard
them screaming at each other in the garden."

Fiona swallowed some lager, looking thoughtful.

"The locals seem to think we're glorified social
workers and often treat us as such," she said finally,
putting her drink back down on the table.

Anne nodded her head.

"Yes, things weren't good between them," she said,
sadly. "I felt sorry for Janey. The poor lass wanted some

financial security and Simon was forever coming up with these crazy projects to make money, but they never worked out. He was driving her nuts, so he was. In the end, Janey's friend got him a job offer at the distillery, but apparently Simon wasn't keen on that, either."

All three of them saw the look of surprise on Richard's face and burst out laughing.

"Bro, everyone knows everyone else's business on this island. It's just the way it is," Stu said to Richard. "I sometimes wish it wasn't this way, but it is. Most of us go back a long way. See Anne, here. She probably knows my second cousin, Archie, who lives up in Stornoway."

The other two nodded.

Then they began a long discussion about extended families in Harris, which seemed to Richard to include a member of every clan in Scotland.

Richard drank his Coke and bided his time.

"What about the name 'Langley'?" asked Anne. "Where does that name come from?"

Richard shrugged.

"It's very common I'm afraid. It's meant to have some roots in an Old Norse female name 'Langlif,' but mainly it's from an Anglo-Saxon tribe living in Langley, which means long wood or clearing. The Langley family crest is pretty hideous. Green and white stripes on it."

Fiona smiled at Richard in sympathy.

"My surname, Mitchell, is meant to be derived from Hebrew and Anglo-Saxon. It's not easy to pin down your roots these days unless you're willing to spend the time and the money."

"You could have some Viking blood in you, Richard,

if your name came from an Old Norse name," said Anne, looking interested.

Richard chuckled.

"Well, if that's the case, I'm in the right place. The Vikings had quite a presence on these islands. It really didn't surprise me at all to hear there'd been some Viking treasure found up here."

"There's no treasure here, man," said Stu, shaking his head. "Wild goose chase if you ask me."

Fiona nodded.

"It's true. We know what's going on in these islands. If there was treasure, believe me, we'd all know about it. I just hope your trip here hasn't been a waste of time."

Richard shrugged.

"I'm sure it won't be the first, or last, time that someone suspects treasure has been found when it doesn't actually exist," he said. "But we still have to look into it."

"Indeed, you do... No one's arguing with that. Let me get you another drink, Richard," said Fiona, seeing his empty glass and getting up.

"No, honestly, I'll go myself," insisted Richard.

Stu laid a restraining hand on Richard.

"You really don't want to get talking to Oliver, the barman, Richard. Or David, for that matter. He'll keep you there blathering until he finds out everything about you. It'll be closing time before you get away."

"OK. Then at least let me give you some money," said Richard, feeling embarrassed by Fiona's generosity.

He pulled out his wallet.

Fiona waved his offer of money away and walked off to the bar.

"She gets the drinks on the house, Richard, so don't worry about it," reassured Anne, in a quiet voice.

Richard heard a curious tapping noise cutting through the pub's background music and chat. He turned around, and saw it was the elderly man who'd spoken to him earlier.

He was walking past their table, making his way to the exit.

As Richard caught his eye, he stopped.

"Cosying up tae th' polis ur we," the man said to Richard in a satisfied voice, as though he expected no less of him.

"Oh, bugger off, Willie. You giving Richard a sample of your Scottish charm and hospitality, are you?" said Stu. "We wouldn't have a single visitor return to the island if they had the misfortune to cross your path. Get out of here, now."

Willie spat on the floor, but seeing Stu stand up in anger, he turned and hurried past them, his stick tapping an even faster beat on the floor.

"Bloody bastard. Ignore him. He's the town's Grouch," said Stu, sitting back down with a black frown on his face.

"He's also Simon's stepfather," added Anne.

"Simon Buchanon's stepfather?" repeated Richard in surprise.

"Yeah," said Stu, in a confiding voice. "He was married to Simon's mum, Frances, but she had an affair. Got pregnant with Simon. Willie wasn't his real dad. She never told Simon about it until he married Janey, but I think it came as a relief to Simon. He never got on well with Willie. You can hardly blame him, though, can you?"

Richard shook his head.

"It was a huge shock for the community. Poor Frances. I felt sorry for her. Some people judged her badly, but I think most felt sympathy. I know I'd have had an affair if I was married to that old sourpuss," said Anne, looking angry.

"It's a real soap opera here in Harris, Richard. You should stick around and see for yourself. It just gets better and better. And you never know, if you stay here long enough you might be able to take a part in it yourself," said Stu, finishing his drink.

"Sounds like too much drama for me," admitted Richard. "And there I was thinking London was bad."

"Well, as we've agreed, some of us islanders have Norse blood in us," said Stu, as though this explained away all the excitement.

He pursed his lips and looked thoughtful for a moment.

"Aye, we're a feisty lot," he remarked, in a confidential voice. "Did you know our Viking heritage is one of the reasons they've been doing the Viking fire festival every year in the Shetland Islands? Have you heard of it? They say it's the biggest Viking fire festival in Europe. You should go and see it. Well worth a visit. Also, on Lewis, if you're into that stuff, you can visit the Norse Mill and Kiln. It's been reconstructed and restored for the tourists."

Stu leaned back on his seat and crossed his arms.

"I reckon Viking blood explains an awful lot about us islanders. I mean, the Vikings were a bloodthirsty lot, weren't they? Full of passion, too."

"Yes, they seemed to be a pretty ferocious bunch," agreed Richard, surprised by Stu's interest in the

Vikings. "Very effective warriors and rampant slave traders by many accounts."

"But well-travelled, cosmopolitan and cultured, too," he added. "People tend to forget that."

Stu nodded.

"I watch the Viking series on Sky. It's good. If you haven't seen it, you should give it a go."

"Thanks for the suggestion," said Richard, starting to warm to Stu. "I might well do that."

Fiona arrived at the table with the drinks.

Richard gave her a nod of thanks.

For some reason, he was starting to feel strangely mellow. Maybe he was beginning to relax at last.

The Harris effect, he thought, smiling to himself.

The space inside the pub was dark, lit mostly by the candles on the tables and dimmed light fixtures in the wall sconces, creating an intimate atmosphere.

Within the enclosed area, the music and the noise of the other pubgoers echoed in Richard's ears like the distant roar of the sea.

He leaned forward to listen to the others.

For the next hour, they filled Richard in on some hilarious anecdotes from the island. He soon lost track of the stories, most of which seemed to involve livestock of one kind or another.

It appeared there was one highlight to the year so far, a case involving a man with a child support claim brought against him by his pregnant mistress. The police were called out to his address after he was attacked by his wife, who'd been trying for the last eight years to fall pregnant.

As the conversation progressed, Richard started to

feel dazed and a sudden desire to leave the premises overwhelmed him.

During a lull in conversation, he pushed his glass away and smiled at the others.

"I'm afraid I'm feeling a little weary this evening. I think it might be time for me to head home."

"What, already?" asked Stu, in shock.

Richard looked at his watch, but as his vision was blurry and the room was dark he couldn't see the time on it.

"Yes, I'm sorry. I'm not feeling too good."

The others looked at him in concern.

"Maybe we should call and get someone to take you home," said Fiona, worried.

Richard shook his head, holding on to the table as he became dizzy. He felt beads of sweat gathering on his forehead.

"No, I'm sure I'll be fine, once I'm out in the fresh air."

He stood up and swayed.

Stu grabbed hold of his elbow and looked at Fiona.

"I think you're best to call someone to drive him home, Fi. I'll take him outside."

Fiona nodded, and opening her bag, pulled out her mobile phone.

Richard didn't remember much else from that evening.

What he did recall, though, was Eilidh's face of mingled outrage and concern when Stu helped him through the door of the cottage they were staying in.

And, bizarrely, he also remembered Eilidh tugging his shoes off after he'd collapsed onto the bed, fully clothed.

7

Eilidh

Eilidh drew back the curtains and looked across at Richard who was wincing in the bright light, his hand in front of his eyes.

She brought a glass of water over to him.

He took it from her gratefully.

Lifting his head, he drank it up, the water disappearing in seconds.

Sitting on the edge of the bed, Eilidh noted the shadows under Richard's eyes and their red rims.

He's going to end up with a cracking headache, she thought.

"Mind telling me what happened last night?" she asked him.

"Your guess is as good as mine."

There was silence while Eilidh pondered this unsatisfactory reply to her question.

"I take it you managed to get hammered with your new pals, then," she said, at last. "That's going to get our investigation off to a flying start, I must say."

Richard rubbed his eyes.

"I had two Cokes, one of which I didn't even finish."

Surprised, Eilidh stared at him.

"Are you telling me they spiked your drinks?"

Richard looked at her and frowned.

"Don't be ridiculous. With just two Cokes? There'd have to be so much gin in them that I'd be practically drinking it neat."

"GHB?"

Richard considered this.

"Possibly."

"But who?"

"I don't know. Fiona Mitchell bought the drinks."

Eilidh's eyes widened.

"Seriously?"

"There were two barmen on duty, too, before you go diving off the deep end."

Eilidh stood up.

"Right, come on, Richard. Get yourself dressed. I'm going to call and make a doctor's appointment. We'll get them to take a blood test."

"No."

"What? Are you kidding me?"

Richard flinched at her raised voice.

"No, I'm not, Eilidh. I'm not going for a blood test. What are you going to do if it comes back positive for GHB? Are we then going to start a big investigation into that, too? There's no proof and we haven't even scratched the surface with our search for any possible treasure. I'm not wasting any time on this."

Eilidh couldn't help it. She felt a wave of fury hit her. That he should put some ancient artefacts ahead of his own wellbeing and safety didn't make sense to her.

What's more, it wasn't the first time she'd questioned exactly where Richard's priorities lay.

She took a deep breath.

"We're going to the GP this morning," she said, firmly.

"No, we're not."

"Bloody hell, Richard. Have you lost your mind? Someone's done some serious shit to you, probably knowing you're a policeman, too. You can't let this pass you by."

Richard rubbed his face.

"I'm not ignoring this, believe me, but even if we do get a positive result for GHB, there's no identifying who did it. What it does tell us is that something's seriously out of kilter here. The pub was a hell of a weird place, for a start. The more time I spend here, the more I'm getting the feeling the treasure's real. After what happened last night, I'm more inclined than ever to believe Janey's side of things."

Richard stared down at his crumpled clothes, as though seeing them for the first time.

He wrinkled his nose in disgust and then looked up at Eilidh.

Eilidh didn't trust herself to say anything. Hormonal with her pregnancy, she felt overwhelmed with a sense of helplessness. It was not a feeling she liked having.

"We must keep an eye on Fiona Mitchell," continued Richard, oblivious to Eilidh's silent despair. "She's the one who saw Simon Buchanon the day he went to the police station with the treasure, and she's the one who got me the drinks last night. I was told she's in some kind of a relationship with the pub landlord, too. But in my opinion, we need to put all our efforts into finding the rest of the treasure. In my mind, that's more important. They're trying to find the remainder of the treasure, too, and sooner or later, I'm sure our paths will cross again, and hopefully we'll get our evidence then."

Eilidh walked across to the window and looked out at the sea lapping gently at the rocks by the shore.

It was such a peaceful view.

She pulled the sides of her dressing gown round her.

What the hell was going on in Lewis and Harris? It was as though beneath the beauty of it all there was a very ugly human element to the island. It brought to her mind the book *Lord of the Flies.*

She smiled.

Hopefully, they wouldn't get to the level of degradation and savagery described in the book, but she did wonder for a moment how it was all going to end. If there ever was an ending to what was feeling more and more like a wild goose chase.

Shaking her head, she pulled herself together.

"When's Mike arriving?" she asked.

"I don't know. He hasn't responded to any of my texts. I'm sure we'll hear from him sooner or later."

Eilidh turned around to face him, resigned to the situation.

"I had Janey here last night. She drew up a list of Simon's closest friends and acquaintances. It's quite a small list, really. We could easily get started on that."

"Yes, let's," said Richard, pushing the duvet away and standing up.

He put a hand to his forehead and grimaced.

"Nothing to worry about," he said, quickly, seeing the concern on Eilidh's face.

He picked up his glass of water.

"Some more water, a shower, and a coffee, and I'll be right as rain."

Eilidh rolled her eyes.

She gave up.

The man was insanely driven by his love of art and artefacts. *On his head be it*, she thought to herself.

"OK," she said. "I'll make you some coffee. Then we can decide where we're going to make a start."

With that, she made her way to the kitchen.

She filled up the kettle and while she waited for it to boil stared out of the window.

Another beautiful day.

Dawn came early this far north and she was forever checking the view when she woke up. Every morning she hoped to catch a sight of the local otters, gambolling along the burn and drying their fur on the grass. Otters needed fresh water and, according to the house manual, they had established a holt near the house. So far, though, she hadn't spotted them. No doubt they were too smart to be seen.

She made herself a cup of tea and left a cafetiere of coffee for Richard on the worktop.

Opening the front door, she went out into the garden and sat at the picnic table, with Janey's list of people tucked into her book as a bookmark.

She closed her eyes for a while, enjoying the feel of the fresh sea breeze on her skin.

Her anxiety began to ebb away.

Facing the vast expanse of the ocean brought her some much-needed perspective. It made her realise that in the whole scheme of things her purpose and existence was irrelevant. As far as the natural world was concerned their presence on Harris was of little importance and their investigation a trivial thing. The wild creatures and plants on the island were occupied with the daily business of survival. Life and death.

And long, long after Richard and Eilidh had gone back to London, the waves would continue licking at the rocks on the shoreline, as they had done for many hundreds of years.

Eilidh opened up her book, but before she could get stuck in she was startled by the sound of a car driving down the hill to their house.

Turning around, she recognised Janey's red Vauxhall.

The car came to a stop on the gravel driveway of their house and Eilidh got up from the picnic table to meet her.

"Janey, is everything OK?"

Janey shook her head as she got up from the driver's seat.

"No, it isn't. I've had it, I'm afraid, Eilidh. I'm booked to leave the day after tomorrow," she said, her voice cracking.

Eilidh couldn't help herself. She leaned forward and gave Janey a hug.

"Why don't you come and take a seat at the picnic table. I'll pop into the kitchen and make you a cup of tea. I'll just be a minute."

"Black coffee for me, please."

Eilidh nodded and made her way to the kitchen as Janey sat herself down on the bench.

She found Richard, who was freshly showered and dressed, seated on a bar stool and drinking his coffee.

His wet hair was starting to curl around the nape of his neck and she could smell the shower gel on him. So much more appetising than the mingled smell of smoke and sweat that had come off him the night before.

Eilidh felt the embers of her desire stirring and firmly suppressed it.

Seeing he'd drunk most of the coffee, she reached across and started filling up the kettle from the tap.

Once it was switched on, she turned to face Richard.

She smiled at him, pleased to see him looking so much better.

"Janey's outside," she explained to Richard.

"Again?"

"Yes. Says she's leaving the day after tomorrow."

They stared at each other.

"For Pete's sake, what's happened now?" asked Richard, sounding fed up.

Eilidh didn't blame him.

She had a distinct feeling that somewhere in the background there was a weird puppet master pulling on all their strings. It was time Richard and she got a break and turned the tables back on them.

"I honestly don't know, but I think you'd better get out there and find out," she said in a calm voice, concealing her misgivings.

However, Richard stayed put and made up a fresh cafetiere, before carrying it out to the picnic table for her.

I could get used to this, thought Eilidh, smiling as she followed him out of the house.

Since she'd become pregnant Richard had been fussing over her like a mother hen. She supposed the feminist in her should resent the attention Richard was giving her, but she'd felt strangely vulnerable during her pregnancy and she appreciated the extra care. She was hoping her feelings of inadequacy would pass or she was going to end up next to useless as a police officer, among other things.

She also didn't think pregnancy was an experience she'd ever want to repeat. She was looking forward to meeting her little boy, but already she sensed he was going to turn her ordered world upside down.

Richard sat down and poured Janey a coffee.

"It's good to see you, Janey. Eilidh's just told me you're leaving soon. Would you mind telling us what's made you want to leave early?" asked Richard, concerned, as he sat down at the picnic table.

Janey wrapped her hands around the mug, hugging it to her as though she needed the comfort.

"I'm sorry to let you guys down, I really am, but I can't stay here any longer. Things are getting out of hand again. You've only started your investigation. God knows how long it's going to take you to get to the bottom of it all. Meanwhile, this person, or these people, are out there causing me problems and I don't feel safe. I've to think of my safety first. I've got kids that need me."

"Of course, Janey. We understand how important it is for you to feel safe. You've been of great help to us already," said Eilidh, smiling reassuringly at her.

Janey let out a sigh, as though she was letting out the weight of the world with it

"For Simon's sake, though, please don't give up on

your search for the treasure," she said, earnestly. "I really don't want those bastards to get it. They've got my husband's blood on their hands. My life might have been difficult when Simon was alive, but it's hell now. As for the kids... where do I begin? They're going to be carrying lifelong scars from losing their dad at such a young age."

Janey brushed the long tendrils of her hair, which were dancing in the wind as if they had a life of their own, away from her face.

Vulnerable and forlorn, she cut a lonely figure, and Eilidh felt tempted to hug her again.

"They broke in," Janey informed them, turning to look at the sea in front of them.

Richard and Eilidh stared at her in disbelief.

"Again?" asked Richard.

Janey nodded, still gazing out to sea.

"Yes. Yet they left the house completely untouched while I was away. At least, as far as I can tell. Want to try and figure out why they then decide to break in when I'm on the premises?"

Her eyes swivelled round to them, challenging them to believe her.

"I take it you reported it to the police officers in Tarbert?" asked Eilidh, worried.

"Yeah, I did. They're going to send a forensics team to the house. They'll do the whole fingerprint thing, but they won't find anything, I can guarantee you."

Janey swallowed some of her coffee.

"To be honest with you, I was kind of expecting something like this," she admitted. "I was prepared. I got myself a rope ladder, so I could let myself down from the bedroom window. Our house hasn't got an alarm, but then again, I don't think anyone in Harris has one. Many of us have left keys under a stone, or pot, by the front door. That's the kind of place Harris is—or was," she corrected.

She sighed.

"I'm a light sleeper; always have been. I woke up at half two this morning and heard someone banging on one of the dining room windows, at the back of the house. It has the view, you see, but it's also hidden from the neighbours..." Janey drank some more coffee. "Anyway, I got myself out of there super-fast and ran over to my neighbour. She came back to my house with me this morning, but I've really had enough of this crap. I want you to sort it out, I really do, but I can't hang around waiting for that to happen. My sister's suggesting I move permanently near them, and I'm seriously considering it now."

"And you're saying nothing was taken from the house?" asked Eilidh, puzzled.

Janey shook her head.

"They didn't. I've gone through the house with my neighbour. Nothing was taken."

Eilidh wondered if whoever had broken in was looking for Janey. It wasn't a pleasant thought but it was viable. After all, from what she'd told them they'd tried to chase her away from the island before. At this point, Eilidh no longer had any doubts about Janey's truthfulness.

"Let us at least take you to the airport," offered Richard.

Eilidh agreed with him on this. They had, after all, asked Janey to come back to Harris, at a significant emotional and psychological cost to her.

"Thanks," said Janey, gratefully accepting his offer. "It'll save my friends having to take time off work to take me there. I haven't been able to get hold of Patrick, either, who would normally be more than happy to oblige."

"Simon's dad?" asked Eilidh, wondering if something had happened to him too. Nothing seemed to be beyond the realm of possibility any more, or at least that was the impression she was getting on this strange island.

"Yeah. He's not answering the house phone, but that's normal. He does that sometimes. He's a painter, and he has a habit of taking off when he's in the mood. Sometimes he camps, other times he stays with a friend."

She shrugged.

"He's very much a free spirit."

Eilidh smiled at her.

She understood. Richard was a free spirit, too. It was something he had to keep in check, working as he did for the police force.

"Right," said Janey, pushing away her mug. "I'd best leave you both to it."

She stood up and looked down at them, the wind teasing her hair out of its hairband and pulling gently on her jacket.

There was a certain dignity and strength about Janey that made Eilidh think of the goddess from Greek mythology, Hera.

Maltreated, suffering, but strong, unbroken, and seeking revenge on those who had disrupted her life.

Eilidh smiled to herself.

The goddess Hera? What on earth was her mind on

about? What had she turned into since joining Richard's department?

She didn't recognise herself any more.

Her art history studies had turned her brain to mush, she thought. That was Richard's fault, if anyone's. He was far too interesting a tutor.

"Let me know if I can do anything to help you before I leave," Janey said, moving on to the practicalities. "My flight leaves at three on Wednesday. I'll drop by here at one, if that's OK with you. Make use of my car when I'm away, if you like. You've only got the one car and public transport around here is crap. It's going to take me some time to find a buyer for it. Simon's van sold pretty fast, which was a blessed relief, but I don't think my old Vauxhall's going to be as easy to shift."

Seeing their faces, she smiled.

"Honestly, it's only got scrap worth. But it has its MOT and insurance up to date."

Eilidh looked at Richard.

He nodded.

"Thank you, Janey. That might be helpful in the short term. I wonder if you'd be willing to come with us when we go to see Simon's friends?" asked Eilidh, looking at the list she and Janey had drawn up the night before. "We narrowed down his closest friendships to three. We might be able to cover them all tomorrow?"

Janey nodded in agreement.

"We could at least try. Actually, why don't you come with me now?" she suggested, suddenly. "I've got to say my goodbyes to them, anyway. Mark's surveying the repairs needed for Eilean Glas lighthouse on Scalpay. It was going to take him at least a week to finish. Findley's going to be a trickier proposition. He's always away early, fishing. Sam will be at the office in Tarbert during the day."

"Sounds like a plan. Speaking to Mark and Sam will be a good start," said Richard, pleased.

He turned to Eilidh.

"Are you OK to go now?"

"Yes, sure. Just give me a moment to get my bag."

"Don't forget your walking boots!" called out Janey, as they both made their way back into the house.

It was needless advice. Richard and Eilidh hadn't worn anything else since arriving on the island. There didn't seem any point wearing normal shoes in such a rugged landscape, even when walking about Tarbert.

Eilidh left her book in the kitchen.

Before she went to change her shoes, she removed the list from it and had another look.

There was one name that stood out for her among all the others: Patrick McQuire.

They were going to have to speak to Patrick McQuire as a matter of urgency. As Simon's real dad, there wasn't going to be any relationship on the list as close or important as that one.

8

Mike

Holding his pint close to his chest, Mike watched the screen above him.

The white snooker ball hit the black.

The black snooker ball shot across the green baize and fell neatly into the pocket.

Mike sighed with relief.

He was glued to the World Snooker Championship, enjoying some down time after a busy couple of weeks.

Apart from a few diehards like himself, the Blue Moon pub in Hackney had few customers that afternoon.

It was too sunny for indoor customers.

The air outside the pub was balmy and the skies were blue. Most people on such a day would be looking for an outdoor bar for a congenial drink, rather than a dark and dingy pub, whose tasteless décor was last updated in the 1970s by the looks of it.

Mike was a regular at the Blue Moon. A creature of habit, he'd only move on to somewhere else if the pub changed hands or if it underwent major refurbishment, heaven forbid.

There were many things he liked about the Blue Moon. He liked the sticky table surfaces and the way the faint smell of weed blended in with body odour and exhaust fumes from the busy road outside. He liked the wooden floor, covered with decades of stiletto marks and spilt wine stains. The black and white framed pictures of The Marcels and Elvis Presley, hanging on the walls had grown on him, too, even though his favourite version of *Blue Moon* was sung by Diane Shaw's dulcet tones.

He liked the clientele. There were the elderly alcoholics who told him about their younger years and their imaginary girlfriends, as well as the divorcées, hanging around in close-knit groups and bitching about their men.

A few members of a Brixton gang haunted the Blue Moon from time to time. They never caused any bother, followed the pub rules, and kept themselves to themselves as they huddled over their tables, darting suspicious glances at anyone who walked close to them.

The workmen formed another crowd, dropping by on their way home from work, covered in bits of plaster, cement, paint or sawdust. Often monosyllabic with tiredness, their conversation was usually limited to what they'd seen that day. In a series of grunts, their chat ranged from page three of *The Sun* newspaper to a celebrity stopping at the traffic lights in the latest Porsche to a pretty woman refusing to look up after one of them was brave enough to wolf-whistle at her.

Then there was "mother Marie," gregarious and friendly. She was a retired local who always turned up at the Blue Moon on her own. She joined any table she fancied on the night, on a rotating basis. She was tolerated by everyone as a fixture at the pub. She wore her long hair down, favoured tent dresses in vivid colours, and had a habit of looking at people over the tops of her glasses, reminding Mike uncomfortably of a former school mistress.

Most of all, Mike liked the way regulars at the Blue Moon went silent and turned around whenever a newcomer walked in.

It made him feel safe.

He had a soft spot for the bar staff, too.

Yes, even those nervous students tending the bar on Friday and Saturday nights, who often as not got his order wrong.

Meanwhile, the long-time members of staff, such as Davie, were like brothers-in-arms. Davie acted as if he owned the place and always served his favourite punters first.

It was Jim, the owner, who was the star of the show in Mike's opinion. The Blue Moon was never dull when Jim was behind the bar, directing operations on a busy evening. Jim would break up any anti-social behaviour in the pub by threatening to smash a bottle of cheap gin over the miscreants' heads—gin being Jim's least favourite drink. Nobody ever doubted he'd stick to his word, either.

Mike took another sip of his lager and watched as the red snooker ball hit the side of the table and rebounded, missing the pocket.

Davie, the barman, came and stood in front of Mike.

When Mike didn't register his presence, Davie cleared his throat.

"Mike, I've someone on our landline for you."

Mike tore his eyes away from the screen and looked at Davie.

"For me?"

"Yep."

Surprised, Mike pushed away his pint.

"Who?"

"Wouldn't tell me, I'm afraid."

"OK. Where's your phone?"

"It's in our back office. If you'll come with me."

Mike nodded and followed Davie through a beaded door curtain to a small office situated by the stairs.

The stairs led up to Jim's flat which was situated above the pub.

Jim, who was a night owl, never made an appearance in the pub before seven in the evening.

"I'll leave you to it," said Davie, pointing to the receiver lying on the desk.

He closed the door behind him.

The level of trust shown by the barman wasn't as odd as it looked. Mike had been a regular at the pub for over twenty years and he was well known to the staff who worked there.

Having helped Jim recover four stolen crates of Dom Pérignon champagne a year and a half ago, Mike was now treated as a VIP member whenever he happened to drop by. VIP in the Blue Moon meant that he had the run of the place and his first pint of lager was always free. Not something that everyone would appreciate, but Mike thought it was a good deal and was quite happy with it.

"Hello?" asked Mike, as he cradled the receiver next to his ear.

"Hi, Mike."

"Hello, Mariella. You keeping tabs on me?"

"Well, what do you expect after your latest stunt?"

"I don't know what you mean."

Mariella snorted angrily.

"Cut the crap, Mike."

Mike smiled to himself.

"Fair enough. I get that you're mad as hell, but at the end of the day, I did you a favour. As long as you had the stuff with you, you were going to be in danger."

"Oh, how sweet. So, you were just trying to take care of me? It's strange I didn't pick up on your good intentions," said Mariella, in a dulcet voice.

"Don't be sarcastic with me, Mariella. It doesn't suit you," admonished Mike. "Loads of people in your line of trade knew about the treasure. The big sharks, too, which should've had you worried. Take Peter Knight and Kev Taylor, for example. They've been sniffing around this, too, and you don't mess with people like them. Stop bloody burying your head in the sand and smell the roses. If it hadn't been me, it would've been someone else."

There was a long silence on the phone.

"And I did try to negotiate with you," added Mike, for good measure.

"Your problem is that you can't take no for an answer, Mike. Your fucking ego's too big for that. Be warned, you're going to regret what you did. As well as the financial cost, you've managed to irreparably damage my business reputation and I'm never, ever going to forgive you for that..." Mariella laughed in what Mike felt was a distinctly sinister manner. "My dear, you know fine well you broke the code and you owe me big time. I'll be calling up the favours very soon, don't you worry, *mio caro*. But do tell me, where are the goods now?"

"The British Museum is keeping them in storage at the moment."

"How much did they give you?"

"I was given a retainer fee to look into the matter. Guess they don't have much faith in the police."

"Surprise, surprise. Well, a little birdie has told me there's more where that came from. So, I might have to go up there and take a look myself. I've always had a desire to explore the north of Scotland. They tell me it's a beautiful country."

Mike felt his heart sink. The last thing he wanted was Mariella knocking about the Isle of Harris and getting her clutches on yet more treasure, but he appreciated her need for revenge. He would have done the same in her shoes. After all, she was out of pocket now.

He wondered how much she'd paid the police officer in Harris for the cup and the torc. A small fortune, no doubt.

"Come on, have you nothing else to say?" demanded Mariella impatiently.

"What do you want me to say?" asked Mike, feeling cornered.

"Idiot! How about 'I'm sorry' or 'I won't do it again.' Or even better, 'I'll make it up to you.'"

"I've never apologised for anything I've done and I'm not about to start now," growled Mike.

"More fool you."

The phone line went dead.

Mike looked at the receiver and placed it back on its cradle.

He walked back through to the bar area and sat on his stool again.

Glumly drinking his lukewarm lager, he thought about Mariella's comments.

He heard a cheer and looked up at the screen to catch the replay.

By now, there were only the brown, pink, blue, and black balls left to pot and win the frame.

As he watched the frame reach its conclusion, his thoughts started to wander back to Mariella.

Damn Mariella.

She was a woman of her word. If she said she was going to hunt for the rest of the treasure in Harris, she bloody well would.

He decided he'd better get up to Harris as soon as possible.

What a pain.

He'd planned to go to Venice next week as well.

He groaned.

Venice in spring was beautiful.

La Primavera.

A couple of weeks ago, the National Archaeological Museum of Venice had requested his services in locating a number of missing Egyptian artefacts and his research had already indicated some of the artefacts were being advertised for sale in Rome.

The quickest way to getting results, though, was to interview the staff members at the Museum in Venice. At least one of them had to be involved in the theft, and in his experience, museum staff cracked easily under pressure.

He grinned to himself.

Or maybe it was just his methods were slightly more unorthodox and direct than those of the local police. He wasn't above hiring some hard men to accompany him and encourage a little more discourse. All done in the comfort and safety of their home, of course. That's what he liked about the Italians, especially those from the south. They understood how these things worked.

It wasn't that he'd given up on finding the Harris treasure by agreeing to take on work in Venice. Far from it. But for now, Richard Langley was up in Harris sniffing around and Mike hadn't felt his presence was going to be needed for a while yet. He was quite happy to let Richard do some of the groundwork for him, during which time he could pursue more lucrative contracts abroad. He couldn't be in more than one place at once, so inevitably his professional life consisted of prioritising the many demands on his time.

Mariella had now thrown a spanner in the works. He might as well accept it and put off his visit to Venice. His excuses to the museum weren't going to go down well and it was going to look very unprofessional, given he'd agreed to be there next week. Gossip among these institutions was rife and his last-minute cancellation could end up earning him some black marks in art circles.

At this late stage in his career, though, he wasn't too bothered. He could take it.

He sighed again and drank the remainder of his pint, forgetting completely about the snooker match.

He tried to get his thoughts in order.

First up, he should warn Richard that Mariella was planning to make an appearance in Harris.

Putting the empty glass down on the bar, he pulled his mobile phone out of his pocket and dialled Richard's number.

It picked up on the third ring.

"Hello?"

"Hi, Richard. I'm afraid I've got some bad news for you. An old acquaintance of mine is heading up to Harris to track down the rest of the treasure. You'll need to keep an eye on her when she's up there. She's the one who got her hands on the chalice and the torc."

Richard groaned.

"Fantastic. Just what we need when we're making next to no progress. What's her name?"

"She's called Mariella Giuseppi, but she won't be there under that name. I'll send you a photo. I wasn't planning on going up to Harris right away, but I'm going to have to now. Mariella's efficient and capable of causing a lot of trouble."

"Well, we're always happy to see you, Mike. Just so long as you stay on the right side of the law, of course."

Mike smirked.

He always broke the law if he had to, and what's more, Richard knew that. Who was Richard kidding? That's how he got results.

"Yeah, whatever, Richard. If I were you, I'd ask the ferry operators to keep you updated with their passenger lists. She won't fly up because she's shit-scared of flying."

"Will do."

"How are you doing with the case, anyway?"

Richard sighed.

"Not great, to be honest with you, but we're plodding on."

Mike smiled.

"You'll get there in the end."

"Possibly," said Richard, not sounding convinced.

Mike was bemused by Richard's despondency. What the hell was going on up there? It wasn't like Richard to sound so downbeat. He decided against probing him further. It wasn't the time or place to have that kind of conversation, and if there was anything wrong he would find out soon enough.

"I'll let you know when I'm in Harris."

"Yes, please do. I'm not sure Mariella's the only one we should be keeping an eye on."

Mike laughed out loud.

"Come on, Richard. Don't forget we work well together. I'm good at bringing down the predators. You know what I mean. The sharks, the killer whales, and the leopard seals."

"Yes, you're like a cannibal. Good at eating your own kind," remarked Richard, recovering his sense of humour. "I look forward to seeing you in action."

"Exactly. See you soon."

Mike hung up.

He looked at his empty glass.

"Davie!" he called.

Davie came over to him, his eyes half-fixed on the snooker game on the screen above them.

"Yes?"

"Get me a whisky, would you? Johnnie Walker."

"Sure thing."

When in Rome prepare to do as the Romans do,

thought Mike. It wouldn't be long before he reached Scotland, after all.

Davie plonked the glass of whisky in front of him.

"Cheers," said Mike, swigging a mouthful.

"Bad news?" asked Davie, leaning on the counter.

"You could say that. My ex is giving me grief."

Davie whistled between his teeth.

"Tell me about it. I've been taken to the cleaners by my ex-wife. Sucked dry by her, is what I am. She got the house and I'm stuck in a shitty bedsit now. Where's the justice in that?"

Mike nodded in agreement.

"Big mistake getting married, Davie. You won't catch me getting hitched."

"It won't be up to you," said Davie, with authority. "Trust me, girls always want the ring on their finger. Don't know why, but it's a fact."

Mike shrugged.

"I've never had that problem. My relationships don't last very long."

He smiled.

"I reckon I'm not an attractive long-term proposition for most women. Maybe it's a good thing."

At this, Davie turned his eyes away from the television and looked at him, incredulous.

"Come off it, Mike. You must be loaded. The kind of work you do, as well."

Mike made a face.

"I get by," he acknowledged. "I'm not dumb enough to let anyone know what I've got stashed away. And I can assure you I'm not vain enough to assume a beautiful girl is with me just for my good looks and charm, especially if I'm splashing the cash around. Let's face it, at my age, I've got wrinkles and all." He patted his stomach fondly. "And the middle age spread. Truth is, Davie, I'm no oil painting. Cash aside, I prefer to be loved for myself."

"Well, in that case, could be a while before you find a girlfriend," agreed Davie, chuckling.

Mike grinned back at him.

"It could indeed."

He downed the glass of whisky in two gulps, and then withdrew a roll of banknotes from his trouser pocket.

"Get yourself a drink, mate. You look like you could do with one."

He peeled off four twenties, and left them on the counter.

"Cheers, Mike," said Davie, gratefully picking them up.

Mike waved a hand before he disappeared through the entrance of the pub.

Outside, in the bright sunshine, he came to a sharp stop and blinked.

The Blue Moon was like an underground burrow, with no windows or daylight, and it always took him a while to adjust to the outdoors after a lengthy stint in there.

Once he'd grown accustomed to the daylight, Mike looked up the nearest Waterstones bookshop on his mobile phone and started to make his way to it.

His home was on Hemingford Road, in Islington, but he wanted to purchase a map of Harris first.

A short time later, after hunting through several bookshelves at Waterstones, he found a detailed map of the Isle of Lewis and Harris.

It had been tucked away between a map of Jersey and one of Andalusia in Spain. The staff at Waterstones were needing to put their maps in order, he thought, but given the pressures high street bookshops were under since Amazon made an appearance, he wouldn't be surprised if they were understaffed.

He paid for the map and walked home, his mind whirring with plans.

By the time he reached his front door he was reading the emails on his phone.

He absentmindedly unlocked his door and then reached up to disable the alarm.

Shutting the door behind him, he noticed a pile of letters on the door mat.

He bent down and picked up the post, then walked through to the kitchen at the back of the house.

Leaving the mail and the map on the kitchen island, he filled the kettle with water and set it to boil.

If he was going to make proper plans, he was going to need a clear head. A black coffee was definitely in order.

He started opening his letters.

Most were junk mail from charities.

Ever since he'd set up a direct debit to The Rock Trust, a homeless charity working with young teens, he'd been inundated with letters from multiple charities. Did any of them ever make any money from posting out unrequested letters, he wondered. All it did was nark him right off.

He picked up a letter in a cream envelope.

The address was handwritten.

He looked at it closely.

The writing seemed vaguely familiar to him but he couldn't place it.

He opened the envelope and removed the single sheet of paper inside of it.

Spreading it out on the kitchen island he saw it had a message:

> *Stay away from Harris, Mike.*
>> *Time for you to retire.*
>> *If you visit Harris, there'll be no retirement for you. Harris will be your deathbed.*

Mike sniffed.

He was used to receiving threats by mail. He was also used to dismissing them. They came with the territory.

However, this was the first time a threat had landed on his doorstep in Islington and not at his office in Putney.

9

Richard

Janey parked her car at the side of the road, up on a grassy kerb.

"Here we go," she said, as she switched off the ignition. "It's not a long walk. About twenty minutes or so."

Richard and Eilidh got out of the car and gazed at their surroundings.

The only buildings to be seen were two small bungalows, one of them with a couple of yellow canoes laid out in an untidy front garden.

Right next to their car, in front of a metal gate and cattle grid leading to the lighthouse walk, was a black Nissan.

Nobody else seemed to be in the area.

A red sign above them indicated the Eilean Glas lighthouse was 2.1 km away.

The start of the path leading to the lighthouse looked uninspiring, to say the least.

Overgrown grass covered the hillside in front of them.

Past the metal gate, the narrow, tarmacked road

meandered over a rocky, empty landscape, before disappearing into the distance.

Coupled with the overcast sky above them, the overall impression was one of dreariness.

Grey upon grey upon grey, thought Richard.

"Vitamin D, vitamin D," Janey had chanted to them earlier on, when rain drops began to pelt down on the car's windscreen. "Doctors in Scotland recommend everyone take vitamin D supplements because of the lack of daylight here. It's a bloody serious problem. You see, there's an established link between low vitamin D and high levels of the disease multiple sclerosis in Scotland."

"I guess the weather at least stops Scotland being subjected to mass tourism and the likes of Ibiza or Magaluf popping up on its beautiful beaches," said Eilidh.

"Yes, that's true," Janey had agreed. "What I love about Scotland is you can go for long nature walks in the Highlands and not meet another soul. Our wilderness isn't overcrowded like it is in England. I went to the Lake District one year and couldn't believe the crowds down there. The people who run the canoe club in Harris came up here to escape the mobs in Cornwall."

But Richard wasn't a nature boffin, he was an art aficionado. As far as the weather in Scotland went, he had to admit he now had a new perspective on Scottish art since visiting Harris.

How Scotland managed to give birth to the wonderful art of the Scottish Colourists, when there was so little bright sunlight to be seen, was becoming a mystery to him.

The paintings created by the Scottish Colourists were full of vibrant colours. Candy apple red, lemon yellow, aqua blue, ebony black, and brilliant white. Their paintings deserved to be the product of the Italian Riviera, rather than the damp, 'dreich' Scottish weather.

Then again, the four Scottish Colourist artists, Peploe, Cadell, Hunter, and Fergusson, had spent a considerable amount of time in France, so maybe France had been the primary influence in their artwork.

Richard resolved to study the Scottish Colourists in more depth when he next had some spare time on his hands.

At the back of his mind he could also hear Eilidh's sarcastic voice saying: "Spare time? With a baby? You've got to be kidding me!"

"Richard? Are you alright?" asked Eilidh, looking at him concerned.

"Yes, fine. Why?" he answered.

"You looked like you were a million miles away."

"I was."

Used to his vagaries and daydreaming, Eilidh rolled her eyes and chuckled.

Richard saw Janey had opened the metal gate and was waiting patiently for them to pass through it.

Without saying another word, he took Eilidh's hand and they started the walk.

Within the space of five minutes, they found themselves surrounded by peat and bog.

There were deep grooves crisscrossing the strange landscape, and water could be seen lying in stagnant puddles between pockets of heather and grass.

A large pond appeared on their right-hand side, its reeds rustling gently in the breeze.

Across the entire area, the woolly heads of cotton grass were dispersed. Looking like bits of sheep fluff, the white balls were pulled on one side, misshapen and twisted by the harsh northern wind.

The tarmacked road soon turned into a chalky, gravel path.

The path was dry and secure enough, providing a firm foothold in what looked to Richard to be a bumpy and treacherous terrain, with unexpected pockets of water and bulging hillocks of heather for the unwary foot.

For a while, Richard and Eilidh walked through the undulating land in silence, too busy examining the view to chit chat.

There wasn't a soul to be seen but the stillness was broken now and again by a curlew calling out as it flew across the land.

They trudged onwards.

After a while, Richard spotted a buzzard hovering above the bog.

The buzzard ignored their presence.

Balancing itself on gusts of air, its eyes were focused on something directly beneath it.

It dropped down into the undergrowth and then quickly flew off, carrying a field mouse in its claws.

Despite being in the midst of so much natural beauty, Richard felt depressed.

Janey's mood was affecting him. Her face and posture were revealing her heaviness of spirit and inner pain. Her forehead was furrowed, her lips set in a grim line, and her shoulders had risen up in a defensive posture.

Did she even realise her hands were clenched, wondered Richard, watching her.

It was as though Janey had sunk into a deep vortex of sorrow and it surrounded her like a thick cloud of flies, following her along the winding path.

Lost as she was in her black thoughts, Janey appeared to have no appreciation of the striking scenery around them. She simply gazed unseeing into the distance as she walked, as though trying to find a brighter future somewhere ahead of her.

Of course, the hardest part of leaving the island for her would be separating herself from her friends and family, not severing herself from its natural beauty, thought Richard. Her indifference to their surroundings was unsurprising.

Richard questioned if Janey was going to have the strength to say her goodbyes to everybody. It was going to be difficult for her to do so when she didn't know when, or even if, she would be returning to the island.

Ruefully aware of the enormity of their mission, he hoped their visit to the lighthouse was going to be successful in extracting some useful information. There wasn't much time left before he'd have to decide whether they should abandon their visit to Harris and make their way home to London, tails between their legs. Resources in his department were already stretched, and he couldn't see Lionel licensing an indefinite stay on Harris, based on the slim evidence of one overwrought woman.

On and on they walked, with only the sound of

shoes, scuffing at the gravel on the path, breaking the silence.

Born and bred in an overcrowded city, Richard was finding the silence unnerving. He'd never been in a situation where you walked for hours without seeing another human being. It was most odd.

Crime rates seemed to be low in Harris, and he reckoned it was probably due to the lack of population density. Which was just as well because it would be very hard to monitor any crime with such huge areas of uninhabited terrain. Even so, from what Fiona Mitchell was saying it was easy to track down any persons of interest because of the limited transport options to and from the islands.

But with so many coves and an extensive coastline, someone with a small boat could easily come and go unseen in Harris, thought Richard. Again, he felt a strong desire to explore the coastline and find the beaches where Simon did his scallop fishing. Janey was adamant Simon had been scallop fishing the morning he found the treasure, and he felt that would be a good place to start in their search for the missing items, even if they had been moved elsewhere by now.

The path led them to an ancient wall, stretching on either side as far as the eye could see. The wall had been built up with irregular-sized grey stones placed in uneven patterns. The builder had expertly placed one stone next to the other in an ingenious jigsaw, and his efforts had withstood the test of time and the weather.

Marbled across the wall surface were streaks of orange and white algae, clinging to the stones despite the inhospitable climate.

They walked through a small gate set in the wall

and saw ahead of them for the first time the sea and an impressive rocky outcrop with the Eilean Glas lighthouse perched on the top of it.

The bold red and white stripes of the lighthouse contrasted with the frosting of green grass on the summit. Beneath the thin icing of grass was solid rock, leading down to the sea.

Richard stared admiringly at the lighthouse.

Every lighthouse seemed to him to be a feat of engineering. In the Victorian age, countless workers lost their lives building them.

Given the landscape they'd passed through, the lighthouse's red and white stripes seemed garish next to the more muted hues of rock, heather and sea. The colours were bold and brash, but then they were meant to be so. Although Richard's artistic side didn't like the palette in front of him, he was sure the majority of visitors to Eilean Glas would disagree with him. Most people had a soft spot for lighthouses.

Several sheep were scattered about on the terrain leading to the lighthouse.

Their black faces turned to watch them, calm and unafraid, as they walked past.

Were these the sheep responsible for the making the famous Harris Tweed, Richard wondered, looking at their shaggy wool coats. Richard hadn't seen any sheep like them before, but their little horns, which were curled tightly against their skulls, reminded him of the deer heads in the Time or Tide.

Not wanting to dwell on his memories of the pub, he averted his eyes and looked out towards the sea instead.

"This lighthouse was one of the first four lighthouses to be built in Scotland," commented Janey in a flat voice, breaking the silence.

"Is it still in use?" asked Eilidh, gazing at it.

"Yes, it sure is. The lighthouse building itself is owned and operated by the Northern Lighthouse Board, but it's a complicated relationship. You see, the smaller buildings around the lighthouse don't belong to the Northern Lighthouse Board. Those belong the North Harris Trust and the Eilean Glas Trust."

Janey looked at them.

"I don't know if you heard of the community buy out on the island?"

Richard and Eilidh shook their heads.

"The North Harris estate belonged to the Earl of Dunmore, but was purchased by the entire community in 2003. It now calls itself the North Harris Trust."

"I like the sound of that," remarked Eilidh. "Seems like a good idea to have the people who live here own and manage the land."

Janey nodded, but her thoughts seemed to have gone elsewhere again.

They walked across to the outcrop, Richard keeping a wary eye on Eilidh in case she tripped up as she clambered over the rocks.

When they came close to the lighthouse, Janey suddenly stuck two fingers in her mouth and let out a piercing whistle.

Richard and Eilidh jumped and turned to look at her in surprise.

A tall man, dressed in blue overalls and a hard hat, appeared from behind the lighthouse.

"That's Mark," said Janey, a small smile on her face.

"Hoy, Janey!" Mark called out, waving a hand.

He took his hat off and walked across to where they were standing.

"Janey! Janey! It's so good to see you!" enthused Mark.

He gave her a bear hug, shutting his eyes briefly as he rested his head on hers.

Watching with interest, Richard sensed Mark had a deep emotional connection with Janey. Was it on Simon's behalf or his own?

Richard had no idea.

They really didn't have long enough on the island to uncover all the complicated threads running throughout the tight-knit community on Harris. And yet he was sure somewhere in the midst of Simon's interconnecting relationships on the island would lie the answers to the treasure's whereabouts, and maybe even the answers to his death.

"What are you doing here? I thought you were away down south?" Mark asked Janey, looking down at her with affectionate eyes.

Janey pulled away from him.

A faint blush mottled her cheeks, but she seemed calm enough.

"I was, Mark. I've come home for a quick visit, but I'm afraid I'm away again tomorrow."

"Seriously? But why?" asked Mark, looking confused and upset at the news.

Janey turned and signalled Richard and Eilidh.

"I've been trying to help these police officers with their enquiries, but it's now time for me to get back to the kids. They're from the Art and Antiquities Unit in London. This is DCI Richard Langley and DI Eilidh Simmons."

Mark appeared stunned by her introduction.

Eilidh and Richard smiled politely at him, both of them used to the public's extreme and different reactions when introduced to members of the police force.

"A pleasure to meet you," said Mark at last, regarding Richard and Eilidh as though they were aliens from outer space.

"Same here," responded Richard, starting to feel amused.

Mark, it turned out, was as transparent as a running stream. He revealed his feelings with a child-like lack of guile, and right then his expression was one of complete and utter bemusement.

Mark turned to Janey, a question in his eyes.

"They're here because of something Simon discovered when he was out scallop hunting," explained Janey quickly. "Mark, did Simon ever tell you anything about the stuff he found when he was out scallop diving, or even where he found it?"

Mark shook his head.

"No. What kind of 'stuff' are we talking about? He never told me anything about that, the sly old dog."

"Viking items, apparently," said Janey.

Mark stroked his thick black beard thoughtfully and then laughed out loud.

"Viking treasure, hey? I'd heard rumours, but I thought it was all part and parcel of Tarbert's gossip mongers. Sounds to me like Simon's been a wee bit of a dark horse. Nothing new there, that's for sure..."

He pursed his lips for a minute as he mulled things over.

The others waited patiently for him to speak.

"You know what, Janey? Findley was the one who

knew every single one of Simon's haunts. After all, they
often went out fishing together. He'd be able to tell you
the places where Simon went scallop diving."

Janey made a face.

"True, but it's going to be difficult to track him
down because he'll be out on his boat a lot at this time
of year. I doubt he'll be in until much later on, if at all,"
remarked Janey, in a defeated voice.

Mark nodded in agreement.

"True enough. He'll be out a lot at this time of
year."

"Maybe we could get the harbour office to ask him
to come in and speak to us," suggested Eilidh.

"Yes, that would be possible, I think," said Mark,
nodding again. "You'd have to contact the Fisheries Pier
office at Scalpay North Harbour. That's where he keeps
his boat when he's back on land."

Eilidh nodded, taking a mental note of the harbour.

Mark and Janey looked at each other, their eyes
exchanging messages Eilidh and Richard were at a loss
to decipher.

Watching them, Richard wondered yet again what
was going on under the surface between the two of
them, but whatever it was, it wasn't something he was
going to be able to get to grips with in the short time
available. After all, Janey was leaving soon.

"Eilidh, why don't we go and take a look at the
view," he suggested, thinking Janey deserved some
private time with an old friend when she was leaving
the very next day.

Eilidh smiled at him and nodded, her warm brown
eyes crinkling at the edges.

"Good idea."

She'd understood his prompting, and Richard felt an outpouring of love for her, thinking to himself how wonderful it was when you were so close to someone they could read your mind.

Eilidh walked on ahead, making her way towards the lighthouse buildings, with Richard following close behind.

Just as he reached the lighthouse buildings, Richard heard Mark say, "Janey, please don't leave again. I can't bear it."

He didn't hear what Janey's reply was.

He went out to the head of the rock and watched in alarm as Eilidh, balancing on a rock, shielded her eyes and stared out to sea.

"Eilidh! For heaven's sake, stand back from the edge," he called out, hurrying up to her.

Reaching her, he wrapped his arms protectively around her.

Eilidh gave him a playful slap.

"For Pete's sake, calm down, Richard. It's OK. Look, I'm back from the edge. There's plenty of room and barely any breeze today."

She pointed to the blue expanse in front of them.

"Look at it! It's beautiful. Stunning!" she cried out, her face lit up with excitement.

Richard followed her gaze.

She was right.

The ocean extended to the horizon, with its surface covered in shifting ripples.

What struck Richard was the space. Vast and open. No wonder the old navigators were convinced the earth was flat. The edge of the sea seemed to stretch out to infinity.

Resting his chin on Eilidh's shoulder, he smiled to himself.

Only a few days ago he'd been crammed into an underground carriage and gliding along dark tunnels far beneath the streets of London. He didn't think he'd ever feel the same about travelling on the underground again.

Waves were lapping and sucking gently at the rocks below them.

A rusty fishing boat chugged by, heading inland. The man at the wheel waved at them. Richard wondered if Findley had a boat like that. Hopefully, he'd soon find out.

Richard and Eilidh stood there for a long time, mesmerised by the movement of the water.

"There you are!" said Janey, sounding relieved to see them.

She came over to their side of the rock, with Mark in tow.

Richard turned and studied Mark's face.

He didn't look as distressed as he had earlier. If anything, he seemed to be at peace. The charged exchange between him and Janey appeared to be resolved.

Mark raised his hand to his forehead and narrowed his eyes as he gazed at the ocean.

"Nothing's taking me from this," he muttered, his brow furrowed. "Couldn't live without it."

Janey said nothing.

"You know, you have to learn to slow down here in the Outer Hebrides," commented Mark as he scanned the horizon. "It's a place for waiting and watching. You can't be a slave to time if you want to catch the real experience. A quarter of the world's whale and dolphin species have been recorded in our waters, and this lighthouse is part of the tourist Whale Trail, but I have to keep telling people, nature works at its own pace. This isn't like a zoo. If you're prepared to wait a little, I guarantee you we'll spot some form of wildlife. But you have to wait."

Eilidh smiled with delight.

"We have time," she said.

Richard sighed.

"Well, in that case, I think I'll sit down," he said, resigned to the situation.

"I'll bring you all some tea and milk. Mark, you should stay here in case you spot anything," instructed Janey.

She walked off towards the lighthouse.

Mark sat down next to Richard and Eilidh, his eyes focused on the sea.

"How do you know where to look?" asked Eilidh, following his gaze.

"There are clues. You can look for where the seabirds are feeding or for any changes in water patterns. Sometimes, if you see dark patches in the water, it could be a shoal of fish or something else. But in my personal opinion, it's mostly luck, pure and simple. This is a good time of year for sightings, though. The warmer weather brings us more wildlife."

Richard surreptitiously looked at his watch. He was prepared to give it an hour, but any longer and his stomach would be craving some lunch.

Janey appeared with a Thermos flask of tea, as well as one of hot milk, and some plastic cups. The lighthouse was well prepared for wildlife watching it seemed.

To Richard's satisfaction, Janey also produced a packet of Borders Dark Chocolate Ginger biscuits from her jacket pocket.

Knowing Mark was keeping watch, Richard and Eilidh helped themselves to refreshments.

"How did Findley and Simon know each other?" asked Richard, licking the chocolate from a biscuit off his fingers.

"School," said Mark and Eilidh in unison and then laughed.

"There's only one school in Tarbert," explained Mark. "The Sir E. Scott School. There was only just over a hundred of us attending it back then. You get to know each other pretty well. Findley dropped out early, before he sat any national exams, and his dad then set him up with his fishing business."

"Findley was bright," said Janey defensively. "Brighter than the rest of us. He was bullied, though, and up here, if that happens, you can't escape it. You're just stuck with it. I know of kids who've committed suicide at the school in Stornoway because of bullying. There's no other way out on a small island."

Mark nodded.

"Simon was Findley's protector at school, but you can't be around all the time. Sooner or later, they're going to catch up with you if you're in their line of sight. Nobody at that age wants to be known as a grass, so these things stay hidden, out of sight."

"That's surprising. If he's a fisherman, I imagine he's fairly strong physically," commented Richard.

Mark looked at him.

"Doesn't make any difference, Richard. Sorry to disagree with you, but physical strength is of no use if you aren't willing to use it."

He tapped his head.

"It's all in here. The bullies mess with your mind."

"Why do you think they picked on him?" asked Eilidh, curious.

Mark and Janey exchanged glances.

"Findley's gay," said Janey finally. "That's why the bastards targeted him."

"I see," said Richard, feeling sad.

Human nature never seemed to change, no matter where you went.

"Don't you go feeling sorry for him," said Mark. "He's living the best life as a fisherman. Loves it. He's also had a couple of books published about his life as a Harris fisherman. He's like a minor celebrity in Tarbert. He's doing good."

"And the bullies?" asked Eilidh.

There was silence.

"What about them?" asked Janey, looking none too happy.

"Are they still around?" persisted Eilidh.

"Yes, they are," stated Mark shortly.

There was another uncomfortable silence.

Richard decided it was useless to probe any further. He wished Eilidh hadn't continued questioning Mark and Janey over Findley's school life. There was so much more they needed to find out about Simon and Findley in recent times, but they weren't going to get any information now. A wall of secrecy had been erected and Richard had no doubt this would be happening time and time again in such a tight-knit community. At the end of the day, they were the outsiders.

He helped himself to another cup of tea and faced the ocean again.

After a few minutes of desultory chat, Mark patted Eilidh's shoulder to get her attention and pointed to a spot where the surface of the ocean was churning with foam.

"Can you see that? I suspect it's a Minke whale."

Richard and Eilidh fixed their eyes to where he was pointing, and before long, they were rewarded.

A dark shape parted the water and then flopped backwards with a huge splash.

The four of them watched the area until it was obvious the whale had moved on.

"Well, that's a first," said Richard, grinning.

"If you spend enough time here, you'll see all kinds of wonderful creatures," Mark told them. "Common and grey seals. Orca, Basking sharks, dolphins and porpoises... pilot whales. It's absolutely beautiful and so far, unspoilt. We're hoping the Scottish government keeps it that way. The tourism up here is getting a bit much these days."

"I doubt the crofters renting out their homes for a fortune during the summer would agree with you," remarked Janey.

Mark smiled ruefully.

"True," he agreed. "Money always wins the day."

"Well, I guess it's time for us to get going," said Janey, looking at Richard and Eilidh for confirmation.

They nodded and stood up.

Carrying the Thermos flasks and cups, they started to make their way back up to the lighthouse.

Richard didn't think Mark had any idea about the treasure's whereabouts, assuming there was treasure hidden somewhere on the island. And speaking of hiding, Mark himself seemed to have nothing to hide. Lacking in guile, his feelings were plain to see to everyone around him. Richard had spent years interviewing people in the search for artworks and he was as sure as he could be Mark knew nothing about the treasure.

Had the sighting of the Minke whale made their trip to the Eilean Glas lighthouse worth it?

Maybe it had, Richard thought, but that wasn't why they were on the island. They needed some results soon, because Lionel was going to be in a foul temper if they came back empty-handed from their trip to the Outer Hebrides. Their lack of success would only convince him further that the Art and Antiquities Unit needed private funding because it was a waste of taxpayers" money.

The clock was ticking.

10

Mike

Mike tried on a red tweed Trapper hat, brown fur attached to its flaps, and looked at himself in the shop's mirror.

"Mike, you look a total twat in that. Don't buy it," said a familiar voice, making him jump.

"Mariella," he said, pulling the hat off and turning to look at her.

"Yours truly," she said, making a mock-curtsey.

Mariella was dressed in a fetching white anorak, belted at the waist, and a pair of wide-legged black trousers. Black, wedge ankle boots were giving her some height.

The Italians always did have an innate sense of fashion, thought Mike.

"When did you get here?" asked Mike, tossing the hat back onto the pile next to him.

"Yesterday. Listen, I've got a proposition for you."

"You have?" asked Mike, looking doubtfully at her.

"Yes, come on, let's get what they call a 'dram' at the Time or Tide and I'll tell you all about it," said Mariella, taking Mike by the elbow and leading him out of the shop.

One day and she already knew where the local pub was. Impressive, thought Mike.

Mike walked across to the Time or Tide, with Mariella's hand tucked firmly into his arm. Somehow, he found himself reliving a time from his misbegotten youth when he was marched into a police station by an officer following a street fight.

He was feeling trapped, and what's more, he wasn't at all sure he wanted to hear Mariella's "proposition."

But his sense of fair play had kicked in. Given his poor behaviour in Birmingham, he felt he owed her one, even though he was positive he was going to regret letting Mariella have her say.

Nothing was ever simple or clear cut with Mariella, unfortunately. She was a complicated woman, who always had self-interest behind any request. Not that different to himself, he had to admit.

They walked into the pub and looked around in silence.

They caught each other's eye, both of them wondering the same thing. What kind of a weirdo had come up with the crazy notion to stick animal skulls on the wall of a pub?

Mariella looked away quickly and bit her lip.

Mike, meanwhile, grimaced with distaste and walked across to the bar to get their drinks.

"Can I have a triple Scotch, please, and a single," he said to the young barman.

"Sure," said the barman, turning to fetch the drinks.

"Where are you from?" the barman asked as he poured out the drinks.

"London."

"We're a long way from there."

"Yep. Sure are," said Mike, with feeling. "You been to London?"

"No. Too many people. It's claustrophobic. Besides, the air isn't clean down there, nor the water, either. Can't beat clean, Scottish water."

Mike nodded.

"We've got a few of you arriving on the island these days," carried on the barman. "Reckon you all must be escaping the big smog."

"Yes and no. London's not such a bad place. Never boring."

"You finding Harris boring?" asked the barman, a slight edge to his voice.

Mike raised his hands in surrender.

"Mate, I don't know Harris, full stop. Only just arrived. I'm not going to argue with you."

The barman nodded.

"It's OK. One man's trash is another man's treasure."

"Very true, mate. Very true," said Mike, with heart-felt sincerity.

"The country isn't for everyone," continued the barman, looking smug. "But don't you go thinking it's boring. Believe me, anything but, my friend, anything but."

Mike grinned at him.

"I'll take your word for that."

He paid for the drinks and took them across to the table Mariella had sat down at.

It was late morning and the rest of the pub was empty.

Mariella had chosen the table that was closest to the entrance of the pub.

Maybe she was hoping to make their visit as short as possible.

When he spotted the pile of bones underneath their table he didn't blame her for not wanting to stay. In his view, there was nothing aesthetically pleasing about bones. He'd already encountered too many bones working as a police officer to see the novelty factor about them. He just thought it was poor taste.

Sitting down, he noticed Mariella had taken her coat off.

She had on a fetching red shirt, which was accentuating her curves and small waist. Mariella was looking extremely pretty, which worried him. He didn't want to get distracted while she bartered with him. Tigers might be beautiful and everything, he thought, but not when sharing the same enclosed space.

"What are you staring at, Mike?" asked Mariella, lifting a hand to her mouth to check she hadn't smudged her lipstick.

"I was looking at your necklace," said Mike, thinking on his feet.

"This?" asked Mariella, in surprise, picking up a gold pendant. "Why would you be interested in this? I bet you don't even know what it signifies."

"A butterfly pendant? Let me guess. New beginnings? A new start?"

"Well done. Right the first time. Given to me by my boyfriend."

"Cheapskate, is he?" asked Mike, unmoved.

"No, unlike you, he's not," shot back Mariella, visibly trying to control her temper.

"That's good, then. Although you should know those don't look like real sapphires to me."

Mariella scowled.

"They're the real deal. Are you daring to question my judgement as a jeweller?"

"No. I'm questioning the judgement of your boyfriend. Real or not, those sapphires look totally fake. It's simply a question of having no finesse."

"Ha! Finesse," growled Mariella. "Says the man who dresses like a buffoon."

Mike grinned.

"Fair point. Touché."

Mike pushed her drink across the table.

"Here you go," he said, cheerfully. "At least this time I didn't say I'd forgotten my wallet."

Mariella's face cleared and she chortled at the memory of their first date.

"I really don't know how I put up with you for so long back then."

"Me, neither," said Mike, in all sincerity.

"I must've had poor self-esteem," continued Mariella, trying for a dig.

It bounced off Mike.

"Drink up, Mariella, I haven't got all day."

Mike watched with satisfaction as Mariella's generous chest rose in anger.

"Come on, Mariella. You know I'm only winding you up."

"Yes, you're a wind-up merchant," agreed Mariella, reaching for her whisky.

She raised her glass to touch his.

"Thank you," she said, sweetly. "Cheers."

Mike watched her suspiciously from the corner of his eyes and took a mouthful of his tipple.

He couldn't figure out why she was trying to be so nice to him. The old Mariella would've stormed out by now given his level of provocation.

"Come on, Mike, stop looking at me as if I've sprouted horns, for Christ's sake. Can't we call a truce?" remonstrated Mariella, putting her drink down.

"Oh, alright," said Mike, flopping back on his seat, defeated.

"Look, I know I was a bit het up the last time we met. I can't say you didn't deserve it, because you've treated me like shit. Even you have to admit that."

Mike nodded.

"Anyway, I've given it some thought and decided I'll be the bigger person and put my animosity aside for the sake of tracking down the rest of the treasure. We'd make a pretty good team, don't you think, between the pair of us? We could also split the proceeds from the find."

"Ah."

Mike swallowed the rest of his whisky, buying himself some time.

Mariella looked at him expectantly.

"I like working on my own," he said, at last.

"If you think I'm not going to know what you're up to on the island, you're mistaken. I've Nico with me, too."

Mike groaned.

"He's going to stick out like a sore thumb."

"He's useful. He has my back."

"Didn't have your back the night you had the torc and chalice stolen from you."

Mariella's eyes lit up with sudden rage.

"How long are you planning to stay up here for?" he asked, before she exploded.

"As long as it takes. My business takes care of itself."

Mike raised his eyebrows.

"It could take a while, and there's a good chance we won't find anything," he said.

Mariella smiled indulgently.

"You wouldn't be up here if that's what you truly believed."

She placed her empty whisky glass in front of Mike.

"That's hardly enough. A Cosmo this time, please."

Mike got up and walked to the bar.

"Back for more already, mate?" asked the barman, with a smirk.

"Yes. The lady would like a Cosmo, please."

The barman began to prepare Mariella's drink.

"Always the same with the ladies," he commented. "Cosmos. Safe choice. Don't know why they won't try something more adventurous. We serve a few cracking cocktails here. The Anna Banana, for example. Sherry mixed with Drambuie, crème de banane, and Monkey Shoulder. That's an American one..."

He poured out some cranberry juice, added the lime, and then started to shake the cocktail.

"Or there's the Suffering Bastard. Ginger beer, gin, bourbon, lime juice, and angostura bitters. Then there's Bacon Me Angry or Ruby Queen. Ruby Queen is our speciality. Beet juice mixed with whisky."

Mike made a face.

"It actually works very well," insisted the barman,

carefully pouring the drink into a cocktail glass and passing the Cosmo over to Mike.

"I'm sure it does," agreed Mike. "Tell you what, while you're at it, why don't you make me up the Suffering Bastard one?"

The barman grinned at him and went to prepare the drink.

"I worked at the Merchant Hotel in Belfast where they still use the original rum used for the first Mai Tai cocktail in 1944," the barman informed him. "Costs a bomb, though. A month of my salary gone just like that," he clicked his fingers, "on a drink. Crazy, man."

"Sounds it," agreed Mike.

"People from all over the world used to drop by for that drink. The Merchant Hotel drew them in."

He sighed.

"Miss it, do you?" asked Mike.

"Me? Nah. I miss the tips for sure, but Harris is home for me. All of us want to come back here after we've been away for a while."

"What's your name?" asked Mike, thinking he might come in useful at some point during his stay.

"Oliver Rust. Yours?"

"Mike. Mike Telford."

"Nice to meet you."

"Likewise," said Mike.

"What's your staple tipple?" asked the barman. "It's not whisky, is it? I can tell."

"Nope. I drink lager when back home. Always fancy a change, though, when I'm away."

Mike turned and saw that Mariella was watching him from across the room, wondering what was taking him so long.

Waving reassuringly at her, he fished his wallet out of his back pocket, and once both drinks were sitting on the counter, paid for them.

"What took you so long?" demanded Mariella as he placed the Cosmo in front of her.

"The barman has done a doctorate in cocktails, by the looks of it. I think he would have happily listed every single cocktail they make here, if I'd given him the encouragement."

"Not what you expect in a provincial pub," remarked Mariella.

"No, that's true," said Mike, thoughtfully. "I wonder who owns this joint. He clearly hasn't spent his entire life on the island, either."

Mariella shrugged.

"It doesn't really matter to us."

"Well, it might. Spoke to Richard when I was travelling up here. He had a very strange experience in here a few nights ago. Seems to think his drinks were spiked. Not like him to be fanciful, either."

Mariella pursed her lips for a moment.

"Don't see why they would do that. Daft thing to do."

"I agree. He was telling me things don't add up here. Many of the relationships on the island are very interconnected, as you'd expect in a small community. One of the policewomen here in Tarbert, Fiona Mitchell, is in some sort of relationship with the bar owner. And he suspects she's the one who took the three pieces of treasure."

Mariella nodded.

"She was."

Mike looked at her, his face impassive.

"Anything else you care to tell me?" he asked.

"Are we joining forces, then?"

Mike shrugged.

Better the devil you know, he thought to himself. At least working with Mariella meant he could keep an eye on her.

"I don't see any harm in that."

"Are you going to seal the deal?"

Mike stared at her.

"How?" he asked, feeling nervous again.

"You give me your signet ring as a sign of trust," said Mariella. "I know what it means to you. I need to have something from you before I can commit myself. You've broken my trust too many times."

Mike took a deep breath in, as he glanced down at his signet ring.

Lifting his head and looking into Mariella's dark-blue eyes, he suddenly realised he didn't mind handing over the only thing left to him by his debt-ridden father.

Towards the end, crushed by debt from a chronic gambling habit, his father had sold everything of value he had. Except for his gold signet ring, which belonged to his mother's family and had their coat of arms engraved on it. It was the one item Mike's father left to him from his once-prosperous estate and proud family lineage. All in all, it was a desperately sad legacy from a man who'd garnered an excellent reputation as a savvy antiques dealer during his lifetime. His fame had extended far beyond Lavenham, where they lived.

"OK," Mike said heavily. "Here you go."

He took the ring off his little finger and placed it in front of Mariella, who seemed astonished he'd agreed to her request.

She picked it up and tried it on the third finger of her right hand.

It fit perfectly.

"Great!" she said, smiling at him.

She took a sip of her Cosmo, ignoring the desolate expression on Mike's face.

"So, you were going to tell me about Fiona Mitchell," Mike reminded her.

"Ah, yes. Of course. Well, in the middle of April I had a visitor to the workshop and Nico tried to fob her off, as he usually does when someone hasn't scheduled a visit through my secretary."

Mike nodded, remembering his encounter with Nico at the entrance to The Midas Touch.

"She then told Nico that she'd been advised by Peter Smithfield to get in contact with me. You know the man. High-end dealer of antiques and collectibles. Owner of Pegasus Antiques in Manchester."

"I do."

"Yes, well, because of her connection with Peter Smithfield, I allowed her to come up to the studio. First of all, she showed me the Two Emperor coin. I've dealt with the coin once before, but I've never heard of a Two Emperor coin found that far north."

Mike scratched his ear.

"I don't think it's that odd. The Vikings were great traders and collected artefacts from as far away as the Middle East, didn't they? The Galloway Hoard had Anglo-Saxon brooches and an Anglo-Saxon crucifix in it, so I would say finding a Two Emperor coin up here isn't as strange as it looks."

He drank some of his Suffering Bastard cocktail, feeling the alcohol kicking in and mellowing him.

"I often think about the beautiful Anglo-Saxon arte-facts that the Vikings plundered and then melted down for silver ingots," he added. "It was a silver economy they ran, but it's really quite tragic when you think of the Anglo-Saxon craftsmanship lost."

If Mariella was surprised by his nostalgia, she didn't show it.

"Let's not lose focus, Mike. As I was saying," she continued, determined to stick to the point. "That's when she showed me the torc, the cup, and the cat pin. I declined the pin after studying it because of its poor quality. The stone in the centre was amber and it was badly chipped. The gold claws holding the amber in place were scratched, and besides, the workmanship wasn't very good. I wasn't convinced I'd get an easy sale from it despite the fact it was so unusual."

"Stupid move that," chipped in Mike, unable to resist giving his opinion.

Mariella glared at him.

"What? It's true, and you know it. You let go of what was probably the most unique item in the collection."

"You didn't see the bloody pin, Mike, so get off your high horse. I deal in quick and fast sales. That's where my priorities lie, not in saving objects for the good of the nation. Stop patronising me, or we'll end up falling out."

Mike looked amused.

"You should be able to take some home truths, you know," he remarked.

"Yes, and how do home truths go down with you, Mike? Do all those dealers you've shafted over your long career keep you awake at night?"

"No, not at all."

Mariella stared at him.

"You said we should keep focused," Mike reminded her.

Mariella laughed bitterly.

"You never change, do you? Try and see if you can keep your trap shut long enough to let me finish my piece, OK? Or I'll lose my temper. What I wanted to say was that the piece that won me over was the cup. It was similar to the Jelling Cup, with animal designs engraved into it. Beautiful. As you already know, of course," she added, drily.

Mike nodded in agreement.

The Jelling Cup was a cup found in Jelling, Denmark, and was presumed to be one of the few items left behind in the burial chamber of the Danish monarch, King Gorm the Old. In his opinion, the cup found in Harris demonstrated superior craftsmanship.

"Yes, it was impressive."

"I agreed to purchase the torc and the cup. Fiona Mitchell wanted the money in cash, and we agreed on a two-week deadline to do the deal."

"She gave you her real name?" asked Mike in disbelief.

"No, of course not. She wasn't as clever as she liked to make out, though. She let fall enough detail about the find and how she managed to get her hands on it for me and Nico to identify who she was. It wasn't hard."

"Tell me, which one of you two grassed her identity to the others?"

"Neither. If we managed to find out, others would've done so easy enough. I'm sure we weren't first on her list."

Mike shook his head.

"If it wasn't you, it was Nico. The news spread too fast. If I were you, I'd keep an eye on that boy. Not good to have a leaker around."

"When I want your advice, Mike, I'll ask for it," she snapped, her chest heaving with anger again.

There was silence while Mike drank some more of his cocktail and Mariella folded her arms.

Mike took a peek at her as he tilted his glass for another sip.

Watching him, Mariella giggled.

"Could you please stop winding me up and behave like a grown-up? I feel like I'm in kindergarten again."

"Nothing wrong with kindergarten," said Mike, solemnly. "Plenty of lessons to be learned there."

Mariella groaned.

"I give up. You're a hopeless case. I told you to keep it zipped, didn't I? More importantly, Fiona hinted to me there was more treasure around and said she would be in touch in the near future. She was very vague about the details, but what this tells us is that Simon must have told her there was more of it."

"Yes, we know that," said Mike, impatiently. "The problem we all have is nobody knows where the rest of the damn treasure is. Simon's dead. Richard says Simon's wife doesn't have a clue where it is, which seems a little odd to me, but Richard's a very experienced officer and I reckon he'd know if she was lying to him. We're basically at a dead end."

"Maybe they didn't get on that well or trust each other," remarked Mariella. "I know exactly how that feels, don't I, Mike? Maybe he didn't say anything to his wife because he wanted to do things his way."

Mike shrugged.

"Either way, we're stuck."

"Talking of stuck, you need to stick close to Richard Langley and make sure you learn as much as you can from him."

"Yes, I don't think that'll be a problem. I reckon he's reached the point where he's happy to get any help he can on this one." Mike rubbed his chin. "He's really not acting like himself. I don't know, might be because his partner's pregnant or maybe he has other things on his mind back in London. Haven't seen him like this before. I reckon he'll be pleased to get this resolved and find himself back at New Scotland Yard."

"Well, it all works in our favour."

Mike nodded.

"It certainly does. How do I get in touch with you, by the way?"

"I'm staying at the Hotel Hebrides."

"Nice," said Mike, looking impressed.

"Where are you staying?"

"An Airbnb studio flat at 4 Tobair Mairi."

"You always were a tightwad."

"True. I'll wear that as a badge of honour. What about a mobile number?"

"You've got my mobile number. I haven't changed it."

"Might have to unblock it," commented Mike, enjoying watching Mariella bristle again.

"Bastard."

"Not sure mobile phone coverage will be great across the island," said Mike, thoughtfully. "It might end up being a problem but we'll see how we go."

"Have you finished with your drink?" she asked

impatiently. "I suggest you hook up with Richard as soon as you can and get the ball rolling."

Mike looked down at his half-empty Suffering Bastard and pushed it away.

"Not as good as it's cracked up to be," he said. "Let's go."

11

Eilidh

Ringing the doorbell for a second time, Eilidh let out a sigh of exasperation.

Patrick McQuire wasn't in.

Damn it.

Nothing was going to plan in their investigation and it felt that at every turn they were thwarted.

So far, the situation for them had only gone from bad to worse. Beginning with Richard arriving, almost comatose, from his night out to Janey's house getting broken into. Eilidh was feeling increasingly suspicious of the people around them and hoped she wasn't edging into paranoia.

Slowly but surely, she sensed things were escalating since their arrival in Harris.

While she was trying to track down Patrick at his house, Richard had run Janey up to Stornoway Airport in Lewis.

However, the elusive Patrick McQuire, Simon's real father, was not in.

Her phone calls to Patrick had gone unanswered.

She'd been told that he was an artist and was often out and about painting, even in the rain, but that didn't explain why he hadn't called her back after she'd left three messages on his answering machine.

Richard had told her all about his encounter with Willie, Simon's stepdad, at the Time or Tide pub. They had mutually agreed to let the man be, unless it was strictly necessary to speak with him. Given Simon had a difficult relationship with Willie, it was unlikely he would have confided in him about the treasure.

Eilidh hoped Patrick didn't have Willie's antipathy towards the English, otherwise getting any information from him would be nigh on impossible, but her gut feeling after viewing his house and garden was that Patrick was a cheerier character than Willie.

Patrick's house was unusual, with its roughcast walls painted bright yellow and his wooden door and windowsills coloured a soft grey.

Bunting was attached to the slate roof of the house, its brightly coloured triangles fluttering in the sea breeze.

The garden was stacked full of sculptures—sculptures made entirely, it seemed, from painted pieces of plastic and steel rods cemented into the ground.

A sunflower was standing upright, next to an enormous brown bear. In another corner there was a wigwam, made of three steel rods, with a sheet of plastic scales over the top.

And as the *pièce de résistance*, there was a life-size Pocahontas, whose plastic dress was decorated with beads and pieces of glass.

Lying next to the front gate was a huge whale skull.

It must've been dragged there from a nearby beach some time ago.

Tangled daisies had grown through its eye sockets, their yellow stamens incongruous against the bone.

With a sigh, Eilidh walked back out of the garden.

Outside Patrick's gate, there was a plastic table selling plants for £2.50, with an honesty box for the cash.

In keeping with the eccentricity of the garden, several of the plants were Venus flytraps, which would need to be kept indoors to survive.

Feeling like a child again, Eilidh touched the trigger hairs on one of the flytraps and watched as the lids shut.

Patrick would have done better to attract youthful buyers by placing a small piece of rotting meat close to the Venus flytraps to attract the flies, but as this apparently was a very quiet part of the world it seemed pointless. Eilidh didn't think there would be many passersby or custom for his plants.

She turned and looked around.

Aside from the small grouping of eight houses, there was nothing else in sight but grassy wilderness, covered in a patchwork of yellow, white, pink and purple flowers.

Patrick's house was the last in the row, situated next to a path that led across the grassland to Tràigh na Cleabhaig beach.

Eilidh's guidebook stated Tràigh na Cleabhaig was situated further down from the famous Luskentyre Sands and was a lesser known beauty spot.

Far in the distance, Eilidh could see the periwinkle blue of the sea.

Gazing across at the sea, she decided she might as

well do some sightseeing. Otherwise, her trip there would be a complete waste of her time.

She put her sunglasses back on and made her way through the gate and onto the path leading to the beach.

It was warm, and she soon had her jacket sleeves tied around her neck as she walked.

All around her she could hear insects thrumming, the noise vibrating like the chords on a stringed instrument.

Flowers of every shape dotted the landscape like confetti, creating a rich tapestry against the green grass.

This was the machair, remembered Eilidh. In Harris, the wild grassland was called machair. In England, she reckoned something similar would be called meadowland.

She bent down and touched a small flower next to the path. It had a distinctive purple-pink, bulbous head and looked like an orchid.

She resisted the urge to pluck it and walked on.

Small birds were dipping in and out of the machair, chasing insects, all of them too occupied with their incessant desire for food to pay her any attention.

Eilidh wished she knew more about wildlife. She doubted she'd be able to identify a single flower, bird, or insect around her. She was beginning to realise how sheltered from the natural world her life in London was and felt this wasn't a good thing.

She walked past the carcass of a car, slumped a short distance from the path with its rusting wheels deep in the mud.

The first sign of human life and an ugly one at that, thought Eilidh.

Stepping up her pace, it didn't take her long to

reach the edge of Tràigh na Cleabhaig. It was, like many of Harris's scenic spots, a beautiful white, sandy beach.

An azure sea was lapping at the edge of it.

The scene should've been tranquil, but the beach was noisy with the screeching of seabirds.

A large number of them were gathered on the sand, distinctive with their white bodies, black heads, and red beaks.

Several more of them were out at sea, skimming the waves. Some were returning back to the beach from the sea, their catch dangling from their beaks.

Eilidh was about to step onto the beach when she heard a loud shout behind her.

Alarmed, she turned around, trying to locate where the call came from.

In the far distance, camouflaged among the grass, was seated an old man in khaki army fatigues.

He was facing the sea.

In one hand he was holding a sketch pad and with the other he was waving at her.

Puzzled, she made her way across the machair to where he was seated.

He turned out to be a tall man with broad shoulders and a thick, white beard. His skin had been toasted to a rich walnut colour by the sun and the wrinkles on his face made interesting patterns on his skin. His eyes were a light ice-blue.

Seeing the laughter lines on his face, Eilidh relaxed.

The man stood up from his camping seat and with old-fashioned courtesy, offered a hand.

She shook it.

"Hello," she said smiling.

"I hope you don't mind my shouting at you," said the man apologetically, clasping his golf hat to his chest. "But you were about to cross over that beach and the Arctic terns are nesting there right now. They can get quite aggressive, you know. They'd have begun to attack you if you tried to walk across their patch. Only protecting their own, of course."

Eilidh turned to look at the beach.

The terns continued to shriek to each other as they went about their business.

"Ah, I see."

"You can take the path skirting the beach. It'll take you to the same place. I mean, I assume you're looking for the ruined chapel like most people?"

"I was just exploring the area to be honest with you. I didn't have a specific destination in mind," admitted Eilidh, smiling. "I was looking for Patrick McQuire, who lives nearby, but he wasn't in. It seemed a shame to waste a trip out here so I thought I'd go for a stroll instead."

A wary look crept into the old man's piercing blue eyes.

"And may I ask why you've come all this way to look for Patrick?"

Eilidh took off her sunglasses and stared at him.

"Don't tell me you're Patrick McQuire."

The man hesitated, then nodded.

"I'm Eilidh Simmons," Eilidh said, softly. For some reason, her instinct was telling her it wouldn't take much to alarm Patrick. "I work for Scotland Yard and we're visiting Harris at the request of Simon's wife, Janey."

An expression of deep sorrow flickered momentarily over Patrick's face.

Eilidh had seen similar looks on the faces of the bereaved parents she'd comforted during her time working at the Homicide Unit. There was no pain quite like it. Losing a child seemed to go against the natural order of things; parents always expected to die before their children.

"I'm sorry for your loss, Patrick."

He bowed his head.

"Yes, thank you, it hasn't been easy," he said quietly.

They stood still for a minute while the wind whipped through the clumps of sea grass edging the beach, shaking their stiff strands and making them rattle. Incongruously, the noise reminded Eilidh of the rustle of a porcupine's spines.

Patrick broke the silence.

"Why am I a person of interest to Scotland Yard?" he asked, a quizzical gleam in his eyes.

"It's about Simon. We've been told you're his father and we wanted to ask you if you knew anything about some treasure Simon supposedly uncovered on the island. As you probably know, any treasure find in the UK needs to be declared to the state. Janey seems to be convinced Simon made a significant find up here. I'm currently working for the Art and Antiquities Unit in London so this is in our purview," explained Eilidh.

Patrick looked at her, his eyes sad.

"Gold brings interest from every quarter, it appears," he murmured.

"Why? Have you had others question you about it?" she asked sharply.

Patrick didn't reply.

Instead, he turned to face the sea.

"One life's already been lost," he said, watching the waves. "I don't want to see any more lost. We shouldn't be disturbing the possessions of the dead. Simon paid for it. The dead have a stronger ownership over their belongings than we realise. Keep away from it. Treasure should always stay buried where the dead left it."

He looked at Eilidh again.

"Otherwise it just becomes a curse."

Eilidh shivered suddenly.

The old man was behaving like an oracle from the past.

She put on her jacket and zipped it up.

"Patrick, if you believe Simon died as a result of having found the treasure, surely you'd want us to locate it as soon as possible. There'll be others chasing it down. Sooner or later, it'll be found."

Patrick laughed out loud.

"I've heard it all now."

Eilidh stared at him, confused.

Patrick smiled.

"It won't be found, lassie. It won't be found," he assured her.

"So, you do know where it is?" asked Eilidh, trying to pin him down.

"No, I don't. I don't. I don't want anything to do with it," growled Patrick, avoiding her eyes.

She could tell he was lying, but what could she do about it? It wasn't as if they were having a formal police interview under caution.

She turned and looked out to sea, watching the waves curling onto the sand.

The sea seemed to be at peace, but she knew in the

blink of an eye it could turn into something quite different. The quiet was deceptive, for the ocean was always a temperamental entity, prey to different weather fronts and currents.

There seemed to be many underlying currents within the community in Harris, too, and she doubted they'd have enough time to decipher them in any meaningful way.

She sighed to herself.

"I didn't come here to cause you any distress," she said gently. "We're trying to get to the bottom of things because it's a little bit more complicated than just recovering the treasure. Some pieces have been sold by many accounts, and it's illegal to not declare treasure and sell it."

Patrick shrugged.

"I don't know anything about treasure getting sold."

"But you knew Simon," urged Eilidh.

Patrick nodded.

"Yes, I did, and I can tell you he'd never have knowingly done anything illegal. It's preposterous to suggest otherwise."

Eilidh smiled wearily.

Round and round we go, she thought.

Patrick patted the camping chair.

"Take a seat. You look like you could use one."

"Thank you," said Eilidh, genuinely grateful for the offer.

She sat down, feeling some relief at taking the weight off her legs.

Patrick sat down a little distance from her and retrieved his sketchbook from the grass.

He picked up a pencil and began to work on his half-finished drawing.

Looking across at his sketchbook, Eilidh was surprised to see how accomplished his drawing was. The unusual sculptures in Patrick's garden had given her some preconceived notions about his artistic ability. Not good ones, it had to be said.

"I understand you want to track down the treasure," commented Patrick, popping his head up and down to look at the sea as he drew. "But you might as well give up. I'm afraid it's not going to be easy for anyone to find now."

"I think we've established that," agreed Eilidh. "We've already been told by the police here it's a wild goose chase."

Patrick raised his eyebrows.

"I wouldn't say so. The treasure was real enough."

Eilidh sat up.

"You saw it?"

Patrick shook his head.

"No, I didn't."

This time it seemed he wasn't lying.

Disappointed, she slumped back on the chair again.

"Simon wasn't a liar," insisted Patrick. "He told me he'd found treasure. I knew Simon. He was telling me the truth."

"And do you have any idea where he'd have left it?"

"Not with Janey. That's for sure," he said dryly.

He continued to draw, moving the pencil in bold strokes across the page.

Reaching down, Eilidh plucked a pink flower from the machair.

"Sea pink," said Patrick, glancing at her. "Thrift's

another name for it. As for this wilderness round about, it's called machair. A real Scottish word, that."

"That's what I was told. Machair," repeated Eilidh with a lazy smile. "It's absolutely stunning with the wildflowers."

Patrick nodded and returned to his sketching.

"Good time of year to visit Harris," he stated, his head bent low over his drawing. "The flowers are in full bloom just now."

Eilidh closed her eyes, enjoying the feel of the fresh sea breeze stroking her face.

Right then, she felt she couldn't care less about the location of the treasure. She just wanted to fall asleep. The sun was shining and she was sleepy. Everything around her was inducing her to relax: the oxygenated air, the movement of the sea with the terns balancing over it, the profusion of wildflowers all around them, the soft sand gleaming in the sunlight.

For a short time, she dozed, with her head back and her hands resting loosely on her thighs.

She was woken by the sound of a grunt next to her.

"Look over there," said Patrick, his voice sharp.

Eilidh reluctantly opened her eyes.

Patrick was frowning.

"To your right, lass," he muttered under his breath. "To your right."

She turned her head to the right and looked.

In the far distance, a sharp light was flashing.

She lifted a hand to shield her eyes, straining to see it.

"What the hell is it?"

"Binoculars."

"*Binoculars?*"

"Yes, you see, you're not the only one interested in my movements," Patrick informed her. "Seen those binoculars plenty of times recently. Started up when Simon died."

He was focused on his sketch once more, but his strokes now held more urgency, shifting rapidly across the page.

Eilidh wondered if they were all becoming a little paranoid. The treasure seemed to be having that effect on them.

"Told you, no good's going to come of the treasure," Patrick added, his head bent. "The best thing's to stay out of it."

Eilidh watched him for a minute.

"You know where the treasure is, don't you?" she asked softly.

"Begging your pardon, miss, but even if I do know the treasure's whereabouts, the secret will be going to the grave with me," he said firmly.

"Aren't you worried that sooner or later they'll catch up with you? Wouldn't it be easier to clear it up with the police once and for all? Make sure it ends up in the right hands?" she asked, still trying to persuade him.

"The police? I'll never have anything to do with *them*," said Patrick in a disgusted voice. "You're alright, lass, but in general I don't have faith in the police force. As for the others, they can try. Was hard enough for you to track me down, wasn't it? I'll be staying out of the way soon. Next Tuesday, I'm planning a trip to Lewis. I've a pal who has a croft by Uig beach. It'll give me a welcome break from the unwanted attention."

The pencil was flying across the page now, manic in its movements.

Patrick added some more shading and then let out a sigh of satisfaction.

"What do you think?" he asked, holding up the sketch.

"I think it's beautiful," said Eilidh sincerely.

Patrick had captured the essence of the beach and the birds in the sketch. The waves were breaking up with foam on the sand, a cloudy sky floating above it.

The drawing was charmingly executed, his pencil lines bold and confident like those of a professional artist.

He ripped out the sketch and handed it to her.

Surprised, she held it in her hands.

"Take it. Art should always find its way to a loving home," he said, smiling. "These drawings are like my children now. Worth more than any treasure to me."

"Thank you," said Eilidh, moved.

He folded his sketchbook and stood up.

"Now, if you don't mind, I think I'll head back to the house," he said.

"Of course," said Eilidh, getting up. "Thank you for the rest."

She watched as Patrick folded up the camp chair.

"Could we come and speak to you again some-time?" she asked, knowing Richard would want a word with Patrick given her dismal success in interviewing him.

Patrick's blue eyes bored into her.

"You can."

He nodded.

"If you can find me," he added, picking up his belongings and making his way across the machair to his house.

Eilidh carefully rolled up the drawing, and holding onto it, walked along the coast path leading to the ruined chapel.

She wanted to have a look at the chapel and then head back to her car. She was going to need a cup of tea and a scone shortly, and the afternoon was passing her by.

Eilidh ambled past another beach and giggled when she saw a few black-faced sheep resting on the sand, acting as though it was the most normal thing in the world. Where else would you see sheep straying onto an empty beach? Harris definitely had a uniqueness of its own.

She clambered up to the top of the hill where the chapel stood and looked back.

A couple of walkers were walking onto the beach occupied by the Artic terns.

She watched as the terns started to screech in alarm.

Before long, the birds were dive bombing the walkers, who began to run for it, stumbling clumsily across the sand dunes.

Eilidh felt relieved Patrick had saved her from the terns. With her bulk, she couldn't run like she used to.

She stroked her belly, wondering why she was finding it so hard to get used to carrying the extra weight. It would be a huge consolation to her if she knew for certain she was going to recover her svelte shape post-pregnancy. She wasn't kidding herself, though. Looking down at her bump, it didn't seem possible.

Trying to distract herself from morose thoughts, she looked at the land around the ruined chapel.

Surely, she thought, if anyone was going to go metal detecting on the island they should do so around this ancient chapel. Wouldn't it be possible for treasure to be found right there, where she was standing?

She had a vision in her mind of wild Vikings arriving on the Harris coast in spring, and a monk hurriedly burying the chapel's holy relics in the grounds, trying to keep them safe from pillaging. A murdered monk might carry the secret location of those relics with him to the next world, much as Simon seemed to have done.

She studied the chapel once more.

She probably had the wrong era. The chapel might well be more recent than the Viking era.

Smiling to herself, she could hear Richard's prosaic voice in her head, scolding her for being several hundred years out in her estimation of the chapel's age.

Lifting a hand, she stroked the rough surface of its worn grey stones.

White and orange algae shredded under her hand.

That's what she was feeling on this island, she decided, caressing the solid stone. A sense of time and history. It was everywhere. In the unspoilt beaches, in the machair's wildness, the old crofts, and the very rocks on the island. There were reminders everywhere on the island of its past history, and the treasure, if they found it, was going to be yet another reminder of a bygone age.

Inside the chapel, she took a photo with her phone of the view through the narrow window, which was open to the elements.

The slit which stood for the window of the chapel was facing what she now called the tern's beach, with the green, white, and blue of the view in sharp contrast to the chapel's dull grey stone. Whoever built the chapel chose the view from the window well.

With the roof on, the inside of the chapel would have been a dark, dank place. She could imagine candles lit during mass and the smell of incense clearing the air of foul odours.

She walked outside.

After watching the rough waves breaking against the rocks below, she stepped back from the chapel and made her way back down to the path.

It was time to head home.

The walk back seemed to take a very long time and she had nearly reached her car when she saw a blonde lady, wearing ripped jeans and a T-shirt, approaching her.

"Eilidh Simmons?"

Eilidh stopped, surprised.

"Yes?"

"Hi. I'm Fiona Mitchell."

"Oh! Yes. Nice to meet you, Fiona."

"Likewise. You've been enjoying a walk, I see," said Fiona, smiling at her.

"Yes, very much so."

"It's truly beautiful in places such as this. We're very lucky to live here."

"Yes," agreed Eilidh.

There was an awkward silence.

Eilidh, who wanted to get away, put her hands in her jacket pockets and looked longingly at her car.

"I met Richard the other night. Isn't he with you today?"

Eilidh's eyes snapped back to Fiona.

She was unable to prevent an intense dislike of Fiona rising within her. Fiona might've had nothing to do with Richard's drugging, but she'd been the one who'd fetched the drinks on that notorious night.

In any case, she didn't want to be reminded of it by Fiona.

"No, Richard's trying to catch up on some work this morning," she lied.

"Ah, I see. I assume he's given up trying to track down the non-existent treasure."

"Not at all," said Eilidh with a forced smile. "The investigation's still ongoing. We'll get results soon enough, I'm sure."

Eilidh peered down at Fiona's walking boots.

"Have you been for a walk yourself?"

Fiona nodded.

"Yes, my home's only twenty minutes' drive away and I quite often stop here for a walk. You have to go for walks in Harris." She shrugged. "Not much else to do, if you hadn't noticed."

Eilidh looked at her in surprise.

"Must get a bit dull in the winter, I suppose."

"It does. Very," Fiona said, with some bitterness in her voice. "But my partner and I get away on some nice trips. Antigua last year."

Eilidh made a suitably impressed noise.

"It's alright for you London officers," remarked Fiona. "You get to see it all down there in London, no doubt. Plenty of excitement to keep you going."

"Nothing's stopping you applying for a post in London," retorted Eilidh, irritated for some reason by her remarks. Fiona seemed to have a chip on her shoulder about something, but whatever it was had nothing to do with her.

Fiona chuckled.

"London's way too expensive for me. I doubt my three-bedroom bungalow would even get me a small studio flat on the very outskirts of London."

She waved her hands at the scenery.

"Anyway, who'd want to leave all this beauty behind?" she asked.

"Certainly not me," agreed Eilidh. "I think Harris is a place once seen, never forgotten."

Eilidh took her car keys out of her jacket pocket.

"If you don't mind, Fiona, I'm going to head off. I'm desperately needing a cup of tea and a toilet."

Fiona nodded.

"If you turn left at the junction and drive on for five minutes, you'll come across a large grocer's shop called The Rhubarb," she said helpfully. "They've a tea shop at the back of it. They do great homemade baking, too."

"Sounds perfect," said Eilidh, glad it was so nearby. "Catch you later, no doubt."

"Oh, definitely. I'm sure of it," said Fiona without a hint of irony.

After waving goodbye, Eilidh got into her car and reversed.

She was making her way down the narrow road leading to the main junction, when she caught sight of Fiona in her rear-view mirror.

Fiona was standing rigid as a statue in the middle of the car park, watching her departure.

12

Richard

"I'm not sure this was such a good idea," said Richard, watching as Findley made his preparations prior to them leaving.

He was wearing a red life jacket and clinging to the edge of the boat, even though they hadn't set off yet.

"Don't be ridiculous, Richard," said Mike impatiently.

"Everything OK?" asked Findley, walking over to them with a concerned look on his face.

Findley was a large man with a mop of dark, curly hair, who was surprisingly nimble walking around the tight confines of the inflatable boat.

"Everything's fine, Findley," replied Mike, with what Richard felt was a callous disregard for his friend's wellbeing. "Richard's just going to take some time to find his sea legs."

Findley's brown eyes swivelled round to Richard.

"This boat's safe as houses, if that's what you're worried about. I've been taking it out every summer for the last eight years. It's not as sturdy and solid as my fishing boat, of course, but it's strong. I've never come to grief in it."

"That's good to know," admitted Richard.

"We can head back at any point. As I said, there's only three places Simon would go hunting for scallops. It shouldn't take us too long."

"Excellent," said Mike.

Excellent, thought Richard, biting his lips. He could think of many words for the trip, but excellent wasn't one of them.

Gazing at the white crests out at sea, he had a nasty feeling their boat trip wasn't going to be comparable to one on the Thames river boat.

Findley undid the landing rope and cranked the motor.

They started chugging out of the harbour.

Richard looked ahead stoutly and silently resolved to try and enjoy the trip.

Mike, meantime, was seated next to Findley as he steered the boat, deep in conversation. He appeared to be in his element.

Mike was a dark horse, decided Richard, wondering how well he really knew the guy. Who'd have guessed Mike would have felt so at home on a boat of all things?

The boat turned out of the harbour and into the open sea with a lurch.

Some of Richard's breakfast made its way up his esophagus and left him with the taste of bile in his mouth.

Wishing with all his heart he hadn't eaten, he leaned his head over the boat's side.

Fifteen minutes later, he'd discharged the majority of his breakfast into the sea but felt a little better.

Mike came and sat next to him.

"Mate, the best thing you can do is sit in the middle of the boat. A little less movement there. And keep your eyes fixed to the horizon."

Richard was so washed out by then, he obeyed Mike's instructions without protest.

He sat on the bench, hoping his stomach would grow accustomed to the movement of the sea or it was going to seem like a very long day.

The things he did for the sake of antiquities, he thought to himself. Literally, beyond belief.

"Simon did the right thing diving for scallops. Hand diving for scallops is the way to go these days," said Findley, voice raised above the roar of the engine. "Much better for the marine environment, and sustainable, too. Most of the scallops in Scotland are dredged by boats and dredging destroys the seabed. When the diver picks up the scallops, he can let the undersized ones go and it gives them a chance to grow and spawn. That doesn't happen with dredging. There's so much dead waste with dredging."

"Do you catch enough fish to make a good living?" asked Richard, looking out to sea.

"Yes, I do well enough. There's plenty of fish in these seas. That's why we get so many seals, whales, and other sea life here. Rich in nutrients, the water is. But in the summer, I make more money taking out snorkelling parties on this thing. People pay a good deal of cash for that. It's a growing market. Cold water swimming has become all the rage these days. Everyone's doing it."

He was silent for a moment.

"Simon and I were planning to start up a business venture together."

"Really?" asked Richard.

Findley nodded.

"Yes."

"With snorkelling parties?"

"Yes. The Scottish Wildlife Trust has set up snorkelling trails for tourists, but Simon and I know the coast inside out. We'd have taken them to the quieter beauty spots," said Findley, his voice breaking.

Findley raised an arm and wiped his face.

Richard and Mike looked at each other.

"I'm sorry. His death must've been a big upset to you," said Richard, stating the obvious.

He felt like kicking himself over the banality of his words, but he wanted to dig deeper into Findley's friendship with Simon.

Or was it more than a friendship? Findley's tears meant he and Simon were very close, but how close exactly?

Mike was uncharacteristically silent, listening to the conversation with interest.

"Yeah, it was," agreed Findley, pulling himself together. "We'd been friends since school, you see. We both loved the ocean."

The boat rocked up and down on the waves.

Richard hurriedly turned his eyes back to the horizon in front of him.

"We were very close," continued Findley. "I loved him, to tell the truth. He was straight, though." He smiled bitterly. "I never was lucky in love."

Turning to look at him again, Richard read the genuine sadness on his face.

Unrequited love. He could remember what it felt like when Eilidh had been indifferent to his interest in her. It wasn't a nice position to be in.

"But I still have this," said Findley, nodding to the water around them. "Until the day I die, the ocean will remain with me. Even my home looks out onto it. My life's always going to be on the water, and I consider that a privilege."

Each to their own, thought Richard.

"Was Simon's death a surprise to you?" asked Mike, suddenly.

Findley mulled this over.

"Both you and Simon seem very competent seamen," continued Mike. "And Janey thinks they deliberately emptied the air in his tank."

"I have to say I agree with her," affirmed Findley at last. "Simon was one of the most experienced divers you could find on the island. He wouldn't make a rookie mistake like that. I do think someone sabotaged his tank."

"Why would they do that, do you think?" asked Mike, straight to the point as always.

Both Mike and Richard watched for Findley's response.

Finley stared back at them.

"There's rumours he found treasure," said Findley. "Isn't this why the pair of you are here? Isn't this why you've asked me to take you to the beaches he used to snorkel at?"

Richard smiled and nodded.

"I'm not a fool," said Findley, voice sharp. "So please don't treat me like one."

Scratching his chin, which was growing a five

o'clock shadow, Richard hoped they wouldn't end up alienating Findley with their questions.

"I understand," he said. "You're right, we're keen to see if we can find the site where he supposedly found the treasure. If you two were close, I assume he told you about his find?"

"No, he didn't," said Findley curtly. "Even Janey doesn't know what he did with it. He died within three days of finding that treasure, according to her. I never saw him during that time. I'm out at sea most of the week. But if Simon said he found treasure, he found treasure. He was very truthful. It's just the way he was."

"The thing is, Findley," said Mike, leaning back on the side of the boat, his legs splayed out, "if Simon's death was murder, the only way we're going to get any kind of justice is if we can prove the murderers are illegally withholding the treasure or hunting for it. If there's a motive, they'll look at Simon's case again. We don't have this proof, so far. The police here are denying the treasure exists."

Findley snorted.

"Those dopey dogs haven't got a clue about anything. They think they're the kings of the island, so they do, when in reality they're totally incompetent."

He looked out to sea, his face raging.

"The police here will be easy to manipulate into silence," he remarked. "They won't want any problems, and they've been trained to sing off the same hymn sheet."

Mike folded his arms.

"We know two pieces have been sold to a buyer via a corrupt police officer, but because it's been done illegally no buyer's going to confess to the identity of the seller. And there's not enough evidence of foul play to get the police on the island to request a second look at Simon's death, sadly."

Richard was surprised at Mike's candour. There was something about the three of them on a boat, surrounded by sea, that seemed to encourage intimacy. He wondered for the first time if fishermen, too, established close bonds during their trips out at sea. He remembered how in Hemingway's book *The Old Man and the Sea* the old man, far out at sea, starts to feel an emotional attachment to the marlin he catches.

For his part, Mike seemed to have decided, given Findley's relationship with Simon, that there was a chance Findley would do everything possible to help them track down the treasure.

"He's right, you know," said Richard, breaking the silence. "The only way to bring the murderers to account is to find definitive proof of who took the treasure Simon left at the police station, and we don't have that. It's been a game of 'he says, she says.' Who's the more credible witness? The police are saying they never received it. And Janey says it was left there. Let's face it, it was well known Janey had a tense relationship with Simon, and now she's grieving for him nobody's going to take her testimony as reliable."

"If no one knows where the rest of the treasure is, then it's unlikely you'll find the culprits," observed Findley.

There was that, too, thought Richard.

"From what Janey has told us, it does seem the guilty party is trying very hard to locate the rest of the treasure," said Richard, trying to inject some hope into the conversation. "Treasure which Simon seems to have taken and hidden somewhere. Sooner or later, those hunting for it will give themselves away. Meanwhile, it's a race against time for us to beat them to it."

Findley looked thoughtful.

"I doubt very much Simon would've left the treasure where he found it," he said.

Richard sighed.

"I know. I agree. It's a crying shame he didn't leave it where he found it, but there we are."

"He was probably worried someone else would get their hands on it," remarked Mike, who, as Richard well knew, had his own trust issues with his fellow men.

"Isn't this trip a waste of time for you both, then?" suggested Findley, looking at them both with an amused smile on his face.

For Findley, of course, the day wasn't a complete waste of time because he was getting handsomely compensated by Mike and Richard for his help. He could afford to enjoy himself at their expense.

Richard smiled back at him.

"No, I think looking at the site could still be very helpful and interesting. It'll help us establish whether the treasure was part of an actual burial mound or just a Viking stash, hidden centuries ago for safety, ready to be picked up later on. And in turn, that'll give us a few clues as to what the rest of the treasure might consist of," said Richard.

In the back of his mind, though, he was thinking, *do you really think I'd be on this wretched boat if I thought it was going to be a waste of my time?*

He shivered and tucked his hands in his pockets. He wished he'd brought a pair of gloves with him.

The boat rounded the headland and a large and beautiful beach came into sight.

The sea near the beach was a stunning shade of green-blue, and underneath its surface the sand was pristine white.

If it weren't for the awful weather, thought Richard, *this could be the Seychelles.*

"Seilebost Bay," announced Findley. "Quieter than Luskentyre Bay, but neither is ever that busy."

Finley pointed to the beach.

"See how white the sand is? The sand in Harris is rich in calcium from crushed seashells. In winter, the winds blow this sand over the island's machair, or grassland as you'd call it, enriching the soil for a multitude of plants. Calcium is a key nutrient for plants and here it keeps the machair rich and fertile. You can find as many as six species of orchid growing in the machair in the summer."

Mike grinned at him.

"Bet you have that well-rehearsed for the tourists."

Findley laughed.

"You're right, I do. But you should know this beach has been voted one of the top ten beaches in the world, so it's an honour to visit it," Findley informed them. "It's no ordinary place."

Findley brought the boat as close as he could to the beach and then lifted the motor out of the water.

"It's a boggy walk down to the beach from the road," he said. "It's far easier to bring the boat in."

He hopped out, wearing his fishing waders, and dragged the inflatable boat up onto the beach.

He held onto the craft as Mike and Richard disembarked.

For a moment Richard felt so grateful to be back on land, he was tempted to sink to his knees and kiss the sand, just like the Pope had been known to do in the past. He remembered the Pope's representative saying "He kisses the ground out of respect for the country and the earth. It is the terra firma we all live on." Well, Richard had learnt the hard way he was happier on terra firma than on any ocean in the world.

"This bay was Simon's favourite haunt for scallop fishing," Findley explained. "I suspect the campers at the campsite might have already come across Simon's dig before us though, if it was located here. I mean, his discovery was made a while ago, wasn't it?"

Richard and Mike didn't bother to respond to this.

If they lived their professional lives with negativity and pessimism none of their investigations would ever reach a conclusion. As a detective, whether in the police or as a private investigator, you had to be dogged in your searches or you never achieved anything. What's more, pursuing lost causes was often part of the job description in art theft cases.

Mike rocked backwards and forwards on his feet as he scanned the beach.

"Right, Richard, why don't you start at the right-hand side of the beach and I'll begin at the left. We can meet somewhere in the middle," he suggested.

Richard nodded and made his way to his section.

There was no need to explain what to look for. They were both going to be looking for the shape of a mound or any signs of disturbance at the edges of the beach. For the treasure to have survived intact for so many centuries it must have been buried far away from the tide line, near to where the seagrass had a gained a foothold.

For a good hour Richard scanned the landscape, often bent double to look closer at the semblance of a mound or an area of dug up sand and earth. He didn't bother looking through vegetation extending up the slope above him. The vegetation was mature and showed no signs of having been uprooted or flattened, other than where the path ran down the slope to the beach.

The end result, after an hour of searching on the beach, was the unearthing of three empty crisp packets, a can of beer, a bottle of sunscreen, and a nappy.

Richard stretched his back to ease its stiffness.

Trying to think of what Simon would have done, he looked up at the road.

Assuming Simon had parked up on the edge of the road, the most obvious way to access the beach was via the path.

He decided to focus his search to the areas on either side of the path.

He looked at his watch. At this rate, they weren't going to be able to reach the other two beaches Simon went scallop diving in.

Heaving a sigh, he shrugged and bent down again to carry on the search.

There were several rabbit holes at the bottom of the slope, looking disused.

There was also one large, sandy crater, looking out of place, about seven metres from the path.

It was far too big to be a rabbit hole and the vegetation around it had been uprooted.

It also looked as though there had been a recent

attempt to cover it up with sand, but part of the sand had sunk down into the tunnel, creating a crater and revealing its circular shape.

Richard stood up, put two fingers in his mouth and whistled loudly, startling a family who were walking on the beach.

Mike jogged across the beach to where Richard was waiting.

Most people would have called Mike's movements a fast stride and not a jog, but for Mike it was the closest thing to a run he was capable of.

Findley didn't move from the rock he was sitting on, keeping watch on the boat.

Apart from a cursory look at Richard, he showed no curiosity whatsoever in what Richard had discovered.

Mike reached Richard and bent over, his hands on his thighs.

"Well, Richard, what have we got?" he asked, panting.

"It looks as though fairly recently someone has tried to cover up a big hole here," explained Richard, pointing to the crater.

Mike looked at it and smiled.

"By Jove, you're right. Very odd."

He inched closer to examine it.

"If it's what we're looking for, then we're not looking at a burial mound," he stated.

"I agree."

"Well, let's get to it. Nothing for it but to dig."

Richard had to agree with him. How he wished he had brought an archaeological team from some university to do the job properly, though.

He handed Mike a pair of plastic gloves.

Both men fell to their knees on either side of the crater and started to push the sand out carefully from the centre of it.

Richard was hoping they weren't going to find something unsavoury like another nappy or worse.

The further down they dug, the more the sand shifted down the tunnel.

For the next half hour, they emptied the tunnel of sand, taking care they weren't missing any object in the process.

In the end, they were left with an empty hole a metre and a half deep and a metre wide. They had uncovered a piece of cord, some sort of tusk, a glass vial, six beads, and several fragments of material.

"Look at this, Mike," said Richard, examining one of the cloth fragments. "It's literally disintegrating under my fingers. This is old. The colour has gone from it completely."

Mike grunted in agreement as he studied their find.

Richard removed a number of clear plastic bags from his jacket pocket and carefully placed the fragments of cloth into one of them.

"What about these," he said, touching the beads with his fingertips.

Mike lifted one of them up and looked at it closely.

"Amber. Amber beads. Handmade, judging by the look of them."

They looked at each other.

In silence, Richard picked up the six amber beads and placed them in another bag.

Mike picked up the glass vial which was missing its lid and had a chip on the side of it.

"This, too, is handmade," he said, holding it up to the light to see it better.

He passed it over to Richard to be sealed in a bag.

"What do you think this is made of?" asked Richard, passing the cord to Mike. "Leather?"

Mike chewed his lower lip as he examined it.

In the end, he shrugged.

"Not sure. Some kind of animal hide, but it doesn't seem like cow hide to me. It's too soft."

He passed it to Richard, who sealed it in another bag.

"Now this is the most revealing piece," said Richard, studying the tusk which had fine lines etched onto it. "Don't they look like runes to you?"

Mike, who'd been looking over his shoulder, nodded.

"Looks like a walrus tusk to me," observed Mike.

"I wouldn't care to hazard a guess on that," said Richard, shrugging his shoulders. "Time will tell."

He placed the tusk in a plastic bag.

They both turned and stared at the hole once again.

"Do we try to dig some more?" asked Richard hopefully.

Mike shook his head.

"We're not going to find anything else in there. We found those bits and pieces in the same part of the hole and then dug well past it."

Richard nodded.

"I'll get what we found couriered to Professor McGill at St. Andrews University," he said. "He's aware of our search, and so I had him on standby for any potential finds. He'll work on getting this stuff radiocarbon dated for us as soon as he can."

"Good idea," agreed Mike.

He looked at his watch.

"I don't know about you, but I'm starving. I wonder if Findley can drop us off at Tarbert before mooring the boat again. Given what we've found, I don't see any point in searching the other beaches, do you? We can wait until the radiocarbon dating is done. If it turns out we're in the wrong era for a Viking find, we can take a look at the other beaches."

"Yes, but at best the radiocarbon dating could take anything between seven and fourteen days to get done."

"I'm not restrained by time like you, Richard, but let's not forget what we're here in Harris for. We're not here to find the treasure site, informative though that might be. I admit, it's useful. If what we've found today is from the Viking era, we've got further proof of a potential treasure find on the island. But let's bypass the crap in this situation. We both know the treasure exists and what we need to figure out is what Simon did with the rest of it. Janey's our most credible witness so far and she's stated he hid the stuff elsewhere."

He crossed his arms and started pacing up and down beside the hole.

"In any case, I wouldn't worry about the wait for radiocarbon dating," he muttered, looking at their dig. "I've got this feeling in my gut that we've found the place where Simon discovered the Viking hoard. Yes, sir, right here in Seilebost Bay."

Richard smiled.

How would gut feelings play out with Lionel? Not very well, he suspected. Richard liked Mike's idiosyncrasies, but with his over-stretched department he had to work with concrete facts.

"It would be too much to believe there's two such locations," admitted Richard.

"Exactly. Plus, there's no way a Viking or Vikings would bury just these small bits and pieces as part of a hidden hoard. If this stuff is Viking and part of a hoard, there'd have been a good deal more of it buried. Which begs the same old question, where is the rest of it now? What on earth did Simon do with it? We need to get inside his mind as soon as we can."

Mike turned to look at Findley.

"Don't you think it's odd?"

"What?" asked Richard, following his gaze.

"The fact he's shown no interest at all in what we're doing."

Findley seemed to be trying to sharpen a fish hook with a stone he'd found on the beach.

"I suppose," said Richard.

But to him, Findley's reaction didn't appear strange. His overall impression of Findley was that of a man whose personality was unaffected by human-made objects. Findley's passion in life seemed to be focused purely on the sea and everything within it.

13

Mike

Mike stretched his legs out and took a sip of his black coffee.

Next to him, on the wall, Sky News was playing on the television screen. The volume was low, almost a murmur, and Mike found himself getting sleepy.

Mariella was late, as usual.

This didn't faze Mike one bit. Knowing her of old, Mariella had a natural Latin flexibility with the concept of time which no amount of years living in Britain had erased from her mindset.

The coffee lounge at the Hotel Hebrides was comfortable enough, with intimate lighting and neutral colours.

There was no one else around that afternoon. It was a sunny day and most of the hotel guests seemed to have chosen to stay outside.

Looking through his emails, Mike noted the work was piling up back home. Maisie, his secretary, was doing a heroic job of manning the fort.

He chewed a nail.

He'd told Richard he had no constraints on his time, but that wasn't strictly true. Odds were high they wouldn't find the missing treasure in Harris, and meanwhile his inbox was filling up with offers for lucrative contracts.

One especially stood out for him.

An Australian businessman was requesting his help in tracing an aboriginal painting by Clifford Possum Tjapaltjarri, which had been stolen from his house.

Aside from the money on offer, Mike had never been to Australia before and visiting the country was high on his bucket list.

He rubbed his chin thoughtfully.

"*Buon pomeriggio*, Mike," said Mariella in her sing-song voice.

He looked up.

She was looking very sprightly, dressed in a green tartan dress and a fitted tweed jacket.

"Trying to blend in with the locals?" asked Mike, with a nod to her dress.

"But of course," said Mariella, sitting down on the armchair next to him. "*When in Rome, do as the Romans do*. Isn't that one of your expressions?"

"Yes, it is."

"You, meanwhile, like to stand out, don't you?"

Mike looked down at his bright-red corduroy trousers and Arran jumper with a pained expression.

"I thought I was looking good today."

Mariella shook her head.

"You look like Santa Claus."

"Ah."

"Never mind, *caro mio*. One day you'll find a

woman and she'll make sure you're dressed appropriately."

Mike looked at her in surprise.

"Yes, I'm sure that'll be the case," he affirmed.

"I meant it nicely for once, Mike, so don't look at me like that. Why don't we get back to business? I've been doing some productive work while you've been occupied with Richard. Nico and I have taken a look at the partner of this Fiona Mitchell," said Mariella, leaning forward on her chair. "David Mackenzie, he's called. I've been to his butcher's shop and bought some meat from him. I've also had a look at his home. Did you know the man owns a yellow Ferrari? Can you imagine? It must be the only such car on the island. He has very expensive tastes. His house, outside Tarbert, looks pricey, too."

She opened an envelope and laid out some photos.

"That's him."

Mike picked a photo up and studied it.

David Mackenzie was a broad, muscular man. He was wearing a short-sleeved T-shirt, of the kind men use to show off their biceps. He had tattoos covering both arms.

"Did you see what his tattoos are of?" asked Mike, squinting at the photo.

"Nothing interesting. Celtic designs, from what I could see," Mariella told him.

David had his hair shaved to the scalp to hide his receding hairline, although his face was still youthful.

He had a long face, with clear bone structure and sunken eyes. There didn't seem to be an ounce of fat on him.

Lucky sod, thought Mike.

"Mind you, to get those muscles the man must spend hours in the gym, lifting weights."

Unintentionally, he'd spoken the words out loud.

"Yes, of course," agreed Mariella. "That look takes a lot of effort. A special diet, too."

Mike shrugged.

Mariella chortled.

"I've never seen you jealous of another man's physique before."

Mike looked at her with dislike.

"I'm not in the least bit jealous," he lied. "I measure people by their brains, not their bodies. Anyway, I don't see where your research gets us. So what if the man has an expensive lifestyle? It doesn't mean he's after the treasure or has anything to do with it."

"Think about it, Mike," said Mariella as she picked up the photos and put them back in the envelope. "Remember when we were in a relationship? We used to work together. We're doing it now, even. It's a natural thing. I suspect David knows about Fiona's involvement in taking the torc and cup from Simon. He probably also knows they were sold to me. I bet you he stands to benefit in the long run. You told me about Janey's experiences, too. Do you not think he sounds just the kind of man to do something like leaving dead, mutilated animals on her doorstep? I mean, look at his pub for goodness sake. If they're working together, we must keep an eye on the two of them."

"I suppose. But let's face it, they're not the ones who know where the rest of the treasure is. The treasure's all I care about at the moment."

Mike reached into his trouser pocket and brought out a folded sheet of paper.

Opening it up, he laid it out on the table in front of them.

Stay away from Harris, Mike.
　　Time for you to retire.
　　If you visit Harris, there'll be no retirement for you. Harris will be your deathbed.

Mariella looked down at it, a frown between her eyes.

"What's this?" asked Mariella.

"You didn't leave this little note in my house, then," said Mike, sounding satisfied.

Whatever doubts he'd had were gone with her reaction.

"No, of course not. Come on, Mike. Don't you remember my handwriting?"

She picked it up.

"Stupid of them to hand write it. Amateurs."

"Yes, I think so," agreed Mike.

Mariella glared at him.

"And you think I'm capable of doing such a stupid thing? You must rate my intelligence very low."

Squirming in his chair, Mike smiled nervously at her.

He wasn't in the mood to cope with a temper tantrum and hoped his comments weren't about to provoke an outburst from her. Mariella wouldn't care who heard or saw them when she was in a rage.

"No, I don't think you're stupid. But if you remember, you were in a fury when I last saw you. I mean, I still have the scar on my neck from when you threw the pliers at me," said Mike, feeling it gingerly with his fingers. "So naturally, having taken the goods from you, I expected you to be apoplectic."

"I imagine the list of people who hate you and wish you dead must be very, very long," responded Mariella, ignoring his woes. "As for this, you'll never be able to trace who wrote the note."

She folded it up and handed it back to him.

"I'll make sure you get a decent funeral," she assured him.

Mike rolled his eyes.

"If I were to take a guess, I'd say it's from Fiona or her beau," he said. "Trying to keep the vultures away. A useless task. And I bet I'm not the only one to receive such a letter."

He looked down at his watch.

Mariella could talk until the cows came home, but he was feeling frustrated by the sluggish pace of the investigation and wanted some action. His patience, never a virtue of his, was starting to wear thin.

"Simon's closest friends have been interviewed by Eilidh and Richard," he said, coming back to the case. "The three of them have turned out to be like the three wise monkeys, who see no evil, hear no evil, and speak no evil. However, Sam works here in Tarbert. I suggest we go and see if we can speak to him this afternoon. He might be prepared to say more to us given we're not affiliated with the police."

"Yes, and there's nothing stopping us speaking to Mark or Findley. You never know, they might let something spill, too."

"Or tell us to fuck off," said Mike, gloomily.

"There's that, too, of course," conceded Mariella.

"You said you felt Findley was hiding something. Maybe we need to ask the others about him."

"What's that got to do with anything? I reckon they're all hiding something. To my mind, they're completely loopy up here. You have a pub full of bones, the police spending their time swilling cups of tea and denying they ever saw any treasure, a friend of Simon's who spends a lot of his time inside a lighthouse, another one who never seems to be off his boat and claims to have had a crush on Simon. Then there's Simon's natural father, disappearing for days at a time on so-called art trips. I mean it's insane. Nobody seems to have a clue as to what the other is doing."

"Unless they're keeping silent about it, my friend," said Mariella. "Remember we're the outsiders. There are remote places like this in Italy, too. Apricale or Chamois, for example. They stick together. It's almost tribal."

"Yes, they might be closing ranks," admitted Mike. "But that never lasts, usually. One or the other cracks at some point and it should've happened by now."

His leg started jiggling with nervous energy.

Mariella stood up.

"Come on, let's go and visit the distillery office. We can see if Sam is in today."

Mike nodded.

Before they left, Mike glanced at the TV screen and saw the news was showing a Roman mosaic floor discovered in Rutland, England.

Mike made a face.

The discovery of a mosaic floor paled into insignificance next to the wonders of a rich Viking hoard.

Putting on his red woolly hat, he followed Mariella out the door.

They walked straight into a brisk breeze, despite the sunshine.

The seagulls, for once, were silent, gliding on the air currents and keeping watch.

Mike and Mariella had already visited the Isle of Harris Distillery in Tarbert as tourists. Mainly because, apart from a few Harris Tweed shops, there didn't seem to be much else to do there.

A local success story producing Scotch whisky and gin, the distillery opened in 2015.

They produced a single malt whisky called The Hearach, which is the Gaelic word for a resident of the Isle of Harris, and its gin, packaged in attractive blue bottles made in Yorkshire, had won Gold at the World Gin Awards in 2021.

Quite an achievement for a small island business, Mike had felt. He'd ordered three boxes of Isle of Harris gin to be sent to his office in London.

A cheerful girl at the entrance of the distillery offered to check and see if Sam was available.

Sam Foster worked in the accounts department, she informed them, but she was sure he'd manage to fit them in.

They waited while she went to speak to him, and five minutes later they were seated on the other side of Sam's desk.

The accounts department turned out to be a narrow room, located in a separate building to the distillery. Floor-to-ceiling walnut cabinets covered one wall, three wooden desks were positioned at a distance to each other, and a plush, cream-coloured rug covered the centre of the oak floor.

The overall impression was one of comfort.

A framed photograph of Loch Lomond was situated above Sam's desk.

"Nice," commented Mike, looking around with interest.

"It is, yes," agreed Sam.

Sam was a thin, fragile-looking man with a head of thick, wiry red hair. Freckles covered the skin on his face in irregular patterns, his lips were barely there, creating the impression of a slit for a mouth, but his eyes, which were luminous, intelligent and sharp, stole the show.

The charisma in his eyes couldn't be underestimated, thought Mike. This was surely a man who could give them an accurate idea of who Simon was and what his movements around the treasure might be.

"How may I help you?" Sam asked, after shaking their hands.

He smiled.

"Or help Janey, for that matter," he added. "I presume it's at her request you're here."

Mike and Mariella nodded.

"We're working alongside Chief Inspector Langley," affirmed Mike.

"I've already spoken to Chief Inspector Langley. I can't imagine what else you think I'd have to add to what I already told him."

"To be honest with you, Sam, we're needing some idea of who Simon was and what his relationship with friends, such as yourself, was. Rumours are out in the open now about the treasure Simon was supposed to have found. We're here, as you know, trying to locate it so the treasure's processed through the legal channels as part of Scotland's heritage and isn't lost to the black market. Others, less scrupulous than us, are on the hunt for it, too, you see."

Sam stretched back on his seat and yawned.

"Chief Inspector Langley said as much."

He leaned forward again.

"It's my personal opinion you'll never find the treasure. I can assure you more than one person, probably, knows where it is, but you'll never get them to talk."

"Why not?" asked Mariella, in a high voice.

Sam shrugged.

"Because people here in Harris take time to trust outsiders with their secrets. Simple as that, I'm afraid. You can't underestimate people's loyalty to Simon, either."

"We were told you were close to Simon," said Mike.

The shutters came down over Sam's face and his eyes became guarded and wary.

"I was, yes," said Sam, a little impatiently. "But I'll not be much use to you because we had a falling out shortly before he died. I already explained this to Inspector Langley. I'd put in a good word for him with my colleagues and, as a result, the owner of the distillery offered him a job working here. Janey and he were in a desperately bad financial situation at the time and I'd already loaned them as much as I could."

He smiled sadly.

"Simon refused the job. I couldn't believe it, of course, and I quarrelled with him. I told him he wouldn't be getting a penny more from me. And that's the last time I spoke to him." He bit his lip. "I do regret parting on those terms, of course I do, but how was I to know he'd be dead barely a week later?"

Mariella reached across and patted his arm.

"I'm so sorry, Sam. That must've been hard."

Sam cleared his throat.

"It was. But it's fine, I've dealt with it."

He sighed.

"I don't think Simon ever got around to telling Janey he'd turned down the job offer. That was Simon for you. He was a bit of a coward."

Mike crossed his arms.

"Assuming Simon found the treasure and wanted someone to take care of it for him, who would he leave it with?"

"No idea," said Sam, without hesitation.

"Who would he trust with the secret?" asked Mariella.

Sam lifted his shoulders.

"I don't honestly know. Maybe his dad, Patrick? I hate to bring the poor man into this, though. I'm sorry, guys, that I can't be of more help. Look, I can just tell you one thing. In small communities like the one on the Isle of Lewis and Harris you see the best of human nature and the worst. There are elements on the island you don't want to mess with. I've come across them even in this job."

Reaching for his papers, Sam began to tidy them up.

"Are you saying what I think you're saying, Sam?" Mike asked, his brow furrowed.

Sam just looked at him.

"Seriously, are you talking extortion?" insisted Mike.

"Attempted extortion," Sam corrected. "They didn't have a chance with the distillery because part of the funding for the enterprise is from the Scottish government and there's more accountability due to that. The accounts here are heavily scrutinised, believe me. I wouldn't say it's the same for some of the other businesses on the island."

"Someone's greedy," remarked Mariella.

"I'd agree with that summary," said Sam, smiling at her. "And it's not just one, I'm afraid. And to our shame, many of us turn a blind eye to fraud and corruption on the island."

"And you've never reported them?" asked Mike.

Sam shook his head slowly, his strange, luminous brown eyes focused on Mike.

"It wouldn't be worth it. Too dangerous. Corruption's multi-layered here. It's not just down to bribery and extortion. There's plenty of drugs, using the island as a staging post to then travel south, too. Just because we're over 600 miles from London doesn't mean we're free of criminals and crime. It's just better hidden within the community up here, I reckon. You learn to stay out of trouble. Everyone knows how to turn a blind eye, everyone learns the limits, and that's the way it's always been."

"Well, the island's definitely deceptive," remarked Mariella. "It seems so sleepy, somehow. Such beautiful nature, too. It's very sad."

"It's a mixed bag but I wouldn't live anywhere else," said Sam firmly. "The beauty of the island will never be touched by any shady dealings. It's been the same for hundreds of years and I hope for hundreds more. There's plenty good eggs living here, too."

Mike nodded and stood up.

"We won't take up any more of your time. It seems we should at least try to speak with Patrick."

"What do you think of David Mackenzie?" asked Mariella suddenly.

The shutters came down on Sam's face again.

"I don't know him very well, I'm afraid, so I can't tell you anything about him," Sam replied.

Mariella picked up her handbag and tucked her hand into Mike's arm as she stood up.

She was developing a bad habit of tucking her hand in his arm, Mike thought to himself. Anyone would assume they were a couple.

He turned to Sam again.

"Did Simon like David Mackenzie?" asked Mike, feeling he was in last chance saloon, and desperate.

Sam looked up from his desk.

"No, I don't believe so," he said calmly. "Simon had a soft side to him. He didn't approve of David's gory interest in bones and dead animals. He refused to set foot in the Time or Tide."

14

Eilidh

As Eilidh got out of the car, she picked up her handbag and a carton of fresh milk.

She walked up to the house and opened the front door.

As she stepped over the threshold she saw a piece of A4 paper lying on the mat, folded over.

Bending down was becoming ever harder so she decided to put the milk in the fridge and dropped her bag on a chair, before returning to the doormat.

She picked up the paper and opened it.

On it was scrawled:

"I have jumped upwards, downwards, backwards and sideways at least four thousand times; and I can't get out: I always get up underneath there, and can't find the hole."

She looked at the back of the paper. There was nothing else written on it.

Puzzled, she walked through to the sitting room,

where Richard was seated in front of his laptop with a grim look on his face.

"Richard, any idea what this is about?" she asked, shoving the paper in front of him.

Richard picked it up.

"No, why?" he asked, frowning

"It was on our door mat," explained Eilidh.

"How odd," muttered Richard. "It doesn't make any sense. It seems to be a quote of some sort."

He scratched his head.

"It sounds to me as though someone's feeling trapped."

He shrugged and handed the sheet of paper back to her.

"At least it's not a death threat or a curse," he said, smiling at her.

"A little strange, don't you think?"

"Yes, it is. Mike said he had a nasty little letter posted to his home in Islington before he came up here. There are lots of 'odd' things happening since we started this case. I wouldn't let it faze you. It seems to me someone's enjoying playing games at our expense, but it'll die down once the novelty wears off."

"I'm not so sure," disagreed Eilidh, looking at the message doubtfully.

"My love, try not to be morbid over it," said Richard, reaching up and massaging her back. "These things do crop up in our line of work from time to time."

For once, Eilidh didn't respond to his caress.

"I just can't figure it out," she said.

"Maybe you're not supposed to," said Richard unhelpfully.

Refusing to be beaten, Eilidh continued to study the bizarre words.

The note was written in pencil, reminding her of Patrick's sketching.

An idea came to her. She walked out of the sitting room and made her way to their bedroom at the front of the house.

Patrick's drawing was laid out on the dressing table.

She looked at his signature and laid the note down next to it.

To her uninformed eye, some of the letters on the note looked very similar to Patrick's signature.

She gazed at the view through the window.

Everything outside the house was peaceful.

In front of her, the sea was smooth as a mirror and reflecting the overhead clouds. The burn, as usual, was trickling down the hillside, and the tumbled rocks at the bottom of the garden brought a sense of timelessness and solidity to the scene.

How she wished their stay in Harris could be on a more solid footing, and as far as time went, they had so little left to get some positive results.

She studied the words on the page.

Something at the back of her mind urged her to take some action.

Picking up the note, she made her way back to the sitting room.

"Richard, we have to go and speak to Patrick about this."

"We will do," said Richard patiently, while at the same time listening in to a Zoom call.

"I mean now," insisted Eilidh in a louder voice.

Richard took off one of his earpieces.

"Love, what's going on?" he asked. "I'm in the middle of a meeting."

"I don't have a good feeling about this. The writing on the note matches the signature on Patrick's drawing. It's Patrick's handwriting."

"Don't let your imagination get carried away with you, Eilidh. Even if it is Patrick, he's probably fine. Look, I have to finish this Zoom call. I'll be done in twenty minutes, and then, if you're still worried, we can head over to Patrick's, OK?"

Eilidh nodded, suddenly embarrassed by her anxiety. Richard had important work to do, and as he seemed to be implying, the note was probably just a cryptic practical joke from Patrick.

But she still couldn't shake off a feeling of dread which persisted, lingering in her mind.

She decided she needed some fresh air.

After putting on her jacket, she picked up her handbag and went out into the front garden.

She proceeded to pace up and down in a bid to work through some of her pent-up worry and release some of the adrenaline she felt building up within her.

The grass was damp from the rain earlier on in the morning and she squelched as she marched, the loose strands of grass beginning to stick in clumps to her boots.

The words *"I can't get out"* spun round and round in her head as she remembered Patrick's hasty retreat back to his house when she'd been with him on Tràigh na Cleabhaig.

A short while later, she heard Richard calling for her.

"I'm out here!" she yelled, and then smiled when

Richard stuck his dishevelled head out the front door and stared at her.

She might look as though she was losing her marbles, but then again, Richard hadn't spent time with Patrick. Patrick had behaved like a hunted man. She'd thought at the time his attitude was brought about by an element of paranoia, but she wasn't so sure now.

Richard sat on the doorstep and put his boots on.

Watching him, Eilidh felt absurdly relieved he wasn't going to dispute with her.

To be fair, their visit to Patrick was long overdue. Richard had been doubtful Patrick would offer up any more information than Eilidh had already garnered from him. Given time was short, he'd been inclined to cover other aspects of the case before going back to interview Patrick again.

As they drove towards Patrick's home, Eilidh remembered the last time she was there and the Venus flytrap plants he had been selling outside of his house.

Had the artist, who by his own account was a free spirit, found himself trapped? Would he be ready to tell them the location of the treasure now, in order to keep the others away from him? Would he accept their help in escaping whatever pressures were bearing down on him?

Her anxiety kept her silent until she'd parked the car.

"Everything looks tranquil enough, wouldn't you say?" she asked hopefully.

Richard smiled at her.

"Absolutely."

They got out of the car and looked at the row of houses.

"Wow! Is that it?" asked Richard, pointing to Patrick's bizarre, brightly coloured garden sculptures.

"Yes," said Eilidh, walking up to the gate.

She opened it and made her way along the path to the front door.

Richard, meanwhile, was distracted by the sculptures. He strolled among the artworks, studying them closely.

Predictable, thought Eilidh, glancing across at him. Any kind of artwork, no matter what its quality, acted like a magnet to Richard. He was a very single-minded man.

She rang the doorbell.

There was no answer.

She tried ringing the doorbell for a second time, a third time, and then a fourth.

"He might be out sketching, Eilidh," suggested Richard after he'd completed his inspection of the garden art.

"We should wait here," said Eilidh.

Richard's face dropped.

She could read his mind. He'd been willing to pander to her whims, but he was reaching the end of the road on that front. He wasn't prepared to sit about for hours when he could be working on something else.

"Eilidh..."

"I know what you're going to say, Richard, but please humour me for a bit. I'm telling you, the man was frightened and I can't help feeling something's wrong."

Richard looked at her and sighed.

"I'm going to try and look in the windows," decided Eilidh, avoiding his eyes.

She started peering through one of the front windows, holding a hand above her eyes to shield them from the outside light.

The room she was looking at held a wooden table and eight chairs. It was cluttered with books, sketchpads, paintbrushes, and other art equipment. The room might have been used as a dining room at one time, but it no longer served that purpose. Sketches were piled up on the table and along the floor.

Eilidh moved across to the two windows on the other side of the front door.

Richard watched her for a minute and then disappeared around the back.

Eilidh presumed he was going to check out the other windows.

She smiled to herself.

If you can't beat them join them was an excellent motto, she thought.

She was having a good nosey at Patrick's kitchen, when she heard a loud shout from Richard.

She took off in its direction.

"What is it?" she asked, arriving out of breath, even with running only a few metres to the back garden.

Richard's face had gone pale.

She turned to look at the window.

"Look," said Richard, pointing through the glass with a shaky hand.

Inside the bedroom, on the floor, there was a foot jutting out at an awkward angle.

Their view was blocked by a double bed, but there was no mistaking the crimson pool of blood which had soaked into the sage-green carpet.

Eilidh grabbed hold of Richard.

"We have to break open the window."

Richard seemed dazed and was staring blankly at her.

In that instant, it occurred to her Richard had never dealt with any injured or dead bodies before. His remit was solely within the Art and Antiquities Unit, whereas she'd spent many years working for one of the Homicide Units at New Scotland Yard. The onus was on her to keep her wits together.

She inspected the window.

It wasn't double-glazed, thankfully.

Looking behind her, she saw a wheelbarrow and spade at the back of the garden.

Straightaway, she went and grabbed the spade, carrying it across to the window where Richard was standing.

Lifting it up, she was braced to smash the window pane when she felt Richard taking the spade off her.

"Stand back, Eilidh," he instructed.

She moved away, and with a hefty swing, Richard broke the glass to the bedroom window.

He chipped away with the spade until as much of it as possible was gone.

Reaching for the thick curtain inside, he tugged hard until it broke free from its plastic hooks.

He pulled the material through the broken window and placed it across the base of the frame.

Then putting the palms of his hands on the edge, he heaved himself up onto the windowsill.

He hovered for a moment on the frame and then tumbled ungracefully into the bedroom.

Eilidh pulled her phone out of her bag and called Tarbert Police Station.

While she was relaying the situation to them, she watched Richard approach the body, taking great care not to tread on the patches of wet blood.

As she spoke to the helpdesk, to her surprise she found herself also praying for Patrick to be alive to any God who'd be willing to listen to her.

Somehow, she knew in her heart it was Patrick's body lying on the floor.

She watched as Richard reached the body, turned around abruptly, and threw up on the carpet.

Patrick was dead.

She ended the call and found she was crying, with the tears streaming down her face.

Brushing them away angrily, she moved closer to the window.

Richard, still bent over, lifted a hand in warning.

"Don't come near it, Eilidh. It's horrific. He's been carved up."

He took in a few deep breaths and then came across to the window.

Their eyes met.

Frustration, anger, upset, and sadness were the emotions they recognised in each other.

In the end, Richard sighed.

"I'd best come out. It's a crime scene now. I'm willing to bet my Alvin vase the police here haven't seen anything like this before."

Hoisting himself up onto the window once more, he jumped down into the garden.

He gently wiped the tears off Eilidh's face and gave her a hug.

Feeling intensely grateful for the support of his arms around her, she clung to him.

Her turbulent emotions had been replaced with a deep feeling of guilt.

She knew it wasn't logical, but she couldn't help thinking back to when she met Patrick at the beach and she wondered whether she could have said something different, something that might have made him open up to her more and enabled her to prevent his brutal, senseless slaughter.

They stood there in silence, standing watch over the window, until they heard voices coming from the front of the house.

When they walked into the front garden, they recognised the burly shape of Rory, who was talking to another officer they didn't know.

Both of them were standing by the front door.

"Won't be any use to you," said Eilidh, making them jump. "The problem's at the back of the house."

"Awight bonny!" said Rory, his face brightening.

"Not really, no, Rory," answered Eilidh.

Rory turned to his colleague.

"Lewis, this is Chief Inspector Langley 'n' Inspector Simmons fae th' Art 'n' Antiquities Unit in London."

"Nice to meet you," said Lewis, smiling shyly.

"Come with us," suggested Richard. "You'll soon understand what we're dealing with."

Rory and Lewis followed them to the broken window.

"Did ye break in?" asked Rory, the disapproval patent in his voice.

Richard rolled his eyes in impatience.

"Will you just take a look through that window, please?" he pleaded.

The two men peered in and stiffened in shock.

"Is that Patrick?" stuttered Rory.

"Yes, I'm afraid so," said Richard. "You'd better call out forensics. Someone's cut him up. Brutal work."

"Ye've bin in thare?" asked Rory in disbelief.

"Yes, we thought he might be injured and in need of urgent help. But he's dead, I'm afraid."

Rory nodded and walked off to make his calls.

Eilidh and Richard turned to Lewis.

He was a small, blond man, with a benign face.

He didn't seem the right fit for a policeman, thought Eilidh. A profession as a university lecturer would better suit him.

"If you don't mind, I'd like to take my partner home," Richard said to Lewis. "She's extremely tired. Rory knows our address. We're happy to make a statement whenever it suits you."

"No problem, sir," said Lewis deferentially.

"These are our phone numbers," added Richard, pulling two cards out of his wallet and handing them over to Lewis. "Rory and Fiona have them in any case. Thank you."

Without further ado, Richard led Eilidh away.

"Richard, shouldn't we wait until the others arrive?"

He shook his head.

"Nope. Not our place, Eilidh. We'll go in and give our statements at the station, but our task is to track the treasure, not deal with homicides on the island."

"But they're bound to be connected."

"Of course, but there's no evidence of that as yet. We can't interfere at this stage. The best thing we can do now is find the wretched treasure. As long as it lies undiscovered unscrupulous people on this island are going to try and get the location from anyone connected to Simon."

"I wonder if Patrick told them where it was. He knew where the treasure was, Richard. I'm a hundred percent certain of that."

Richard shrugged.

"It wouldn't surprise me, given what I saw, if he did tell them. Again, there's not much we can do about that, either."

Tiredness swept over Eilidh. Her energy levels were dipping and she needed some calories to keep her going.

"Richard, can we stop at a tea shop called The Rhubarb? It's very near here. I'd like to get a drink and some food."

"Yes, of course. Would you like me to drive?"

Eilidh shook her head.

Given Richard's appalling sense of direction, they could well end up halfway to Lewis searching for The Rhubarb. She didn't have the energy or patience for that.

A short time later she was tucking into an enormous freshly baked scone when Richard took her by surprise.

"Do you have Patrick's note, Eilidh?"

She put her scone down and stared at him.

"Why?"

"We're going to have to hand in that note when we give our statements to the police. I'd like to have a skim of it before it disappears for good."

Eilidh rummaged around in her handbag and passed the note to Richard.

She watched him with amusement as, completely

oblivious to her, he studied the words on the paper, his mug of coffee growing cold between his hands.

After a few minutes, he took out his mobile phone and began doing a search

"Interesting," he announced at last. "It's a quote from the classic *The Water Babies* by Charles Kingsley.

> '*I have jumped upwards, downwards, backwards, and sideways at least four thousand times; and I can't get out: I always get up underneath there, and can't find the hole.*' It's the part of the book where the lobster is trapped in a lobster pot. '*Tom looked at the trap, and having more wit than the lobster, he saw plainly enough what was the matter, as you may if you will look at a lobster-pot.*'"

He rubbed his chin thoughtfully.

"I know of only one man on this island who would understand anything about lobster-pots. Findley."

15

Richard

"Forgive me, but this seems a little farfetched to me. You receive an anonymous, somewhat cryptic note through the letterbox. Then, you appear to have a eureka moment, and determine the note was written by Patrick McQuire. Do I have that right? And you sense he's in trouble. So, you go over to his house and when he doesn't answer the doorbell you decide to take a look through the windows?"

Detective Inspector John Duncan crossed his arms and waited for their response.

Richard looked at him.

He was a tall man, with an uncompromising face.

His cold, black eyes were staring at them, detached and impersonal.

In other words, he was no walkover and didn't suffer fools gladly.

Richard sighed, feeling despondent.

John Duncan was quite right, of course. It didn't look good.

"Look, my partner's pregnant. She's prone to getting anxious and having strange fancies..."

"Oh, no you don't, Richard," interrupted Eilidh angrily, torpedoing his explanation. "Don't put this on my pregnancy."

She rolled her eyes.

"Men," she said, shaking her head, her short, blonde curls fluttering as she did so.

Richard blushed.

John, meantime, was beginning to look amused.

Seeing signs of a sense of humour in John, Richard felt himself relax.

If they'd managed to introduce a little light relief into the interview, all the better, he thought. It could only help, given their current situation. Those who discovered murdered bodies had to be eliminated as suspects first, and John didn't seem to want to make allowances for the fact Eilidh and Richard were police officers.

"Why don't you tell me the reason you thought Patrick might be in danger?" John suggested to Eilidh.

Richard shut his eyes, dreading Eilidh's answer.

"I knew something was wrong when I read that note. You see, I'd met him once before, and he came across as a disturbed man," she explained, waving her hands in the air for emphasis. "He was anxious, worried even, when I spoke with him."

"I presume you were wanting to speak with him for a reason?"

Eilidh nodded.

"I'd been attempting to get in touch with Patrick because he's Simon's natural father. I thought Simon might have confided in him and told him something, anything really, about the Viking hoard he'd found on the beach, which in turn might be useful and help us in our search for it."

She made a face.

"It was a bloody tiresome task trying to get hold of him," she added. "I'd been calling him on his house phone, and I'd left a number of messages, but he never replied to them. I decided, therefore, to visit him at his house and wait for him to turn up if he wasn't in. This was a while before the murder happened, by the way."

Rory, who was seated slightly behind John, seemed fascinated by her account.

He'd spent the last fifteen minutes chewing the end of his biro and not volunteering a word. Richard thought he looked somewhat out of his depth on this case, which was understandable given the mess the killer had left behind. It wasn't exactly an everyday kind of homicide for the small community in Harris.

"What day did you visit his house?" asked John, scribbling down notes.

"It was just over a week ago, on Thursday. Richard had gone to drop off Janey, Simon's wife, at the airport in Stornoway. I went over to Patrick's home."

"And you met Patrick then, didn't you?"

"Yes, I bumped into him accidently on the beach near his house," agreed Eilidh. "Tràigh na Cleabhaig beach, it was. It's a beautiful beach and Patrick was sketching it. We got chatting and he more or less implied he knew where the treasure was. He also said there were people watching him and, even then, he sounded like he was a trapped man. At one point, he spotted binoculars flashing in the distance and pointed them out to me. He was a lovely man, but after speaking to him I began to think he was getting paranoid."

Eilidh smiled at the memory.

"Anyway, he kindly gave me the drawing he was working on and made his way home soon afterwards... I don't know how to put it. He seemed frightened, but that's just my personal take on it." She shrugged. "I remember he said he was planning to go to a friend's house to get away from being hassled and spied on. I said we might try and get in touch with him again. He seemed fine with that. Once he'd left to go home, I carried on with my walk along the coast."

"And?" prompted John.

"And that was it, until we received the note."

There was silence in the room.

Richard glanced nervously at John.

His face was still looking sceptical.

Richard gathered Eilidh's explanation wasn't faring any better than Richard's in assuaging his doubts.

Weighing things up, Richard felt his pathetic attempt to blame their anxiety for Patrick on Eilidh's pregnancy whims was possibly a safer bet, overall, than to admit they'd believed in Patrick's crazy, irrational fears. Though neither explanation covered them in glory, it had to be said.

The more Eilidh revealed to John Duncan, the more Richard felt she was doing a sterling job of digging a pit deep enough for the pair of them to be buried in. They had to come up with a better reason for visiting Patrick's house on the day of the murder. Saying they bought into Patrick's paranoia wasn't going to cut it with John, and Richard could see unless they came up with a more convincing excuse they'd end up stuck on the Isle of Lewis and Harris for a very long time, with John's investigation unfolding at a snail's pace.

Harris was that kind of a place. Sleepy and slow.

Suddenly, he felt a sharp yearning to be back at their flat in South Kensington, nestled in the centre of London.

At least in London they knew and understood the crime demographic, and it was familiar territory to them. A quiet island, full of weirdness, unexplained happenings, and a small, local population closing ranks against any "outsiders" was not his area of expertise.

"So, when you received the note you decided it was from Patrick?" John asked Eilidh, bringing Richard back down to earth with a bump.

"Yes, the note was written in pencil and it made me immediately think of Patrick because the sketch he'd given me was also done in pencil," said Eilidh. "When I compared the signature on my drawing to the writing on the note, they looked similar to me."

"And neither of you heard the note being posted through the letterbox?"

"No. Eilidh was out of house, fetching some milk," admitted Richard. "And I was working in the sitting room. I certainly didn't hear anything, but even if I'd heard the mail coming through the letterbox, I wouldn't have rushed to the front door to get it, because it's not our house and the mail's never for us. Any mail we receive is always addressed to the landlady. We're only leasing the house for a total of four weeks."

John nodded, accepting this.

"We've found Patrick's fingerprints on the note," he said. "It's a shame we don't have an exact time for him delivering it to you. We might've been able to piece together a timeline for the day he was murdered."

There was another long silence.

"You're here to find this so-called Viking treasure, I understand?" asked John, reading through their statement once more.

Eilidh and Richard nodded.

"I imagine there must be sufficient proof such a treasure exists to bring the head of the Art and Antiquities Unit up here from London," he remarked, rubbing his chin. "Would you care to tell me what evidence you possess regarding the treasure find?"

"Yes, of course," said Richard quickly, before Eilidh opened her mouth. "If you like, I can provide you with the photos I was given by a contact of mine. The photos are of three items belonging to the missing Viking hoard. We were tipped off by a reliable source. He informed us there were rumours circulating in the criminal underworld about a substantial treasure find on Harris, and he subsequently left me with the photos. All three items were being offered for sale on the black market."

Richard rubbed his eyes, feeling weary.

He wondered how many more times he was going to have to justify their presence on the island. And no doubt, when they returned to New Scotland Yard, he was going to have explain their lack of success in finding the treasure over and over again, too.

"It's difficult in these days of government cuts and austerity for us to allocate adequate resources in hunting down stolen or missing artworks," he said, ploughing on manfully. "However, this Viking hoard caught my boss's imagination. As you already know, whoever was trying to sell the Viking treasure on the sly was essentially stealing it from the Scottish nation and breaking the law. It wasn't a given, but my boss at New Scotland Yard was willing to smooth the way for us to come up here to the Isle of Lewis and Harris to hunt down the remaining treasure before it disappeared for good."

"Not that we've got anywhere close to finding it," added Eilidh despondently.

"True," agreed Richard with a rueful smile. "Speed is of the essence in this case, I believe, because more pieces could be sold on the black market. Once it was agreed with the Scottish authorities and we'd received clearance, I was informed by my source that the two pieces we knew of had been sold to a buyer in Birmingham. The buyer was acting as a middleman, as far as I understand. Undeclared to the authorities, of course. My contact, who runs an agency specialising in art recovery, managed to retrieve the two objects before they vanished for good and has handed them over to the British Museum for safe keeping."

He ran a hand through his hair.

"By now, I'd expect for the British Museum to have been in touch with the curators at the National Museum of Scotland regarding the pieces."

Richard slouched back on his chair.

"There's our proof, for what it's worth," he added, wanting to see John wipe the incredulous look off his face. It was beginning to irritate him.

However much he wanted to put John in his place, Richard wasn't going to complicate matters by mentioning Mike Telford. Mike had built up a formidable reputation in his field, indeed he was something of a celebrity in art-world circles, but Richard didn't think it was going to be helpful to bring him into the conversation. He was certain Mike would want to keep a low profile in Harris. It was the way he tended to work.

In any case, it was highly unlikely a Detective Inspector from such a remote place as the Outer Hebrides would have heard of an international art crime expert like Mike Telford.

Richard looked across at Eilidh.

He could tell Eilidh was itching to tell John about Fiona Mitchell and the obvious issue with police corruption on Harris.

However, at this stage, they had no solid proof of Fiona's involvement with the treasure, and he didn't want to start going down that road. It was a red herring because they were "outsiders" and Fiona's words were going to carry more weight with the local police force.

And as far as the treasure was concerned, there were risks in bringing Fiona Mitchell into the conversation. If Fiona felt she was under scrutiny, she might commit any number of rash actions to cover her tracks and any chance of them discovering the treasure's whereabouts could then disappear for good.

Eilidh was glaring at Richard in disapproval, willing him to tell John about Fiona's perfidy, but in the end, she said nothing—much to his relief.

John looked from one to the other.

"I can see there's more to this treasure than meets the eye," he said dryly.

He looked down at his notes, thinking.

"Eilidh, can you tell me once again why you inferred the note was a cry for help?"

Eilidh's large brown eyes looked him over with contempt.

Having spent a great deal of time giving their statement the day before, her patience was beginning to wear thin.

"Didn't you read the note? Doesn't that sound to you like someone who's in trouble? The words '*I can't get out*' seem pretty clear to me."

John nodded.

"Right. Then you decide to go to Patrick's house and find he's not at home," he said, flicking backwards and forwards through their statement. "What made you want to start looking through the windows of the house?"

Eilidh looked confused for a minute.

"My anxiety for him, perhaps?" she offered.

Richard could see from the expression on John's face that he was placing "pregnant woman" and "totally irrational" into the same bracket.

Ha. Maybe, just maybe, they'd be saved from any further uncomfortable and probing questions as a result of this. There was hope for them yet.

"Did forensics find anything in the room?" asked Richard, deciding it was time to go on the offensive.

They were fellow police officers and he'd have expected some openness from John regarding Patrick's murder. Despite the fact it was incredibly rare for police officers to commit murder, they were getting questioned by John as though they were prime suspects in the case.

John needed to sort out his priorities, thought Richard. And soon.

John's inscrutable black eyes looked back at him.

"May I ask what shoe size you are?" he asked Richard.

Richard stared at him in surprise.

"Size 11."

John nodded.

"Would you mind?" he asked, glancing pointedly at his feet.

Startled by the request, Richard bent down, undid the laces of his walking boot and removed it from his foot.

He handed it over to John.

"Thank you," said John, giving the boot a cursory inspection and handing it back to him.

"They found footprints in the blood on the carpet," John informed them, while Richard put his boot back on. "The owner was wearing plastic covers on his feet but we estimate the foot size to be a size 13, which I'm sure you'll agree is exceptionally large."

He crossed his arms.

"We've also found a couple of hairs on the body. Not Patrick's, obviously. The murder was a pretty violent one, so it's not a surprise traces were left behind. The murderer spent a considerable amount of time carving up parts of the body after the death, but the pathologist also thinks Patrick was tortured before he was murdered."

Eilidh flinched at his words.

"The two questions we have to ask ourselves are, were they trying to extract information from him and could it have anything to do with this Viking treasure?" mused John. "It's a bit of a conundrum for us. Murders like this do not happen on this island. They just don't. It's such a small population. We have to factor in that an outsider might have been involved. Just as the treasure brought the two of you up here, it could've attracted some ugly customers from elsewhere as well."

"A professional hit, you mean?" asked Eilidh.

"This isn't a professional job, by any means," disagreed John. "I've limited experience with this kind of murder, but that's my opinion after reading the reports."

He smiled at them, but there was no warmth in his smile, and Richard did not lower his guard for a minute.

"I presume neither of you has any idea why he was killed in such a manner?" John asked.

"No," said Richard.

"Eilidh?" asked John.

"Well, as I've said before, I think Patrick knew what Simon did with the treasure. In fact, I'm almost sure of it. I suspect that's the motive you're looking for."

"Any ideas who might be responsible for murdering Patrick?"

Eilidh and Richard shook their heads.

"None at all?"

Again, they shook their heads.

John sighed.

"OK. Well, thank you for coming in to speak to us today. I'd appreciate it if, as soon as you can, you let us know what your movements are going to be in the near future. For my part, I wouldn't be happy to have the pair of you disappearing back to the mainland any time soon. I'm sure you can understand this."

Richard grimaced at his words.

"Yes, well, I'm afraid our time on Harris is running short," he said apologetically. "But giving you information on our movements over the next couple of weeks should be easy enough."

He sighed.

"We've got less than two weeks left on our rental agreement," he said glumly. "After that, unless there are any major developments, we'll be expected to head straight back to London. I'm not sure my boss will see Patrick's murder as a reason for us to delay our return."

Eilidh looked at him and then turned to John.

"With so few people on the island, wouldn't it be possible to take hair samples from everyone who knew Patrick?" she suggested.

John shook his head.

"Not at the moment, no. We need to unpick the circumstances surrounding Patrick's murder a little more," he countered. "In terms of testing people, we should first establish if there's a possible connection to the murder with someone who lives locally, here on the island."

He smiled at her.

"We're going to have to weigh the pros and cons before we begin doing anything like that. As you rightly pointed out, Harris is a very small community. We're going to have to tread carefully or there'll be a full-blown outcry."

John scratched his head as he looked at his notes.

"There isn't any concrete proof Simon was involved with the Viking items you've located, or even that Patrick's murder was in any way related to them," he said dismissively. "We're going to need a whole lot more evidence, proving the treasure's behind his murder, before we decide to pursue that angle."

He tidied up his notes and leaned back in his chair.

"Right, you're both free to go. Thank you for your time."

Richard and Eilidh pushed their plastic chairs back and stood up.

John looked up at them, his brow furrowed.

"By the way, one last thing. If you do come across any pertinent information in your search for the treasure, I'll be expecting you to report it back to me," he warned, folding his hands on the table. "Don't forget your official presence here is solely due to the indulgence of the Scottish police force. That can always change."

"Sure thing," responded Richard, giving Eilidh a gentle prod in the back towards the door.

He wanted them out of there as soon as possible.

The interview had been his first experience of being treated like a suspect and he hadn't enjoyed it one little bit. Added to that had been the agonising worry that Eilidh was going to give away too much, in her usual forthright manner. She wasn't one to mince her words.

Rory, who seemed to be intimidated by his superior, nevertheless managed to give them a covert smile, as though wanting to assure them of his good will before they left the room.

Feeling agitated, Richard nibbled at his fingernail as they walked out of the interview room.

At least for today, they'd emerged relatively unscathed from their encounter with Harris officialdom.

John was no fool, though. He knew they were keeping things back from him.

If John turned out to be a persistent man, and

Richard couldn't hazard a guess on this because he didn't know him, he'd be keeping an unobtrusive eye on them while they were in Harris, in the hope something would come to light in terms of the murder.

Well, good luck to him, if that was the case.

Given their complete failure so far to track down the Viking hoard, it was unlikely John would be able to get much from them in terms of his murder investigation, either. The treasure and Patrick's murder were definitely connected, even if John hadn't reached the same conclusions as them yet.

He would in time, though.

Time.

As they walked down the corridor, the word *time* started to run around in circles inside Richard's mind, taunting him.

Time, time, time.

Finding the Viking hoard was entirely a question of time, thought Richard, as they walked out of the police station into a grey drizzle.

And, as far as he was concerned, the lack of time was becoming critical.

It seemed to him the success or failure of their mission on Harris was going to be defined by the parameters of time. They were running out of official time to crack the case, and the longer time flew past without results, the greater the likelihood the valuable treasure would escape their grasp forever.

Time, time, time.

Something had to shift soon or they'd have to admit defeat, relegating the Viking hoard to the rather large pile of unresolved cases sitting on the shelves of his basement office in London. Yet another failure...

Putting up their coat hoods, they both walked over to their car.

As soon as they were back at their cottage, he was going to make some hot cocoa and get the log fire burning, to cheer themselves up.

Even if it was May, it was bloody freezing. London was a tropical oasis in comparison to Harris's chilly climate.

A longing pang for the hustle and bustle of his home city engulfed him again. It came at him like a punch in the solar plexus, making him catch his breath.

He tossed his head and told himself to get a grip.

No doubt they'd be back there soon enough.

All it would take was for Lionel to be reminded of their existence again, because of yet another high-profile art theft case landing on his desk at New Scotland Yard, and they'd be summoned down to London without further ado.

16

Eilidh

Eilidh was rummaging around in a crate at the local mini-market, trying to find a pepper that wasn't shrivelled up and on its last legs.

She didn't know why, but for some reason, the "fresh" fruit and vegetables sold in Tarbert never seemed in reality to be very fresh.

"Overripe" would be a polite way of putting it. "Rotten" would be closer to the truth.

The transportation of perishables to Tarbert seemed to her to be an issue. Given the harsh climate, she thought most of the produce would have to be imported into the island and maybe this was a problem when servicing a tiny, out-of-the-way place like Tarbert.

At least Stornoway, up in Lewis, had a bigger population and better transport links with mainland Scotland. She was sure the fruit and veg arriving there was in better condition compared to Tarbert's days-old deliveries.

There was a big Tesco supermarket, too, in

Stornoway, but it was over an hour away from Tarbert, and far too much of an effort to get to.

As she couldn't find any edible peppers, she gave up and decided to use some tinned tomatoes instead.

She was picking up a couple of tins when she heard an altercation coming from the front of the shop.

A familiar voice was saying: "Breath freshener, man. How come you don't have any? They told me you did."

"No, sir, we don't have any mouth spray. We've mouthwash. The Colgate one."

"That's no good, I keep telling you. I'm not going to walk around outside carrying a bottle of that stuff with me."

Eilidh poked her head around the corner and spotted Mike standing at the counter, smartly dressed in a pair of navy corduroys, a checked shirt, and a bow tie.

He was wearing a conservative wax jacket over this ensemble, but the overall effect was ruined by his stripy white and blue baseball cap.

The shopkeeper, an elderly man, was wearing a red apron over a pair of old jeans and a T-shirt.

He was also looking decidedly fed up and had his hands on his hips.

"What about chewing gum?" suggested the harassed shopkeeper.

"Disgusting," repudiated Mike, looking horrified at the thought. "Do you know how much damage chewing gum does? For goodness sake, didn't you know that gum takes over five hundred years to decompose? Do you have any idea how bad it is for the environment? And let me tell you, sir, eighty to ninety percent of gum isn't disposed of correctly."

The shopkeeper went quiet in the face of this verbal onslaught.

Eilidh seized her chance.

"Mike!"

Mike turned around and smiled.

"Hello, Eilidh. Thought I'd bump into you sooner or later."

"What's the problem?" asked Eilidh.

"The problem's simple. I was told by the pharmacy this shop was guaranteed to have a breath freshener spray. Now he's saying he doesn't have it in stock."

"It's not that I don't have it in stock. I've never had it in stock," chipped in the shopkeeper, his arms crossed in a defensive posture.

Eilidh thought about this for a moment.

"Well, Tarbert's a small place," she said at last, feeling amused. "I wouldn't have thought they'd extend to selling breath freshener in their shops, Mike. Why's it so important, anyway? Are you on the pull or something?"

"No," said Mike unconvincingly. "I finished my breath freshener yesterday. I always carry one around with me. I didn't expect Harris to be such a back-of-beyond place."

"Maybe you should try brushing your teeth a bit more," suggested the shopkeeper in a snarky tone of voice.

Eilidh looked at Mike.

"Why don't I take you for a coffee?" she offered hastily in an effort to provide a diplomatic solution to the impasse.

The colour on Mike's face had turned to a deep shade of crimson.

"In a minute, Eilidh," said Mike.

He turned to the shopkeeper.

"I brush my teeth regularly, thank you very much, and I take my oral hygiene very seriously. Judging by your set of false teeth, you haven't done so."

The shopkeeper stared at him in surprise.

Mike stomped over to the shop door.

"Come on, Eilidh," he called out. "Let's leave this shack."

Eilidh smiled apologetically at the shopkeeper and then followed Mike outside.

"You're making waves in Tarbert already, aren't you?" Eilidh commented, as they walked back up the street.

"No, I'm not. The man was a plonker."

"Suit yourself. Where would you like to stop for coffee?"

"How about The Calanais tea shop?"

Eilidh nodded.

There were only two tea shops in the whole of Tarbert apart from the distillery café: The Calanais and The Herringbone.

They made their way to Manse Road and entered a small but bustling tea room.

The Calanais tea shop was one of those deceptive places which looked tiny from the outside but morphed into something much bigger when you entered it.

The back of the shop opened out onto a large-sized garden and they found themselves a comfortable corner table to sit at, shielded from the persistent breeze but still exposed to the sun. It was also at the extreme end of the garden, a distance away from the other customers.

A buxom lady dropped two menus on their table and then hurried off again.

Eilidh studied the menu. It had a drawing of the Calanais standing stones on the front of it.

She felt some sadness looking at the picture, because she found herself wondering if Patrick McQuire had drawn it for the tea shop.

The curious Neolithic stones, named the Calanais Stones, were based on the Lewis part of the island. She'd been to visit the site with Richard, who was, predictably, fascinated by them.

At an average of three metres high, the Calanais Stones were the island's equivalent of the ancient Neolithic stones at Stonehenge in England.

Situated at opposite ends of the UK, both the stone structures were supposedly used as astronomical observatories by humans in prehistoric times.

The central Calanais monolith weighed approximately seven tonnes and the largest sides of the giant stone were precisely aligned to the north and south.

Both Stonehenge and the Calanais stone circles were constructed thousands of years ago, but the Calanais were said to predate their more famous Stonehenge cousins, and were estimated to be over 5,000 years old. To Eilidh, this was mind-boggling.

Having visited the standing stones only the week before, Eilidh could remember the impact they'd had on her.

Unsure of what to expect, she'd been bowled over by the aura of mystery and majesty that lingered over the area.

They'd seen the Calanais Stones in the evening and the setting sun had created a wonderful backdrop against the uneven stones, extending their shapes with long, black shadows.

The stones themselves had looked to Eilidh like gigantic grey teeth bursting out of the grassy ground. They dominated the area around them, making the sea and hills in the distance seem insignificant and transient.

Placed up on a ridge, the site had uninterrupted views to the distant horizon for a full 360 degrees. Perfect for some prehistoric astronomy.

Maybe she was prejudiced by her affection for the Isle of Lewis and Harris, but she thought the wildness of the landscape on the island transformed the Calanais Stones into a more impressive monument than Stonehenge. The mystical atmosphere surrounding the Calanais Stones, and the beautiful scenery of the island, combined to take her back in time to a different age much more effectively than battling through heavy traffic on the roads around Stonehenge. Stonehenge, after all, was based in such a congested, overpopulated part of the south of England.

The standing stones on Lewis were in keeping with the antiquity of the entire island. In her opinion, the backdrop of the machair, the wild coastline, the old stone walls, and crumbling ruins altogether created the perfect setting for the Calanais Stones to exist in.

According to Eilidh's guidebook, the rock on the Isle of Harris and Lewis was the oldest in Europe and, despite the passage of time, the natural environment on most of the island was unspoilt. Given the human destruction in so many other beauty spots around the world, this was quite an achievement. And the Calanais Stones, unique and prehistoric, were an important part of the untouched heritage on the island.

"Have you visited them?" asked Mike, noticing her lost in the drawing of the stones.

Eilidh put the menu down.

"Yes, I have. They're impressive. What about you?"

Mike shook his head. "No, but I'd like to see them. It's damn amazing to have two such structures survive from the Neolithic times in the UK, especially so when they're situated seven hundred miles apart. It's incredible, really."

Eilidh nodded in agreement and then looked around, wondering when the waitress was going to turn up. She was hungry, and unfortunately the position of their table meant it was easy for them to be overlooked by the café staff.

As though reading her thoughts, the waitress came out into the garden with some drinks for a neighbouring table.

Catching her eye, the waitress came up to Eilidh.

"What would you like, darling?" she asked in a friendly voice.

"A hot chocolate and a slice of carrot cake, please," said Eilidh.

"An Americano and the millionaire's shortbread for me," followed Mike.

The waitress nodded, picked up the menus, and left them to it.

"A little birdie tells me you're running out of time on the Isle of Harris," commented Mike as Eilidh watched the sparrows darting under the tables, searching for dropped crumbs.

Eilidh looked at him and smiled. "Richard?"

"Yes."

Eilidh sighed. "True. We've only got a week and a half left on the house lease. I don't think we're going to get to the bottom of things before then."

Mike rubbed his chin. "It depends, I suppose."

"On what?"

"On whether you're prepared to make things happen."

Eilidh was puzzled. "Meaning?"

"We do know quite a lot already about the thieves, if you think about it." He looked around and lowered his voice. "For one thing, we know Fiona Mitchell's involved and quite possibly that hefty boyfriend of hers. Maybe we should be focusing on them, instead of the treasure."

"I don't see how we can make anything happen with those two. There's absolutely no hard evidence connecting them with the hoard."

"There might be evidence in their homes, though," said Mike, leaning forward and clasping his hands together.

Eilidh stared at him. "You must be mad. Stark raving bonkers."

"We've done it before, remember?"

"Yes, and I was lucky not to end up spending part of the year in a Spanish jail. I'm not repeating that in a hurry."

"For goodness sake, that was ages ago," said Mike, impatiently. "This is a completely different situation. For a start, Fiona and David don't have a house alarm, like many of the houses here in Harris. This place is no metropolis. Trust me, it'll be very easy to break in."

"You've been sussing out the lie of the land already, I see."

"But of course. It makes sense."

Mike looked at her.

"Oh, no," said Eilidh, shaking her head. "You aren't persuading me to get involved. Once bitten, twice shy, remember? Why don't you try it yourself?"

"I might well do so," said Mike, acknowledging her refusal with a smile. "The big question rolling around my mind is which of the two do you think has been the brains behind all of this? David or Fiona?"

"Fiona for sure," said Eilidh, without hesitation. "And I'm not being bitchy when I say that. She was the one negotiating to sell the goods on the black market, wasn't she?"

Mike nodded. "She does come across as a powerful Lady Macbeth figure," he agreed.

"David, meanwhile, strikes me as all brawn and not much brains."

"Now that's a bitchy comment," said Eilidh with a giggle.

The waitress came up to their table and started laying out their drink and food. She departed soon afterwards, called over to another table.

Eilidh picked up a fork and sliced a piece of carrot cake with it. Putting it in her mouth, she savoured the creamy icing and wondered if she'd get sugar withdrawal when she started the inevitable post-pregnancy diet.

She was sure she was going to end up high as a kite on the calories she was consuming, but she would enjoy the kick it gave her, while it lasted. To hell with worrying about her weight gain, she thought.

The pleasure was worth the tighter waistband, and given she was wearing pregnancy clothes her waistband was expandable in any case. She would just increase the notches and nobody would know any different.

"I do understand why you're tempted to have a look inside her house," she said thoughtfully, after drinking some hot chocolate.

She saw Mike looking at her in enquiry.

"None of us know what happened to the third item of treasure left at the police station," she explained. "I guess she could still have it in her possession. What would be even better than looking at her house would be casting an eye over her text messages and emails. Also, her bank account. But, sadly, we don't have enough evidence for that, and even if we had, we'd create a scandal if we requested permission to do to a covert search, because she's one of our own."

"Her being a police officer is a problem," conceded Mike, who'd already wolfed down his millionaire's shortbread in three mouthfuls. "And up here she'll have more contacts within the Scottish police force than you two have. You both should be careful."

"That's rich coming from the master of risk-taking," said Eilidh, amused.

"True. I'm preaching to the converted, though."

Eilidh dropped a few cake crumbs on the ground.

"It's extremely frustrating, given we're certain Patrick's death is somehow connected to the treasure," Eilidh said, feeling depressed. "To leave and declare the case unresolved is really gutting. You know how it is. I'm finding the whole thing demoralising, to be honest with you. Meanwhile, it seems Fiona's pocketed the money and she's free to do whatever she likes."

She sighed. "You couldn't get that lady in Birmingham to admit to Fiona's involvement in the sale?"

Mike shook his head. "You know that's not possible. She'd get into hot water herself."

Eilidh made a face. "Well, it looks as though we're coming to the end of the road, then. Richard's gone to speak to Findley, Simon's fisherman friend, but I doubt he'll get any results there, either. People on the island seem to be very good at keeping things to themselves and behind closed doors."

"Why on earth has he gone to see Findley again?" asked Mike, interested.

Eilidh ate some more of her cake and thought about her answer. They were both on the same side and had little to lose at this stage.

"We received a note from Patrick before he died," she said, at last. "And Richard discovered it was a written quote from a book called *The Water Babies*. It's a Victorian classic. I've never heard of it. Anyway, apart from the note's obvious cry for help, the quote from the book was about a lobster stuck in a lobster pot."

Mike chuckled as he stirred a lump of sugar into his coffee.

"So from a random note, Richard thinks of all things seaward and comes up with Findley? Now, that's a long shot if ever I heard one. I think my suggestion works a lot better than that."

Eilidh nodded. "Probably."

"Are you sure you won't consider coming with me to look at Fiona's house?"

Eilidh smiled. "No, I can't. You got me into a lot of trouble last time. What's more, Mike, you're only asking me out of pure self-interest. It was the same in Madrid.

You were only using my position as a police officer to save yourself."

Their eyes met.

"Fair enough," said Mike, putting his coffee mug down. "I must confess, it would've been helpful to have you there, though. Now I'll have to weigh my options."

"Meaning?"

Mike laughed. "Meaning I'll have to weigh up the risks to myself if you're not willing to join me in this venture."

Eilidh raised her eyes heavenward in despair.

"As a police officer you'd have a legitimate reason to be there," he pointed out. "Given what we know."

"Not without a search warrant," said Eilidh crisply.

"True," he admitted.

"And you know I shouldn't even be having a conversation like this with you," added Eilidh.

"You've become very straight-laced, Eilidh."

"Well, what did you expect? I'm about to become a mum. I've got to be responsible at some point."

"That's disappointing. I always thought you had real potential for undercover work. Ever fancied setting yourself up as a private detective?"

Eilidh giggled at the thought.

"I think I'm going to have my hands full as it is in the near future," she said, placing a hand on her belly. "But I'll admit, the idea is an enticing one. Maybe one day I'll be able to persuade Richard to leave his department, with its tiresome bureaucracy, to set up his own detective business. He's getting more and more irritated by the internal politics going on at New Scotland Yard."

"Don't blame him," commented Mike. "I couldn't hack it."

Mike stretched out his legs and leaned back on his chair, his face tilted to the sun.

"You should know I'm going to be retiring soon. You could both take over my practice."

"And how soon is soon?" asked Eilidh, surprised by his admission.

"Give or take, in the next year or two."

Eilidh smiled as she tried to imagine it.

"Unfortunately, I don't think Richard has the ability to connect with the dodgy characters you meet with on a regular basis," she pointed out.

Mike opened an eye.

"No, he wouldn't. He's too posh. But you'd do OK."

17

Mike

Mike turned off the main road and drove up a narrow driveway.

Just ahead of him was a small, picturesque bungalow surrounded by laurel trees.

The front lawn was neat and manicured, the grass showing even, parallel stripes where the lawnmower had cut it.

The front door was painted a bright shade of yellow and a climbing clematis was shedding its pale-pink petals on the ground in front of it.

Parking his van on the gravel outside Fiona's home, he pulled up the handbrake and reached across for his satchel.

Before getting out, he paused for a moment, satchel on his lap. For some reason, he was feeling an unfamiliar sense of foreboding. He couldn't put a finger on why this was because he'd done his research well enough. Looking out of the van windows, he checked nothing looked different from the other times he'd seen the house.

Richard had been very helpful in assisting Mike with his enquiries and he'd given Mike the location of Fiona's house soon after his arrival in Harris.

Afterwards, Nico had gone along and taken detailed photos of the exterior of Fiona's bungalow, which both Mariella and Mike had studied from top to bottom over cosy mugs of coffee.

And for good measure, a couple of times, when he'd observed Fiona was on duty in Tarbert, Mike had driven out to her home to have a look around it. On those occasions, he'd parked his van further down the road from the bungalow and then walked up the driveway to survey the place, resisting the temptation to break into it there and then. He knew he needed to make sure there was sufficient time to conduct a proper search, and to do so safely, too.

Well, the right day to have a look inside Fiona's bungalow had finally arrived and he was as well prepared as he could be, he reckoned. There should be no surprises in store for him. With a sigh, he got out of the van and made his way along the side of the bungalow to the back door.

It was early afternoon and he had hours of time on his hands. He knew Fiona was meant to be on duty at Tarbert police station until ten o'clock that evening.

This useful tip-off had been helpfully provided by Eilidh, who'd probably used her considerable charm when asking Rory Petrie for a copy of the police rota for the week.

Mike smiled to himself. When giving Mike the rota, Eilidh made a rather pathetic attempt at pretending not to know why he needed it. She really was a terrible actress.

Too bad she'd chickened out from joining him on his search. He could've done with a buddy.

He'd also been told by the friendly barman at Time or Tide that his boss, David, was coming in to help out with the pub's stocktake that afternoon.

With the precious pair fully occupied, the coast was clear. A perfect set-up for his "exploration."

He refused to think of it as a break-in. In the interests of art, anything was permissible, in his view. Especially when he was working on the side of the angels. Unconstrained by the owner's presence, there was a beautiful window of opportunity for him to get stuck into the job and do a thorough search, which was nothing like the kind of grab and dash a typical burglar would do.

He reached the back door and dumped his satchel next to it.

The garden was a long one, extending right down to a stream running at the bottom of it. Several Japanese maple trees shielded him from the neighbours' view on one side of the house. Given the sheer number of trees in the garden, it was obvious Fiona cherished her privacy more than the sunlight. This was a big bonus to Mike because not getting seen by the neighbour next door meant there was one less thing for him to worry about.

Operation Mitchell was about to begin.

He grabbed a pair of plastic foot covers out of his satchel and snapped them on. Mike then pulled a pair of gloves from his pocket and wriggled his fingers into them.

He did a cursory inspection of the deadbolt on the

door and took a power drill out of his satchel, along with a case of drill bits.

After a minute, he found the right bit to match the size of the tiny screws holding the deadlock in place, and secured it onto the tool.

He carefully placed the drill on top of one of the two screws, which were placed on either side of the keyhole, and braced himself.

He drilled deeply into the screw hole, pushing the screw further and further down the shaft, and then did exactly the same for the other one.

When he pulled at the deadbolt, he found it came away easily from the door.

Bingo, he thought. A smooth start.

After dropping the power drill into his satchel and chucking the deadbolt into the undergrowth, he turned the door handle and made his way inside.

He walked into a small utility room, consisting of a washing machine, dryer and sink. Clothes had been hung up to dry on a rack above the sink.

He walked through the door of the utility room into a bright kitchen. As far as he could tell everything looked to be meticulously tidy, which gave him hope in his search for incriminating evidence. He spent a short time going through every kitchen cabinet and drawer and soon realised there was nothing relevant to be found there.

Out in the hallway, there were several doors leading off into other rooms. Mike stuck his head hurriedly into every one of them and ascertained he'd be best to prioritise the study and main bedroom in his search.

Walking into the study, he turned in a slow circle, trying to decide where to begin. An entire wall was taken up with bookshelves. Fiona was certainly very well read. Books on serial killers, dictators, and activists of various kinds jostled for space alongside a few Jack Reacher books and what seemed to Mike to be the entire collection of Dan Brown's books.

On one side of the room there were three plastic storage boxes, which looked interesting. But in front of the window, at the other end of the room, was a desk. It was an imitation Victorian desk, with a dark-green leather worktop.

Mike decided to start with the desk and then move onto the storage boxes afterwards. Crouching down, he began pulling out the desk drawers and sifting through the paraphernalia in them. Most of the papers he found were bills, neatly stapled together, with the odd letter and postcard dotted among them. Very efficiently, each drawer in the desk seemed to section the bills according to the relevant company or utility.

He worked his way through the drawers until he got to the top left-hand-side drawer, which was locked. Taking a pick and a tension wrench out of his satchel, he fiddled with the wafer lock until its locking mechanism shifted. Opening the drawer, he peered inside.

The drawer was empty, except for a small object wrapped in black tissue paper. He lifted the bundle of tissue from the drawer, holding it gingerly in his cupped hand. He carefully opened up the tissue layers and discovered a cat pin he'd seen before.

The body of the cat consisted of an amber stone, held in place with golden claws. The gold head was barely recognisable as a cat's, but the tail of the pin was long, curled, and lifelike. The two feet set at the base of the pin were also realistic cat paws. It was exactly the same pin he'd seen in the photos Farshid had shown him at the Kyoto Garden pond.

He went nearer to the window and held the pin up to the light so he could examine it better. In some ways, he could see why Mariella hadn't wanted to buy it. The cat's face was badly dented, and one of the claws holding the amber stone in place had snapped off.

If it wasn't for its antiquity, nobody would give it a second glance. Despite this, he was convinced she'd been a fool to reject it, because of its uniqueness. Among Viking artefacts, its rarity was going to be undisputed. It was a one-of-a-kind object, and due to its history, it was sure to be worth a load of money, damaged or not.

Wrapping it in tissue again, he placed the pin inside a side pocket of his satchel. Then he turned to look at the storage boxes. He debated whether he should head back out while the going was good. He'd found the missing Viking pin. Was there going to be anything else worth finding in the bungalow?

The arguments to stay or go fought a quick battle in his mind. As ever with Mike, his curiosity won the day. He somehow managed to convince himself he'd find further incriminating evidence if he continued with his search of the house, and maybe even some clues leading to the whereabouts of the remaining Viking treasure.

Sitting down on the floor, he pulled the first storage box towards him and began going through its contents.

It didn't take him long to realise there was nothing of interest to be seen. Lodged inside were mainly photo albums and little else.

He was thankful Fiona was such a tidy person because she was saving him effort and time. He found himself smiling. Exploring Fiona's house was proving easy as pie so far.

Thinking back to his youthful misadventures, he wondered if run-of-the-mill thieves ever broke into a bombsite of a home and felt utter desperation at finding anything of value amongst the mess.

He couldn't remember a time when it had happened to him, but then again, his break-ins had always been focused on upmarket properties. Expensive homes generally had cleaners to tidy away any messiness.

He pulled another storage box towards him and started rummaging through it. A few minutes later, he was done with the last storage box. too. There was nothing in them to get excited about.

The second storage box contained a number of files from various training courses. The third one was full of manuals covering psychology, social studies, leadership skills, teamwork, mental health, and law. Police stuff, in other words.

Mike got up, dusted himself down, and then made his way through to the main bedroom.

Fiona's sportiness was evident in her bedroom because there was an exercise bike and a pair of weights taking up space on the floor. The rest of the furniture was utilitarian in style and made of dark wood.

There was a framed picture of Muhammad Ali on the wall, which Mike felt was an odd choice for a woman's bedroom. But then again, maybe not so strange for someone with a Che Guevara tattoo on their wrist. Although he'd only seen Fiona Mitchell from a distance, both Richard and Eilidh had described her in great detail to him.

Nobody had any proof to show Fiona was guilty of appropriating the treasure Simon had left at the police station, but thanks to Mariella, they all knew she'd been selling the artefacts on the sly. She was their main suspect and therefore of great interest to them.

And we were right, thought Mike, *we were so bloody right.*

He did a quick recon of the room. Like everywhere else in the bungalow, the bedroom was clutter free, but looking out of place on the chest of drawers was a messy pile of old notebooks. Six of them were scattered across the surface, with most of them having been left open.

Mike went over to take a closer look. The notebooks were filled with small pencil sketches, but also plenty of writing. He flicked quickly through one of them and came to the front page where in bold lettering was written the name "Patrick McQuire." He blinked in surprise and whistled to himself.

Incriminating evidence indeed.

Deciding he shouldn't hang around too much longer, Mike picked up the six notebooks and dropped them into his satchel. He proceeded to open and shut every drawer in the room, then had a quick rummage in her cupboard.

Nothing.

Having finished with the bedroom, he decided to go through to the sitting room. He grimaced when he walked into the sitting room. The room gave him the jitters, it had to be said. Who wouldn't be affected by the image of two decomposing heads? Not many, in his view.

Taking up a lot of space on one wall was a print of a

gory painting by the artist Théodore Géricault, called *The Severed Heads.*

Depicted in the painting were two decaying heads, those of a man and a woman.

Mike knew a little about Géricault and the man had a dark side to him. One of the heads had been beheaded and it was rumoured the artist kept severed human remains and corpses in his workspace. Disturbing, when one considered this was in the days before refrigeration was invented.

As far as Mike was concerned, Géricault was a sick, perverted man, and Fiona and her weird sidekick seemed to be living pretty much in the same headspace as the crazy artist. He was convinced people with similar tendencies tended to be attracted to each other, like magnets.

He averted his eyes from the painting, but the rest of the room didn't exactly rock his world, either. If he was to sum up the décor in the room, he'd describe it as a tasteless shrine to *The Day of the Dead.*

Skull cushions nestled against the red sofa and a number of porcelain skull candle holders held red candles in them. The frame of the mirror above the fireplace was painted black with a pattern of white skulls around it.

A large rug on the floor depicted an upside-down dog, with its eyes closed and its tongue hanging out. The dog looked to be sleeping, or quite possibly it was supposed to be dead. Judging by the theme of the rest of the room, Mike thought it was probably the latter.

The *pièce de résistance* in the sitting room, undoubtedly, was the coffee table. It was the strangest thing Mike had ever seen because large papier mâché human feet were supporting the table legs.

Mike pursed his lips in disapproval. Maybe it was meant to be a bit of fun. It was hard to tell. Either way, he thought the coffee table was ugly as sin.

Mike could not by any stretch of the imagination see a convivial gathering of visitors sitting in that lounge, enjoying themselves. But, as he wasn't one to hold sociable events in his own home, perhaps he wasn't in a position to pass comment on Fiona's hospitality habits and décor.

He shrugged.

Each to their own. Live and let live, he thought.

His eyes skimmed over the objects in the room and soon determined there was nothing of note to be searched or looked at.

He popped his head into the spare bedroom. Taking a cursory look through the drawers and cupboard, he decided there was no point lingering there any longer, either.

He was almost done.

He nipped into the small bedroom by the kitchen. There were only two items of furniture in the room. A sofa bed and a bedside table. Except, when he had a closer look at the bedside table, he realised he'd been mistaken. It wasn't a bedside table at all. It was a collector's cabinet.

Excited, he inspected it from every angle, looking for any hidden drawers.

It was waist-high, grey, and consisted of two lots of small drawers, reaching down to the floor.

He opened the first drawer and had a look inside. Sitting on a piece of kitchen towel was a gold ring with a garnet stone. Mike reached in and picked it up. It was definitely handmade, he thought, turning it over on his palm.

He'd seen similar before in a number of museums. The thick shank was engraved with crosses and initials. At a guess, it looked medieval to him, with four stylised eagles holding up the garnet.

He dithered for a moment, debating whether he should confiscate the ring, too. He looked over to the cabinet and chewed his lip. He wondered how many other valuables were stored in it and where Fiona had procured them from.

Would they have been stolen? Odds were high they had been. Even if she'd come by them legitimately, he was certain Fiona hadn't declared any items to Treasure Trove Scotland for assessment. To date, she hadn't shown a good track record in notifying the appropriate authorities of historical finds, as demonstrated by her actions when she had a part of the Viking hoard in her possession.

Mike placed the ring in another pocket of his satchel. He opened a second drawer and found a whale bone comb, badly damaged. But again, it looked to be old.

Glancing at his watch, he decided to take as much as he could with him and figure out the value of the objects later, at his leisure.

Tossing the comb in with the other items inside his bag, he then proceeded to go through the other cabinet drawers at lightning speed. Several coins, a pair of earrings, a harpoon tip, and a pottery figurine all disappeared into his satchel.

He was reaching for one of the lower drawers when he heard a noise coming from the kitchen.

Pure instinct made him freeze on the spot. He slowly straightened up and listened. Voices were whispering in the kitchen. Confused, he glanced at his watch. There was supposed to be plenty of time yet.

He realised the rota information he'd been given by Eilidh had been incorrect, or must have been changed at the last minute. Either that, or Fiona had simply decided to come home early for some reason.

It also dawned on him that he was getting sloppy.

Somewhere along the line he'd miscalculated because he hadn't taken his usual precautions against this kind of a mishap. For a start, he should've made sure he'd had an accomplice with him, to keep watch and warn him of anyone approaching the house.

Damn it.

"David, get the knife," he heard from the doorway.

He turned around.

Blocking his exit was a tall, Scandinavian-looking woman with pale-blue eyes. Those eyes were staring at him mockingly, without a shred of fear. In fact, he could almost swear there was a look of glee in them.

He wasn't surprised by the dangerous look in her eyes. What he'd seen of the house had already made him realise there was a streak of outlandishness in her character.

The problem with unbalanced people, though, was that they were unpredictable and hard to manage. He was going to have to be cautious.

"Hello," he said calmly.

David appeared behind Fiona and she moved aside

to let him into the room. He was indeed carrying a very long and sharp-looking knife.

Damn it, thought Mike, again. One he could probably outwit, two was going to be a harder proposition.

"Give her the bag," instructed David, not beating about the bush.

Mike held out the satchel and Fiona took it. She went through its contents and then looked across at him, her eyes blazing with anger.

"I think you've just signed your death warrant, Mr....who the hell are you, anyway? Don't tell me you're connected to that nerdy detective, Richard."

"My name's Ian McNiesh," Mike whined. "I live over in Tarbert. I was hoping to pick up a few things, so I could put some food on the table. I'm really sorry. Truly, I am. I'm running short of cash, see."

Fiona burst out laughing.

"Really? Your accent's very English."

"There's lots of us up here," protested Mike.

"Good try. I'm afraid I don't believe you. There's been too many newcomers sniffing around the island the last few weeks, hunting for the treasure. Tie him up, David."

"With what exactly?"

"I don't know. Your belt?"

"Don't you have any shoelaces, Fi?"

"Yes. I'll go get some."

Fiona disappeared from the room, leaving David standing in front of Mike, still holding the knife.

There was silence for a minute.

"I like your tattoos," commented Mike in a conversational tone of voice.

David snorted, reminding Mike uncomfortably of

an enraged American footballer. He was sure built like one.

"It's not going to work, you know," David growled.

Mike shrugged.

"It was worth a try."

"No, it wasn't. I'll tighten the cords even more now. Losing the circulation in your hands will soon wipe that smug smile off your chubby face."

Fiona came back in with several shoelaces in hand.

David took them and handed her the knife.

Mike made sure his posture was slouched and unthreatening, but his eyes were watching their every movement. He'd been in tight corners before. Several times. Surely, he could get out of this one?

He was convinced if his brain would just crank up a gear, he could think up something to get himself away from the deadly pair. Unfortunately for him, his brain had decided to go on strike. For some strange reason, it had opted to have a meltdown and wasn't working to its normal capacity. He wasn't sure whether this was due to his age, or simply down to pure bad luck, but he suspected he was heading into retirement territory.

Feeling desperate, he wondered if the punters at the Blue Moon would miss his presence after he was dead and gone. Then he thought of Mariella and felt really pissed. Would she ever find out what had happened to him?

He took a breath and tried to steady himself. He was in deep shit, no doubt about it. How he wished he'd brought Mariella with him when he'd searched the house.

Hindsight was a great thing, of course. But he knew between them they'd have found a way out of the situation. If only he'd been able to trust Mariella more. The problem was, he couldn't.

He was sure if Mariella had discovered the antique items in Fiona's house she'd have disappeared with them and they'd never be seen again. Despite his knack of breaking the law when it suited him, Mike felt a strong degree of loyalty towards the Art and Antiquities Unit and other art institutions—something which Mariella certainly didn't possess.

His loyalty was perhaps misguided, but there it was. Mike shared with Richard a sense of responsibility when it came to cultural treasures. Was his allegiance to the art authorities due to his previous police training kicking in, or was it instilled in him by his antiquarian father?

Who could tell? Not given to great self-awareness Mike wasn't going to speculate on this. But for whatever reason, he believed antiquities belonged to the nation as a whole and not to some ruthless individual who had the money and power to buy them.

He sighed as David yanked his arms behind him and he felt a shoelace go around his wrists.

"Why did you do it?" asked Mike, trying to stay cool.

Fiona stepped forward a pace.

"Do what?"

Mike nodded at the satchel.

"Steal those items and kill Patrick...I'm genuinely interested."

He winced as David tightened the cord unmercifully. It was now cutting deep into his skin.

Fiona's eyes narrowed. "You've given up pretending

to know nothing about it pretty quickly, haven't you?" she said.

Mike nodded. He hoped the gorilla behind him would hurry up and move away from him. But no, he was busy tying another lace around his wrists. As if one wasn't enough.

"It's never going to be your business why we're doing this," said Fiona, moving closer to him. "You're finished."

She slid the tip of the knife down his neck and he felt the burning sensation of cut skin, followed by a trickle of what he could only assume was blood.

He really should learn to keep his big mouth shut, he thought to himself. It would have saved him a tonne of grief with Mariella, too.

Fiona looked into his eyes.

"If you really want to know, we're planning on leaving Harris in the near future. This treasure has been our final lottery win. The icing on the cake. As soon as I saw what Simon had in his rucksack I knew it was very special."

She smiled.

"He was very trusting with it, poor boy. Shame, really. Although maybe I did him and his yappy wife a favour. Only a question of time before those two murdered each other."

She lifted the knife and placed it under his chin. Then she applied some pressure.

"You don't happen to know where the rest of the treasure is?" she asked, watching him.

"No," said Mike, not daring to move his head. He flared his nostrils in disgust.

Her breath smelt of aniseed and beer. A sickly combination.

"We're wanting to find the rest of it, but if it doesn't appear soon we'll be gone in any case," she said. "We've enough put by."

"What's with the other stuff in the drawers?" asked Mike, not breaking eye contact with her.

Fiona smiled again and stepped back, much to his relief. "It's a little side business for me," she said, swinging the knife up and down, slicing at the air. "Buying and selling. Call it a valuable hobby, if you will. Truth is, I would've been a dealer in another life. The antique shops on the mainland often get sold stolen property that's too hot for them to handle. Sometimes the stuff's stolen from right under the nose of the museum staff."

She ran a finger up and down the shaft of the knife.

"I'm what's called a fence. I'm sure you're well aware of what that is. I sell things on to buyers all over the world. Clandestinely, of course. Working for the police force has been an excellent cover, too."

"You're not very good at it," remarked Mike bluntly. "Many of my baseline contacts had heard about your efforts to sell the Viking treasure."

Fiona's expression was scornful.

"What do you know about it? You're hardly in a position to talk. You've botched up a basic break-in. You've no idea what we've put by or how well we do. For your information, we're doing brilliantly. I always manage to hide my tracks. Otherwise, I'd be in the slammer by now, but I'm not, am I? That's because there's never any evidence to be found."

She scowled at him. "I wouldn't be so superior, you

nosy midget. If you don't watch your tongue, you won't just be dead by the morning, you'll also end up skinned alive by a professional butcher. Instead of trying to pick us apart, put that in your pipe and smoke it."

Blinded by her self-belief and ego, thought Mike. Well, pride came before a fall, and he would've loved to see it happen to her. Not that it looked likely he'd be around long enough to do so.

"And you think you're going to get away with what you're doing to me, do you?" asked Mike, watching her. "Others know where I am and they'll be asking a lot of questions if I don't reappear."

She looked at him with pity.

"Yes, I do think we'll get away with it. If you behave, you're going to be another Simon. An accident by a cliffside. A suicide, even. They'll never be able to tell. There's the crystal-clear answer to your question."

She came up to Mike and placed the knife under his chin again. "Enjoy the last dregs of your life, while you have breath to do so," she said, pushing the knife into his skin. "You miscalculated badly coming here, and you'll be gone before the morning. We'll be the ones enjoying our freedom and new life. I hope that gives you satisfaction."

"Not really, no," said Mike, unable to resist squeezing in the last word.

Fiona turned to her accomplice. "David, make sure he can't get untied and lock him up in the spare bedroom."

David nodded. "Come on, chum. You're going to have a wee rest until it gets dark."

He gave Mike a push in the back, making him stumble. Mike obediently walked into the spare bedroom and sat down on the bed. David went to him and checked the knots on his wrist.

"What if I need a toilet break?" asked Mike.

"Bang on the door and I'll take you to it," said David with an ominous smile. "Don't want you making a mess, do we?"

He's a real charmer, thought Mike. He tilted his head to one side as he assessed David. Or possibly, he was a psychopath. Now he could see him up close, it was clear his eyes were pretty much dead as a shark's.

David took the key out of the keyhole and then closed the door behind him. Mike heard him locking the door on the other side. He flopped sideways on the bed and stared at the wall.

He was in real trouble now.

18

Mariella

Nico appeared at the bottom of Fiona's driveway and made his way back to the car, his steps cautious and his head swivelling around as he approached. He opened the boot of the car to extract something. Then, after shutting it, he made his way to the side door.

Mariella noticed he was carrying a spool of rope. As soon as Nico got into the car, Mariella launched herself at him, grabbed his arms, and started shaking him.

"Come on," she pleaded. "You have to save him. What am I paying you for?"

Nico removed her hands. *"Basta!* Settle down, Mariella. He's alive. He saw me looking at him through the window."

He rubbed his eyes. "They've tied him up. I keep telling you, they're not going to do anything to him while he's at their house. They'll not dispose of him in there because it's too risky and messy. They'll wait until it's dark and then leave."

He turned to look at her. "They'll take him some-place where they can push him into the sea and make it look like an accident," he said earnestly. "It's the easiest way to dispose of a body here. There's no fucking CCTV on this part of the island. Nothing to track their movements."

"For Pete's sake, Nico. How can you be so sure? Hasn't it occurred to you they might not have a Mafia upbringing?"

"They're amateurs, certainly," he said, his voice full of scorn. "But they can't risk finishing him off now. Even if they decide to kill him before they chuck him into the sea, it could show in the post mortem. Depending, of course, on when the body's found. She's a policewoman. She knows that."

Mariella covered her face. "What a fucking idiot! He's losing his touch. In the past, he'd never have let himself get caught out like that. He's getting old."

Nico shrugged. He was gazing out of front window, looking bored.

Mariella tried to pull herself together. "What do we do now?" she asked.

Her voice, even to her, sounded pathetically plaintive.

Mike's situation was weighing heavily on her, and yet she couldn't bring herself to admit she had feelings for the stupid man. It was too humiliating after everything he'd put her through.

Nico yawned. "We wait," he said. "It's another hour at least until it gets dark." He put his head back and closed his eyes. "Why don't you take first watch while I catch up on some sleep," he suggested, eyes closed.

"Fair enough," agreed Mariella. She was sitting behind the steering wheel and so would be able to get them moving at short notice.

"Nico?"

"Mmm?"

"How on earth are we going to follow them on these empty roads? They'll see our headlights from miles away!"

"We'll travel with the lights off. I've put a tracker on the van in any case. They'll want to move that van from their house as soon as possible." He opened an eye. "I wonder if they plan to push the van over a cliff, too. It'll be interesting to see what they decide to do with it."

Mariella said nothing, staring doggedly into the distance. Before long Nico was snoring quietly beside her.

She wasn't convinced he'd been a member of the Italian Mafia. Surely a former Mafioso would be on full alert, watching for any unexpected movements, and not sleeping like a baby beside her.

She sighed and looked down at Mike's signet ring. Mike had always seemed to her to be indestructible, impervious to any threat, but today he was proving her wrong.

She hadn't realised, until she was in danger of losing him, how much he meant to her. He wasn't going to slip through her fingers again in future. She'd make sure of that. It looked as though he was soon going to be in her debt anyway.

If she hadn't followed him, suspecting he was up to something untrustworthy, he would've been dead meat by the morning. At least now, thanks to her and Nico, he had a small chance of surviving.

Unable to cope with her fears, she took her phone out of her coat pocket and began to browse the news websites, hoping the usual collection of terrible true-life stories would put Mike's situation into perspective and take her mind off his troubles. She needed some respite.

Nothing happened for a long time.

Harris was far north, and this meant short days in the winter and long days in the summer. At ten in the evening, the sun had barely set.

By the time the sun had disappeared over the horizon, Nico's sleep-ridden head was practically on her shoulder, and she needed the toilet.

She lifted a hand and shook Nico's head. He woke up and blinked blearily at her.

"Nico, I'm sorry, call of nature. I have to exit the car for a bit."

"Sure," he said, rubbing his face.

Mariella got out of the car, carrying her bag with its packet of tissues, and walked further down the road. She found a thick clump of blackberry bushes and crouched behind them, sincerely hoping she wouldn't be caught with her pants down when Mike and his captors left the house.

She was getting too old for this stuff, she thought. Seriously, it was time for her and Mike to retire. She was going to knock some sense into him, assuming she ever managed to get her hands on him again.

When she'd finished she walked back to the car, which was parked neatly out of the way on the grass beside the kerb.

Only a few cars had passed them by while they'd been waiting. She suspected there was no such thing as heavy traffic on the island, unless the sheep or cattle decided to stray onto the road.

Once she was seated in the car again, she decided to look through her emails. She couldn't nod off at a drop of the hat, like Nico seemed to do. She might as well catch up on some business. She'd been away for far too long. She was flicking through her emails, deleting as much as she could, when she came across a message from a man she hadn't heard from in a while.

She felt the goose bumps rise on her forearms.

It was from Kev Taylor.

Mariella, how are you doing?

I was wondering if you were still in contact with Mike Telford? I know you two were an item at one point. I'm trying to get in touch with him. Rumour has it he's disappeared up north to an island called Harris?

If you hear from him or find out where he is, please let me know.

Hope you're doing well.

I have a few pieces you might be interested in seeing. Let me know your availability.

Mariella bit her bottom lip.

He was very eager to track down Mike. Odd. Kev hadn't been in touch with her for many years. She wondered if Kev had been the one who left the note at Mike's house, threatening his life.

She had to be careful.

Hi Kev,

Good to hear from you after so long. No, I do not know of Mike's whereabouts, nor do I want to. He scarpered a long time ago. If you see the fucker, pass on my best regards.

Get in touch on my office number and my PA will slot you into the diary. Busy times!

She looked up. It was pitch dark outside now. Occasionally, she caught glimpses of the clouds scudding past above them. An overcast night meant no moonlight for any length of time. How on earth was she going to drive without the headlights switched on? She was sure they'd end up in a ditch at the side of the road.

"They'll be setting off shortly," commented Nico.

"I hope so. We'll both be getting cramps soon, sitting like this," grumbled Mariella, feeling a painful twinge in her hip. "Do you want to drive?"

"No, it's best you drive. I might have to shoot," stated Nico matter-of-factly.

This wasn't something she wanted to hear.

"You do realise the only way to get off this island is by ferry or plane?"

"Yes, it's very inconvenient," he agreed. "I'm sure we'll find a solution if I'm driven to the extremity of using my gun. Let's hope it doesn't come to that."

Mariella had a sudden vision of the pair of them sitting in a cell at Stornoway, awaiting extradition to the mainland. In the typical manner of a pessimist and worrier, she then progressed in easy stages to imagining her business hitting bankruptcy without her and the entire place getting shut down.

Then, for extra measure, she went on to visualise in her mind's eye a dreary bedsit, with brown walls, brown carpet, brown kitchenette, in fact, brown everything. And in the middle of this brown splendour, herself lying on a tatty bed, too depressed to get up.

Mariella glanced at Nico's inscrutable face. His white scar was gleaming in the darkness.

"Nico, how did you end up in Birmingham?" she asked, trying to distract herself from morbid thoughts.

"It's a very good question. Why does one leave the beauty of Rome and end up in a city such as Birmingham? I mean, for real. The reason is family. Italians need to be with family, as you should know, and I have my brother and parents in Birmingham."

"I wouldn't know. I have no family. Both my parents died young. What does your family do in Birmingham?"

Nico looked shifty. "This and that. They own different businesses. They run a restaurant and they also sell wine imported from Sicily."

"In other words, they're running a money-laundering operation in Birmingham and smuggling in undeclared wine."

"Pretty much," acknowledged Nico. "That's where they found a niche they could fill in the market. It's their turf for now."

"Doesn't working for me seem a little tame to you?"

Nico chuckled. "No, not at all. Some very interesting people visit you. It's given me quite a few new business opportunities, which I much appreciate."

Mariella lifted a hand. "No more, Nico. I don't want to know and I'm sure you don't want me to know, either. The less you tell me, the better."

She could see Nico nodding in agreement and heaved a sigh of relief.

"Where did you get that scar?" she asked, fluttering from one subject to another as was her norm.

"At school. First badge of honour."

"First? There are others?"

"Yes, of course. The Mafia have their rituals. Cuts, broken bones, bruises are a necessary side effect of our business. It's the way it is."

"I see. Well, rather you than me. Are there no women allowed in?"

"No. Women gossip too much. They're a distraction and liability to the business, and after they have children, worse. They become too soft."

Mariella stiffened, feeling deeply offended. What the hell was he doing working for her, then?

"I don't mean any disrespect to you. Please understand," he added hurriedly, sensing her discomfort. "This is just the way the Italian Mafia see it. You do not do so bad in your line of business, here in Britain."

Mariella thought about this.

"Yes, although like Mike I feel I'm losing my touch," she admitted. "The way he snaffled those Viking items from me in Birmingham was crazy. One's luck runs out, sooner or later. I think it's best to quit on a winning streak and I'm giving retirement serious consideration."

"But who will you leave the business to if you leave?" asked Nico, sounding surprised.

Whether he was taken aback at the prospect of her retirement or at her honesty, she couldn't hazard a guess. He was always reserved and scrupulously professional at work. She'd learnt more about him on this short trip to Harris than in eight years of having him as the gatekeeper to her business in Birmingham.

She thought about his question

"Not sure," she said at last. "I'd like it to be another woman, but she has to be a jeweller, of course. I've got one or two in mind. Something to think about when I get back, I suppose."

She sighed to herself. For some reason, the prospect didn't enthral her.

Nico touched her arm. "They're on the move. Listen," he instructed, winding down the window.

Mariella strained to listen and heard a faint scuffling noise, which corresponded with someone getting dragged across the gravel. Her stomach tightened with fear.

She hoped they weren't dragging a dead Mike across the gravel. At the end of the day, how much could she trust to Nico's judgement?

She switched on the engine and left it running.

Thank goodness they'd had the foresight to hire an electric car, keeping noise to a minimum. Harris was an eerily quiet island, almost silent she sometimes thought, if it weren't for the constant breeze.

They heard the sound of van doors slamming shut.

Headlights suddenly came on and shone in two bright arcs down the driveway.

Mike's van left the driveway shortly afterwards and turned right.

Mariella waited until Nico gave the signal and then pulled out onto the road, following the speck of light in the distance.

The chase was on.

The tail lights were the only thing indicating to Mariella where the van was heading. She was grateful there weren't a lot of junctions or roads to negotiate on the island. Many of the roads around the island were single lane, with places to stop and let others pass.

The entire population on the Isle of Harris and

Lewis was around 20,500 people. Populated areas were few and far between. Although mountainous and undulating, Harris had big tracts of open land and so following the van didn't prove too arduous a task for Mariella.

She wondered where the bastards were planning on taking Mike. Not too far, she hoped.

However, she was proved wrong.

Almost an hour and a half later, they found themselves at the other end of the island, in Lewis, and they were crawling along a road following the coastline.

The wind was now howling and buffeting the car.

The wind never seemed to leave the Isle of Lewis and Harris, but here on the exposed cliffs of north-west Lewis, it was a different beast. Hostile, unfettered and powerful.

She could only guess what Mike was thinking during his interminable, and no doubt uncomfortable, journey. At least he'd spotted Nico, though she wasn't sure how much consolation that would have brought him. But, surely he must know they'd do their best to get him freed.

"They're slowing," said Nico in a level voice. "Watch we don't get too close."

A couple of minutes later, he reached for the steering wheel.

"Stop right here. They're going onto the grass now. I'm wondering if they're planning on putting him in the front seat and then rolling the van down the slope and over the cliff edge. It looks that way."

"With his legs and hands tied? Surely that defeats the purpose?"

"I'd knock him out, then remove the ties. Maybe

they'll do that. The cliffs seem very steep here. After a week decomposing on the sea floor, it'll be harder to tell how he died."

Mariella stared at him.

"Shouldn't we get closer?" Mariella asked, alarmed. "Time's ticking."

Her heart was pounding with such ferocity she was certain it was going to burst out of her chest and plop onto her lap.

"You should stay here and not be seen," Nico stated, as he pulled on a balaclava.

He opened the door cautiously, too cautiously in Mariella's opinion, and began walking up to where the van was positioned.

Now the headlights were off, the van was barely visible. The black shape of it created a faint outline against the sky, but that was it.

Ignoring Nico's instructions, Mariella opened her car door. The wind was so strong she could barely get it to swing wide enough to allow her to exit the car.

She managed to get out and began to follow Nico.

She saw the doors at the back of the van were open and both Fiona and David seemed to be having trouble extracting Mike.

He was putting up a good fight, if David's curses were anything to go by.

David and Fiona were so preoccupied with getting Mike out, Mariella and Nico had enough time to reach the van unnoticed.

A minute later, panting heavily, David and Fiona had managed to haul Mike out and dropped him onto the grass.

Mike was no lightweight.

Probably as a result of his fine dining, thought Mariella sourly. He wasn't the type to restrain himself for the sake of his health.

She screwed up her eyes as she tried to see him in the darkness.

He was trussed up like a turkey. She could just about see the whites of his eyes above the material covering his nose and mouth, which reassured her.

David and Fiona were bending down to lift him up, when Nico spoke up.

"Stop there," he said, softly. "I have a gun."

They froze in the posture of a medieval tableau, half bent at the waist, staring out into the darkness at them.

A tense few seconds passed.

"What the fuck do you think you're doing?" asked David explosively.

At this, Mariella lost her rag. The strain of the last few hours was proving too much for her self-control.

"What the fuck are we doing, you headcase? More like what the hell are you two doing," she shrieked at the top of her voice. "You've got my fiancé there and you're going to bloody well pay for it."

Mike's eyes widened in alarm.

For a brief moment, Mariella wondered if he was worried about her interrupting a delicate standoff or was having a minor heart attack at her calling him her fiancé. Knowing Mike, could be either one.

"Mariella, get the rope from the car," said Nico wearily. "This, for me, is a prime example of why the Mafia don't take women. For goodness sake, try and control yourself."

Nico's dispassionate voice seemed to subdue David and Fiona.

This didn't surprise Mariella. His tone was professional and detached, but there was a hint of menace in it nonetheless.

"Bloody hell, Nico. Shut the fuck up. Seriously," said Mariella, at the end of her tether. "I think you sometimes forget the male race wouldn't exist if it wasn't for women. And besides, if everyone acted like the Mafia, they'd be no one left alive on the planet."

"We need the rope please, Mariella," repeated Nico, turning a deaf ear to her comments.

After casting an angry look in their direction, Mariella ran down to the car and picked up the spool of rope.

She was running back to give it to Nico, when she saw one of the two kidnappers making a run for it.

Before she could warn Nico not to fire, there was a gun shot and a dark figure collapsed to the ground.

"No, Nico!" she yelled. "What have you done?"

Her shout was drowned out by a scream from Fiona.

More of a wail than a scream, thought Mariella. It rose up and up like a banshee in full throttle.

It was cut short when Nico shot her, too.

After that, except for the wind and the murmurs from the sea, everything went quiet.

Mariella fell to her knees and covered her face. She was convinced they were done for.

"Did you have to shoot them, Nico?" she asked between her fingers.

"After they'd seen you, I'm afraid so, yes," he said. "You're a liability."

Mariella sobbed.

When she managed to look up again, she saw Nico cutting Mike free with a penknife. Mike was rubbing his wrists, trying to get the circulation going.

Nico came back towards her. "Come on, Mariella. Get up," he said, offering her a hand.

Speechless, she let him pull her up.

Nico patted her back.

"It's OK. Better this way."

His frivolity riled her. "How on earth do you fathom that? What the hell are we going to do with them now?" she asked.

"I'll toss them in the sea."

"But the blood," she stuttered. "There'll be a search for them tomorrow."

"It's fine, Mariella," said Mike, now standing up. "We'll find a way to get him off the island. The police aren't used to this kind of thing up here. It'll take them days to get themselves organised properly. He'll be well away by then."

Mariella thought about this. Nico had indeed been keeping a low profile on the island, camping outdoors a short distance from Tarbert and meeting her at coffee shops, not at her hotel. He hadn't accompanied her to Harris, either. She'd no idea how he'd reached the island, but she knew better than to ask him.

He was always ruthlessly efficient at her office in Birmingham and seemed to know what he was doing. And he'd rescued her from quite a few tricky situations over the last eight years. She must remember that. In her employment, he'd given her no cause for alarm.

They might, just might, be alright.

Nico had walked off into the distance and reappeared carrying a heavy stone which he dropped at the cliff edge.

He then strolled back to the fallen bodies.

She watched as Nico signalled to Mike to help him.

The pair of them lifted David, grunting heavily. They walked to the edge of the cliff, stopping to rest a couple of times. Nico untied the rope coil and sliced it in half. Taking one of the two pieces, he proceeded to tie the rock to David's feet. Once he was satisfied, he called Mike over, who came forward and helped him lift the body up.

Giving David's body a swing, they released it into the empty space.

They stood as close to the edge as they dared to see where it landed. Seeming pleased with its trajectory, they nodded at each other. Turning back, they went and did the same for Fiona.

Mariella watched numbly as Mike then got into the van, started up the engine, and drove it back towards the road.

The headlights were blinding her, but she saw him behind the steering wheel, waving at them as he prepared to leave.

The van rumbled down the road and disappeared.

There was only emptiness where the van had been; everything had returned to its natural form in the blink of an eye.

What remained, to remind them they were still alive, was the distant rumbling of the sea below, the heavy sighs of the wind rustling through the machair and, high above them, the moving cloudscape.

The sea birds, if there were any nearby, weren't tempted to make their presence felt.

The drama of the night had been erased. The desecration they had committed on this part of the coast would soon be but a faint memory to its landscape, and as time went by, every trace they'd left behind would be lost forever.

Mariella imagined the two murders would keep the police occupied for a very long time.

Sooner or later, it was likely the bodies, bloated with gas, would rise to the surface, breaking free of the weights tying them down.

But with the sea you never knew. Countless bodies had gone missing, never to be found again, in the ocean. There was an abundance of sea creatures off this island. It could well be that the corpses would be eaten, instead of slowly decomposing on the seabed. Small fish would feed on them. Lobsters and crabs. Maybe even sharks.

The blood on the grass would be impossible for them to clean up, but in such a quiet location, off road, it might well fade with the rain.

Insects would feast on the blood, too, no doubt.

They were in Lewis now, not Harris, where David and Fiona were from. The swathes of wild terrain on the Isle of Lewis and Harris would make a proper search difficult to resource and time consuming.

There were visible tyre marks where the van had ridden up on the grass, but the machair was tough and would bounce back soon enough.

Mariella felt herself relax.

"Come on, Mariella. It's time to go home," said Nico quietly.

Home. If only.

"Right, let's go," she agreed. "I never, ever, want to be in a situation like this again."

Nico smiled, his scar pulling upwards. "I doubt we'll end up in this position again," he reassured her.

She wasn't convinced, though.

As long as she and Mike continued to work in the business of stolen goods, the risk would always be there.

And they might not survive the next time they found themselves in a tight corner.

19

Eilidh

Eilidh rang the doorbell at Mike's apartment in Tarbert and waited.

"Who is it?" asked a gruff voice.

"Mike, it's me," said Eilidh.

Given he'd asked her to come to his apartment at ten o'clock, she had no idea why he was now asking her to identify herself. She guessed it must be a part of Mike's instinctive training to check who was at the door before letting them in, even when they were residing in what was probably one of the safest places in the UK.

The Isle of Lewis and Harris was quiet and sleepy. There didn't appear to be a need to worry about serious criminal intent. In truth, it seemed to her the only disruption to the peaceful idyll had been brought about by Simon's discovery of the Viking hoard.

It hadn't taken her long to find out that a fair number of the locals in Harris didn't bother locking their front doors. A stark contrast to London where it was estimated burglaries cost insurers approximately 130 million pounds a year.

The door buzzed and Eilidh let herself into a dark stairwell, winding upwards until it reached the third floor.

By the time she reached Mike's flat on the third floor, she was out of breath.

Mike was standing in the doorway, and as he watched her catching her breath he grinned.

"Looks like the little one's taking up your oxygen," he remarked.

"Yes," agreed Eilidh.

She waited a moment more and then followed Mike into the apartment.

The place was impersonal and smelt of cleaning chemicals, which wasn't a surprise given it was available for short-term lets.

"Would you like a drink?" he asked, taking her to the kitchen.

"A glass of water would be just dandy, thank you," she said.

Mike poured her a glass and then led the way to a bright sitting room, which had a pleasant outlook over the town to the Herringbone Café and the candle shop next door.

"Nice view," she commented, peering out of the window.

She turned and took a seat on the sofa.

There were several scruffy notebooks piled on the coffee table and she presumed they hadn't come with the place, but were Mike's property.

Whoever had decorated the flat went for mini-malist appeal. There were no prints or mirrors on its magnolia walls, nor any patterns or stripes on the cream curtains and sofa. The carpet was a plain, mocha colour which matched the dark wood furniture.

Mike sat on an armchair opposite her.

"I thought you might like to take a look at these," said Mike, indicating the notebooks on the coffee table.

Surprised, Eilidh picked up one of the notebooks and scanned through the pages.

She recognised the writing and the style of the drawings.

"Patrick's?"

"Yes," agreed Mike.

"How did you get your hands on these?"

"It's a very long story," said Mike. "I won't bore you with it. I found these notebooks in Fiona Mitchell's house."

He saw the look of surprise in Eilidh's eyes and nodded.

"Yes, it took me aback, too," he agreed.

"What were you doing there?" asked Eilidh, suspiciously. "You decided to break in? I thought you hadn't got around to doing that yet."

"I did. Twice, actually. I had to go back to deep-clean the place and I decided to bring these notebooks to the apartment with me."

Eilidh looked down at the notebook.

"Unless Fiona took these things from Patrick's home to study as part of the murder investigation, it looks as though she might be connected to his death," she said.

Mike nodded.

"I'd agree with your second conclusion. As far as I'm concerned, she's partially responsible for his murder. Her sidekick isn't innocent, either."

"Boy, you like taking risks, don't you? She'll be mad as hell you took them."

"We'll see," said Mike, noncommittally. "Anyway, I thought you might like to keep them and have a browse."

"By that I take it you've already studied these to an inch of their life and found nothing relevant to finding the treasure."

"I have looked through them, that's true. I found nothing of any interest. But Richard told me you had a soft spot for the old man and it would be nice for them to go to a good home."

They caught each other's eye and smiled.

"Why, that's thoughtful of you, Mike. Thank you. I do appreciate the thought, but surely these should be considered part of his estate?"

Looking uneasy, Mike cleared his throat.

"Between you and me, it's best if these aren't handed over to anyone else, Eilidh. If you did, it's possible they'll be handed in to the police as evidence in Patrick's murder investigation. And for reasons I can't explain to you, they can't be."

"Yes, but these could be used as proof Fiona was involved in Patrick's murder," insisted Eilidh.

"Eilidh, these notebooks should be kept by you," said Mike, firmly. "If you want them. If not, I'll dispose of them. It's essential no one official gets a hold of Patrick's notebooks. I must be getting a little sentimental in my old age, otherwise I would've binned the lot by now. They've nice drawings inside of them, though, and I think they're a wonderful thing to remember the old man by."

Eilidh looked at him, trying to understand.

"OK, Mike. I catch your drift," she said slowly. "I can see you've been up to your dirty tricks again. I'm not going to end up in jail, am I, if I take these?"

Mike smiled.

"If you're smart enough to keep quiet about them, no."

Eilidh stroked the cover of the notebook she was holding, thinking hard.

"How about I borrow them to see if I can find something you might have overlooked?" she suggested. "And then I'll bring them back to you."

"If you bring them back to me, they'll end up at the bottom of a container in a waste disposal centre. Just keep them, Eilidh. I know you like his drawings."

"What do you want in return?" she asked as she leaned back on the sofa.

"What do you mean?" he asked, sounding hurt.

"You always want something in exchange. Out with it," said Eilidh, ignoring his pained expression. "And don't give me the puppy-dog look," she added. "You're too ugly to pull it off."

Mike chuckled. "You've developed a fair bit of bite, haven't you? Must come from working with Richard in that dead-end department of his at New Scotland Yard."

He leaned back on the sofa, crossing a leg.

"From what he's told me, you often have to fight like tigers to get the government or Lionel to listen to any advice on art theft cases. But I can see working in that environment's given you a bit of a backbone, Eilidh. I'll have to have a word with Richard about what it's doing to your character."

He chuckled again.

"Cut the crap," said Eilidh reprovingly, though she was smiling, too. "What is it you want from me?"

"I didn't think it was going to be a big deal, but I thought it would be helpful if you didn't mention my asking you for a police rota."

"I've forgotten it already."

"Good. Yes, I thought you might. Cheers for that. It's much appreciated. However, it's all well and good you saying that now. Wait until tomorrow and you'll see all hell break loose. Things are about to blow up big time. The fat is about to hit the fire, if you catch my drift."

"Ah. I see."

"I'm not sure you do. Fiona and David are missing."

"Missing?"

"As we speak."

Eilidh stared at him.

"Are you saying they've been murdered?" she asked, incredulously.

"No, I'm not saying that. All I'm saying is they're missing."

Eilidh frowned.

"I thought you didn't do murder, Mike."

"I don't. It's a complication I don't need."

"But you have a situation here, clearly."

"Yes. It wasn't anything to do with me."

"Sorry, I don't believe you, Mike."

There was silence while Eilidh thought about Mike's tendency to bring trouble and mayhem into her life.

He'd been of significant help to Richard and her in the past, too, of course.

"You went back to Fiona's house to clean up afterwards, didn't you?" she asked at last.

"Look, I swear on my life, I'd nothing to do with any murder. But, yes, because I was in their house for quite some time yesterday evening, I felt I had to make sure I'd left no traces behind."

"Fine. Don't tell me any more," she said, giving up. "As usual, I'm not sure I believe you, Mike. You were definitely involved somewhere along the line, even if you aren't responsible for what's happened to them."

She piled the notebooks up in front of her.

"I'll take the notebooks because we're desperately trying to locate the treasure and our time's going to be up very soon. I'll let you know if I find anything in them."

She reached for her glass of water and swallowed some.

"That's fine," said Mike, more relaxed now. "I certainly didn't see anything in those relevant to finding the treasure, but you met the guy and might have a better grasp on his way of thinking. Half of his writing didn't make sense to me. He's very cryptic. Batty as a moorhen, if you ask me."

"He was eccentric," agreed Eilidh. "But before the treasure find emerged, he struck me as living a very happy and independent life. We'd do well to wish for the same at his age."

"As you say, my dear. I'm not far off getting there."

"You've mentioned that before. Planning your retirement already?" asked Eilidh, with a smile.

She couldn't imagine Mike retiring. He had a restless quality about him. His mind, at least, seemed to be constantly on the go. In some ways, he reminded Eilidh of a mongoose, for he was curious, intelligent, and single-mindedly determined when tracking down artworks.

"I am indeed," he sighed. "Why? Do I look as though I've mellowed?"

Eilidh laughed. "No. Far from it. I'm wondering what kind of trouble you're going to bring to me as you wind the business down. No doubt you'll be passing on to us some of your unresolved cases."

"There are none," said Mike in a confident voice. "None at all. I'm too good, Eilidh. Cases don't stay unresolved with me."

Eilidh decided to ignore his denial. She'd learnt over the years to take Mike's assertions with a hefty pinch of salt.

"There's not a girl involved in this retirement plan is there?" asked Eilidh, trying to figure out what on earth was making him hang up the towel.

"There might be," said Mike, suddenly looking miserable. "An ex. She seems to think she's engaged to me."

"And you don't?"

"No. She'd rule me with a rod of iron, if I let her. But I owe her big time and she's not going to let me forget it."

Eilidh couldn't help smiling.

"Sounds like she has your measure, Mike."

Mike nodded, unhappy.

Eilidh rubbed her eyes and yawned.

"She might find another eligible bachelor," she suggested, feeling weary.

"No. I definitely think she's set her sights on me," insisted Mike, crossing his arms.

Eilidh studied him for a moment.

Looking like the man from the Del Monte advertisement, he was wearing sockless moccasins, a white suit, and shirt. It was an outfit best suited to the Caribbean, not a cold Scottish island.

You had to love him for it.

Nothing was disguising his beer belly, either, or the lines on a face which had seen too many stressful situations unfolding during his years of work, but his eyes were very kind and his personality was endearing.

At times. When he wasn't causing her any grief, amended Eilidh.

She had love handles hanging over the top of her trousers, so she was hardly in a position to judge attractiveness or appearance. At the end of the day, love handles or beer bellies were often the result of a life well lived, rather than a life lived with a narcissistic focus on one's appearance. It was what was inside the person that mattered most.

She was aware she might not be thinking that when she tried on her pre-pregnancy clothes again, but for now, it sounded good.

"You know what, Mike?" she said, gently. "I think you're right. She'll know fine and well she could do a lot worse than you and she'll not want to lose you. I'm not surprised she's fallen for your charms. I reckon there'd be many others in her position, too."

"You think?" asked Mike, brightening.

"Yes, I do, but I'm not a relationship guru. What went wrong with the pair of you before, if I may ask?"

"I was younger than I am now and behaved like a clown."

"In other words, you bailed out and broke her heart."

"Something like that."

Eilidh finished her water.

"Maybe she needs the ring on the finger to believe in your commitment this time around."

"Probably," agreed Mike, looking utterly dejected at the thought.

20

Richard

Richard waited patiently on the dockside.

It was half past five and the early morning light was shimmering across the placid water and reflecting off the white hulls of the boats in the harbour.

It was his third visit to the harbour and his third attempt at tracking down the elusive Findley.

The harbour master had sworn to him Findley would be there first thing in the morning, given the fine weather forecast, and so there Richard was at the crack of dawn, standing by Findley's boat.

Richard looked down under the surface of the water, and saw the brown shapes of fish nibbling at a docking rope.

A sheen of oil coated the top of the water in ugly patches.

He heard footsteps coming along the wooden jetty and turned to see who it was.

"Richard!" exclaimed Findley in surprise. It didn't escape Richard's notice he didn't sound terribly pleased to see him there. "What are you doing here?"

"Hi, Findley. How are you doing?" asked Richard politely, not wanting to launch straight into an explanation for his presence.

Findley ignored his question.

"What are you doing here?" he repeated, frowning.

"I was wondering if you could spare enough time for a coffee?" asked Richard, hopefully.

He wanted to establish the extent of Findley's involvement with the treasure, but he wasn't keen to go out on a boat again unless it was absolutely necessary. He'd prefer to hold the conversation on dry land, even though that morning, for a change, the sea did seem unusually tranquil.

"I was hoping to bring in two catches today. Is it important?" said Findley impatiently.

"It could be very important."

Findley pursed his lips while he thought about this. He was well aware he was under no obligation to speak to Richard.

"OK," he said at last. "Let's grab one back at the harbour office. Just let me dump my gear on the boat."

He clambered onto the boat and deposited the bags he was carrying on the deck.

Jumping nimbly back onto the jetty, he clapped Richard on the back.

"Right, let's go get some black coffee. They do a good one at the café. Great for early morning starts."

They walked to the harbour office, where Richard paid for two take-away black coffees.

Finding a bench overlooking the moored boats, they sat down.

Richard sighed as he looked at the view. He couldn't imagine a more peaceful scene.

The boats were bobbing up and down with the gentle ebb of the seawater, the seagulls were hovering silently in the windless sky, and this early it felt as though they had the harbour entirely to themselves.

"Have you heard what happened to Patrick?" asked Richard, deciding it was time to speak to Findley about his concerns.

"No, why?"

Richard looked at him.

"I'm surprised," said Richard, genuinely startled by his ignorance. "Quite frankly, I thought the news would be racing around the Harris grapevine by now."

"It probably is. You forget I'm out on the boat a lot at this time of year. Like Patrick, I lead a pretty solitary life on Harris, and I'm not one to gossip, either. Has something serious happened to him?" he asked, a worried look on his face.

"Yes, you could say that," said Richard, under-stating the case in his usual reserved manner. "I'm afraid he was murdered in a very unpleasant way. In his home."

Findley stared at Richard in disbelief.

"Are you for real or are you pulling my leg?"

"I'm not making it up. My fiancée's distraught about it. She feels she should've stepped in and done some-thing to prevent it, even though it's anyone's guess what she could have done to stop it."

Findley said nothing for a while.

Processing no doubt, thought Richard, feeling sad. The news was going to be a major shock to the system. He wished he'd had proper training to deal with such situations. Eilidh, with her experience working in the

Homicide Unit at New Scotland Yard, would know exactly what to say.

Richard caught Findley's eye.

"It's really happened. He's gone," he confirmed quietly.

By now, Findley was ashen-faced underneath his tan.

"Bloody hell, this is awful news," he said, miserably.

Was there a tinge of fear in his voice? Richard wasn't sure.

Findley leant forward and rested his arms on his legs, his head hanging down.

"I'm sorry to be the one to break it to you."

Findley didn't bother replying.

Richard decided the best thing he could do, given the circumstances, was to give the man some time.

He looked upwards and watched the seagulls as they circled above them, each one keeping an eye out in the hope some food would end up coming their way.

Findley stood up after a few minutes and walked to the edge of the quay.

"Why did you want to tell me this?" he asked, his back to Richard.

"Because I'm wondering if you might be in danger yourself now this has happened," said Richard, opting to be blunt with him.

Findley turned to face him, suspicion in his eyes.

"And why would that be? What makes you think that?"

Richard smiled a little ruefully

"It's a very good question. Call it an inkling. Patrick left a mysterious note at our house the day he was

killed. You can read it if you like. I have a copy," said
Richard, retrieving the folded note from his coat pocket.

Findley took the note and read it.

By the time he'd finished reading it, he looked
confused.

"I understand if you're puzzled. It's a totally bizarre
note," said Richard, nodding. "But, either he was
completely nuts, or there was some truth in his writing.
I'm inclined to think the latter now, given there's an
element of distress in the words, and given the fact he
was subsequently murdered."

"He was a daft bastard," said Findley, shaking his
head. "He often left messages like this for people. Of
course, some folk thought he was downright mad. I
guess he was Harris's eccentric, alright. But I reckon
writing and saying these things was just a bit of harm-
less fun for him. He had a playful side to him and
enjoyed little pranks to wind people up."

He lifted up the paper and studied it again.

"As for this note...I mean, sure, he sounds trapped,
but what's that got to do with me?"

Richard looked up at him.

"It's a quote out of a book. It's from *The Water
Babies* by Charles Kingsley. And it refers to a lobster
that's stuck inside a lobster pot. Any idea why?"

Findley shook his head. He appeared to be struggling to breathe.

He turned to stare out to sea again.

Richard waited, biding his time.

The quay was getting busier and a few people were
dotted around.

A young couple came across to them and greeted
Findley, before heading off to their boat.

Findley came to the bench and sat down.

"I need to know how much trouble I'll be in over this," he said heavily.

"I'm not interviewing you under caution," Richard replied. "This is an informal, off-duty chat. I don't have any other officers with me today. My interest is only in recovering the treasure for the sake of the many Scots who'd appreciate seeing those items in a museum one day, as part of their heritage and history."

Looking across at Findley, he could tell his trepidation hadn't eased.

"Look, I'm not seeking to lock anyone up or assign any blame," he said, trying to convince him. "My motivation in this case is purely to recover the artefacts and put them through the proper governmental processes. It's the job of the Scottish police force to track down any criminals involved in this, not mine. I'm here in a supporting role."

Findley nodded.

"I see. I was afraid I'd be prosecuted for what I've done, which is why I've remained silent for so long."

"Would you mind telling me what happened? I'm completely in the dark here."

Findley sighed.

"I was asked by Simon to keep the treasure safe. As I told you, we were very close and he trusted me. But when he died, I left it hidden. I wanted it to go to Janey and the kids one day, but I just didn't see how it could be done without me getting into some serious trouble."

"I might be able to help you with that. If we can recover the treasure, I'll not mention your involvement in it. I'm sure you were only trying to help out a friend."

"I was. Simon knew what finding the treasure

meant and all the implications that came with it. Looking back, he knew this better than any of us at the time."

He sighed. "Simon was always a dreamer, but, sadly, most of his dreams tended to fall flat, as you probably know by now. But see, when he found that treasure, he was a changed man. He was full of excitement about the future for him and his family."

Findley leant back on the bench and folded his arms.

"Truth is, he knew finding the treasure on the beach was a huge deal and he was terrified he'd end up robbed if people found out he had it in his home."

"Understandable," agreed Richard. "It does indeed seem as though there's been some attempts to find the Viking hoard at his home, from what Janey has told us."

Findley nodded.

"Yes, I heard about that from Janey. Typical, isn't it? He brought three pieces from the treasure to Tarbert police station, but he didn't particularly trust them, either. Not because he thought they would rob him, necessarily, but because everyone on this island gossips. Can't seem to help themselves. He thought word about him finding treasure would do the rounds and make him a target for robbery."

"Fair enough. So, he thought he'd be better off leaving it with you, did he?"

"Yes, he asked to meet up with me and Patrick, and we discussed the problem. Patrick was the one who came up with the idea of hiding the treasure in a lobster pot and keeping it underwater." He smiled. "I now know where he got the idea from. It wasn't a bad idea. No chance of someone finding it, if it was positioned somewhere out of the way and hidden in the sea. I knew of just the place, of course."

Richard nodded, thinking Simon's caution might indeed have saved the treasure from disappearing altogether.

There was a momentary pause while they finished their coffees.

They were both treading cautiously round each other, as though they realised they'd reached an important crossroads in their discussion.

At least they were both ranged on the same side.

"Findley, I think it's time for us to recover it, don't you? Before anything else happens as a result of this treasure?"

"Yes, I agree. Patrick's murder changes everything. I'm wondering if he confessed before he died. In which case, it won't be long before they decide to come for me."

"I wouldn't blame him if he did confess," said Richard, thinking back to the horrific wounds Patrick had sustained. "They certainly put him through the wringer before he died."

He shook his head dejectedly.

"The pursuit of wealth tends to corrupt the best of people, and it can make the most ordinary person ruthless. Poor Patrick became a consequence of that greed."

Findley looked at him.

"Shall we go?" he asked.

Richard made a face and nodded.

"I suppose so," he said with a forced smile. "It's not my favourite pastime hitching a ride on a boat, but at least it looks pretty calm today."

"It is. A perfect day for it."

They got up, chucked their cups in the recycling bin, and started walking across to Findley's boat.

"Where did you plant the lobster pot?" asked Richard. "I mean, is 'plant' even the right word for it?"

"No," said Findley, chuckling. "I guess it's called lobster potting. And I think the word you're looking for is 'place.' I placed the lobster pot near the Monach Islands. It's one of the many small uninhabited islands around the coast of the Isle of Harris and Lewis. I'm afraid it'll take us a little while to get there."

He wasn't wrong in his prognosis. In future years, when Richard looked back on the trip, all he could remember was how interminable the journey had been. Indeed, during their return voyage, which for Richard was immensely stressful, time seemed to slow to the point that every second felt like a minute.

As treasure keeper, Findley had taken his guardianship to a whole new level. No one would think to search for the treasure in the sea. It seemed to Richard that Findley was a man who took his responsibilities very seriously, and he could only admire the ingenuity of hiding treasure so far away, off shore and underwater. Patrick couldn't have chosen a better hiding place.

It was time to bring things to an end, though.

Time again, thought Richard, smiling to himself as they made their way back to Findley's boat. Time had been his nemesis, but maybe he now stood a chance of beating it to the finish line.

They climbed onto Findley's fishing boat, and soon afterwards were heading out of the harbour, on course for the Monach islands.

Richard glanced at his watch.

It was six in the morning.

Despite the early start, Richard found they were travelling at a sluggish velocity compared to the inflatable boat they'd been on before.

"Can't this boat go any faster?" asked Richard after half an hour, feeling the butterflies in his stomach rising and falling with the boat.

"No, I'm afraid not," said Findley apologetically.

He looked at Richard.

"And I'm afraid I couldn't risk bringing the inflatable this far out, if that's what you're thinking. The weather's meant to change later on this afternoon, and where we're going the currents and sea can be unmanageable with an inflatable. It's too dangerous, I'm afraid."

Richard nodded, bowing to his superior knowledge, and continued gazing into the distance where he could see a small brown dot on the horizon, which, according to Findley, was where the Monach Islands began.

"The Monach Islands are a special place," Findley informed him. "Hand on heart, the best sunsets I've ever witnessed. It's such a romantic setting, I even once considered starting up a business taking photos of tourists on the Monach Islands, but the weather's too unpredictable, sadly. The islands also have the biggest colony of grey seals in the UK, and over a hundred bird species have been recorded there, including the sea eagle. Unsurprisingly, it's a National Nature Reserve."

Richard smiled at his enthusiasm.

"I can't help but feel the extreme contrast between the south of England and remote Scottish places such as the Isle of Lewis and Harris," he said. "I hope the identity of these islands continues to be preserved. It's getting harder and harder to find untouched places in the world."

He blushed.

"And I have the gall to say that as a confirmed London boy. A city slicker."

He chuckled at his hypocrisy.

"But, you know, whatever my background is, it doesn't mean I can't appreciate the importance of places such as these islands."

"Exactly," agreed Findley. "You value and want to preserve ancient artefacts in your job. In other words, you understand uniqueness. For many like myself, these islands are a unique artefact, needing preserved for future generations."

"Yep, that sums it up perfectly."

"What are you going to do when you have the treasure in your hands?" asked Findley, interested.

"Get to Edinburgh as soon as possible, I imagine," said Richard over the roar of the boat's engine. "And hand it over to the National Museum of Scotland with our blessing."

Findley's perceptive eyes looked at him.

"I think we'd best squeeze in a tea break, before we lift the lobster pot out of the water. I can tell you're going to be too excited to think about food and drink after we bring up the treasure."

Richard laughed, feeling the exhilaration in every nerve.

"Very likely," he admitted.

The thought of seeing the Viking hoard was even helping him ignore the queasiness in his stomach. An added bonus.

He turned to face the Monach Islands again.

By mid-morning they were anchored near a secluded cove, accompanied by six grey seals who were lying on the rocks, their whiskered faces staring at them with curiosity.

"Here, Richard, take a hot drink. That was a long ride," said Findley, passing him a cup after pouring it from a thermos flask.

Richard drank it gratefully, feeling the warmth returning to his fingers as he held the cup.

The cove they were next to had water trickling down the sides of it from a small burn above. Like a shining, transparent sheen, the running water polished the walls of the cove and gave them a bright lustre.

Under the clear seawater, different layers of rock could be seen, in pink, cream, and grey colours.

A geologist would have a field day here, thought Richard. How wonderful to be able to spend one's life distinguishing different types of rock and crystal.

Further down under the water, Richard could see a dark forest of seaweed.

"The guardians of the kelp forests are the otters," said Findley, watching him. "They keep a perfect ecological balance in the sea. Without them, the sea urchins get out of control and devour the kelp forest to extinction, along with every sea creature which shelters within it."

He smiled.

"There's really nothing cuter around these parts than a sea otter cub."

Richard nodded his head, rather absentmindedly, as he continued to peer down into the depths.

He suddenly heard a humming noise coming from afar and turned to see where it was coming from.

On the horizon, there was a large speedboat coming towards them, churning up the water behind it.

Findley and Richard tensed up.

"That's odd," commented Findley. "Don't usually see many of those this far out."

The speedboat seemed to be approaching them, but then veered off in a wide arc and came to a stop at quite a distance away.

Richard looked at Findley.

"Joyriders," snorted Findley, shaking his head. "Madness. Bet my bottom dollar they're outsiders, without a clue about how the ocean works."

"Are you sure they're joyriders?" asked Richard doubtfully.

"Yes, of course," said Findley, surprised by his concern. "I see them fairly often during the summer months. Mostly outsiders, they come here for the summer break with their kids."

He offered Richard one of his ham sandwiches.

Richard shook his head. Given they had to head back over the sea, he didn't think his stomach was going to be reliable enough to cope with a sandwich in it.

"Where's the lobster pot?" asked Richard, looking around.

He couldn't see a lobster buoy near them.

"You're very single-minded, aren't you?" commented Findley. "It's five minutes away. Are you ready to go?"

"Yes, of course."

Findley started up the motor and eased the boat out of the cove.

The seals watched them leave, their sad, dog-like

eyes seeming to plead with the two of them to stay and provide them with some entertainment.

They made their way to a headland close by.

Findley cut the engine when they reached an innocent-looking, bright-orange buoy.

"Here it is," said Findley, while the boat rocked gently in the water.

Richard blinked in astonishment.

The reality of millions of pounds worth of treasure sitting on the seabed, at the end of a rope, was beginning to hit home to him.

Findley went to the back of the boat.

"I might need your help, Richard. Put it this way, the treasure's quite a bit heavier than a lobster. Easy to drop down, not so easy to lift. I think we'll have to use the fishing winch to bring it in."

Richard moved to where Findley was mulling over the buoy.

Findley leaned down and tried to lift the buoy by its plastic handle.

"Nope. Not budging," he said at last, panting. "I'll attach the winch. I'll have to find a shackle big enough."

He fiddled with the winch while Richard looked down into the water and tried to catch a glimpse of the lobster pot.

It was impossible to see. Although the water was clear and relatively calm, the rope stretched down a very long way and disappeared out of sight into a forest of seaweed below them.

"How far down is it? I can't see very much," said Richard.

"You won't see anything. It's about 50 metres deep here. Lobster pots can be placed up to 100 metres below the surface, in some cases, and even then, lobsters can go far deeper than that. They like rocks and crannies to hide in. The rocky seaweed beds around this coastal area are a perfect place for them to take shelter."

Findley attached the winch to the buoy and began to wind it up.

"Let's hope the knots on the buoy withstand the pressure," he said calmly.

Richard stared at him.

If the rope broke, it would require a major operation to salvage the lobster pot. They'd have to hire specialised divers to locate it.

Slowly, bit by bit, the rope was pulled in, until at last Richard could see the box-like shape of the lobster pot coming up towards them through the green-blue water.

Findley continued to work the winch until the lobster pot hit the side of the boat with a clunk.

He reached down and tried to hoist it onto the deck.

Richard came to his side and helped him as he strained to lift it.

Between them, they managed to bring it over the side and landed it on the bottom of the boat.

"There we go," said Findley in a satisfied voice.

Taking out a pocket knife, he started cutting through the cords on the lobster pot.

Inside the pot was a sealed, rubbery black bag.

"It was easy dropping things in through the opening of the lobster pot, but it'll be time consuming trying to get them out that way," Findley explained, pulling the cut cords away.

Richard felt himself shaking with pure excitement.

After what had felt like a hiding to nothing with

their trip to Harris, he was finally going to see the mysterious Viking hoard Simon had discovered on a sandy beach.

Findley tossed away the last strands of rope and pulled the bag free of the metal cage.

"It's a waterproof bag," he said. "Very useful in this case. Although I had to place a couple of stones in it for good measure, to make sure it would go down."

He unsealed the flap and then unzipped the bag.

Richard bent down and peered over his shoulder.

Inside of it there were several items, wrapped up in plastic supermarket bags.

"There you go, Richard," he said, removing the plastic bag from one of the items and passing him what looked to be an engraved silver chalice.

Richard held it in his hands and studied it.

He couldn't help making an anguished face.

Simon had decided to give the silver a good polish, rather than leaving it to the experts to do.

He shook his head. Madness.

He turned the chalice over in his hands.

It also seemed to be slightly dented.

Richard suspected the design on the exterior was Byzantine. The decorative styling of it certainly wasn't typical of Anglo-Saxon or Viking craftsmen.

There was a delicate grapevine enacted on its surface, with little birds scattered throughout the leaves. A large cross was in the middle of the vine, a typically Byzantine one.

It was normal for foreign items to be found among Viking possessions. The Vikings were great wanderers and traders, often collecting objects from as far away as the Middle East and Asia.

An utterly special piece of antiquity, Richard thought to himself, lifting the chalice up.

Under the base of the chalice was what looked to Richard like Greek lettering.

He put the chalice down beside him. He was sure its secrets would be researched many times over in the weeks and months to come by the museum entrusted with the Viking hoard.

Findley was laying out other pieces of treasure on the bench beside him for Richard to look at.

There were five large silver ingots, each of them wrapped in plastic.

Seven brooches were laid out next.

Some were clearly Anglo-Saxon, with leering, almost caricature-like faces engraved into the silver. Others had garnets and rock crystals held in place by intricate metalwork.

The brooches were all made of silver. It was often said the Vikings preferred silver to gold. They bartered for their slaves with silver ingots and silver arm rings.

However, amongst the silver in the bag there was a small, gold Anglo-Saxon cross, with a garnet in the middle and golden beadwork encircling the stone.

Picking it up, Richard wondered where it had been plundered from.

Quite possibly from an Anglo-Saxon monastery. The Vikings held no reverence towards Christian houses of worship and stole from them with the same impunity with which they raided Anglo-Saxon villages and towns.

In the Viking age, most of Europe had converted to Christianity, but the Vikings were very satisfied with their own gods and held onto them for a significant period of time. It was only towards the end of the Viking age that the Vikings fully accepted Christianity.

Richard laid down the little cross.

The next item made him catch his breath.

It was a heavily embossed silver box and it was one of the strangest objects Richard had ever seen.

Norse in design, it consisted of a serpent and its coils. The serpent's head on the lid had large, bulging eyes and long fangs.

The serpent's coils were knotted together and stood out from the silver surface as though wishing to break free of its confines.

It was utterly entrancing.

Richard spent a few minutes turning it round and round, gazing at it.

He smiled with pure delight.

Catching Findley looking at him in amusement, he blushed.

Putting the box down, he laughed.

"It's blown me away," he admitted, running a finger over the top of it. "It's a once-in-a-lifetime experience to see something like this."

"These two are nice items," said Findley, passing a couple of neck torcs to him.

Richard took hold of them.

Neither were as beautiful as the torc Mike had rescued from Birmingham, but they did have a charm of their own.

Two thick pieces of silver had been twisted together, and at their ends two amber stones had been embedded in a silver cage.

The workmanship was crude, yet striking.

How anyone could feel comfortable carrying the

heavy weight of the silver on their necks was a mystery to Richard, but back in those days such things were a status symbol. Carrying a lot of silver about your person during Viking times proclaimed your place in the pecking order. Possibly, it was the equivalent to driving a Ferrari or wearing a Rolex watch.

However, he was certain being loaded down with the weight of it couldn't have been a pleasant experience.

"There are a lot of coins," commented Findley, looking into the black bag. "I think it's probably best if we leave these in there for now."

He passed the bag over to Richard.

Richard put his hand inside the bag and picked out a few random coins.

Taking them out, he placed them on his lap.

Most of them, as he expected, were silver penningar, the standard Viking coin.

"Is that it?" asked Richard faintly, feeling so over-whelmed he didn't think he could cope emotionally with any more marvels.

"Not quite," said Findley. "There's two rings left."

He took them out of the plastic bag he was holding and passed them to Richard.

One of them caught Richard's eye at once because the coloured stone in it was engraved. The script was undoubtedly Arabic.

"This is fascinating," he said, holding it up to his eyes. "I'm willing to bet the stone is coloured glass and it comes from the Middle East. I'd love to know what it says. It probably says 'for Allah,' or some such thing. There's one other ring I know like it from the Viking era, discovered in Birka, Sweden."

He picked up the other ring.

It was made of gold and the centre of it had a flower depicted in white and green enamel.

"Beautiful," he muttered to himself. "Definitely Anglo-Saxon, I'd say. The enamel work on this is of excellent quality."

He put it down next to the other items and thought for a moment.

"You know, Findley, I think we'd best put the pieces back in the black bag, as we found them," he said at last. "I wasn't planning to get the police on the Isle of Lewis and Harris involved, but looking at this, I think it's too risky not to. I think I'm going to have to go to Stornoway and take it to the police station there. I imagine the police headquarters in Stornoway is a bigger outfit than Tarbert, given the population's larger, and it'll secure the treasure's protection better. I'm certain they'll want it transferred to Edinburgh as soon as possible, for analysis."

"Whatever you say, boss," said Findley agreeably. "Just, please, don't get me mixed up in this."

"I won't. I promise I'll keep you anonymous. We can even give everything a gentle wipe down before I go there to make sure your prints aren't on them. In truth, the sooner this hoard is out of my hands, the happier I'll be."

"I know exactly what you mean," agreed Findley with heartfelt sincerity.

They wrapped up the items once more and returned them to the black bag.

Findley sealed the bag carefully and left it on the bench.

He then started up the engine again, but as soon as

they began moving, the speedboat, which hadn't shifted during this time, revved up its engine and came towards them.

Findley and Richard looked at each other.

Findley cut the engine as the speedboat got closer.

Soon they were able to make out three men on the speedboat.

"What the fuck are these idiots wanting?" asked Findley, sounding annoyed.

Richard wasn't irritated. He was feeling worried. Decidedly worried.

The speedboat slowed down and came alongside them.

"Hello," said one of the men in a pleasant voice.

He was a broad man, with blond, shoulder-length hair and an oddly pointed face, almost as though someone had squashed both sides of it in a press.

He was wearing a black Dior jumper and a pair of black trousers, as well as an expensive-looking gold watch.

Richard saw Findley's lips curl in distain as he looked him over.

"Hello," said Findley curtly. "How may we help you?"

"You can help us by handing over the parcel we've just seen you fish out of the sea," replied the man, getting straight to the point.

"And who are you?" asked Findley, keeping his cool.

"Kev, to you," said the man with a big smile. "You'll be Findley Thoresby, of course, and this gentleman is the famous art detective, Richard Langley."

"Chief Inspector to you," responded Richard, riled

by the man's attitude. "Do you think it's wise to plan a daylight robbery in front of a senior member of the police force?"

The two men with Kev chuckled.

"You'll never see us again," pointed out Kev, smile still plastered on his face. "We're good at what we do. You needn't worry our paths will cross again, because they won't. We won't be bothering you again. Pass over the bag and we'll get out of your hair in no time."

He lifted a gun from the seat beside him.

"You see, you'll have to cooperate with us because we have guns on us."

"Richard, come over here," said Findley in an urgent voice.

Richard obediently went over to the bench at the back of the boat and sat down.

"Hold on to this," instructed Findley, hoisting the black bag up and balancing it on the very edge of the boat's side.

Richard did as he was told, but he was waiting for a gunshot to kill one or both of them at any second.

What Findley was doing seemed to him to be the height of insanity, but out there, on the sea, Findley was captain. Richard was out of his depth in so many ways, and at this stage he wasn't going to argue with him.

"Take the knife in your other hand," said Findley, passing the opened penknife to him.

Without a word, Richard took the knife in his right hand.

He was beginning to think Findley was turning out to be every bit as eccentric as Patrick. The pair of them were two peas in a pod.

Findley turned to Kev, who was now standing up on his boat.

His gun was raised and it was pointed straight at them.

His obnoxious smile had disappeared.

"We're going to head back to Harris," said Findley in a steady voice. "Any attempt on your part to take that bag off us and Richard will slice it open and toss the contents into the sea. We'd rather do that than let it fall into your hands. Understand? Once it's thrown back into the sea, no one will ever find those items again. It'll take months for professional divers to search through the kelp beds for it and it would be a fruitless task given the weather conditions up here. I can guarantee you, you don't have the resources for it."

Richard felt he was going to have a heart attack.

Findley was absolutely right, though. He'd rather toss the lot into the sea than let those cretins get their hands on it.

Kev turned his eyes to stare at Richard's face.

Richard could tell Kev was trying to assess his commitment to Findley's statement.

He did his best to appear resolute and strong, looking Kev straight in the eye, a stubborn expression on his face.

In reality, of course, he wanted to cry like a baby at the thought of losing the treasure to the sea.

To allay any further doubts in Kev's mind, Richard reached up with the penknife and sliced open the top of the bag.

He then held the bag wide open with both hands, in readiness for emptying it into the sea.

At this, Kev sat back down and signalled to his colleague to move the speedboat.

Findley started up the engine and Richard began to breathe again. But he soon discovered they weren't out of the woods yet.

As the fishing boat chugged away, the speedboat stayed close behind them, trailing them like a shark tracking its prey.

Findley turned around to look at them and grimaced.

"I'm going to call the harbour master and get some help. It could get messy when we get closer to land," he said.

Richard nodded his agreement.

While Findley put the call through, Richard crouched down, as low as possible, and kept an eye on the speedboat.

His job was clear; to make sure the treasure was kept from the guys on the motorboat, at any cost, but also to hold onto it for dear life.

He wondered where Kev and his men had come from. Kev's accent had a strong Mancunian undertone to it, although accents didn't signify anything these days. It only indicated Kev's roots were in Manchester, nothing else.

Mike had told him word of Viking treasure had gone around the criminal circles known to him. But even so, for them to attempt daylight piracy seemed to Richard completely insane.

He realised they must have been keeping a watch on his movements, which wouldn't be hard on such an isolated island.

Suddenly, Richard wished Mike was with them.

Mike was known to be a fast thinker and hard as nails. He also thought very much like a criminal, which in Richard's opinion was a useful skill to possess in situations such as theirs. Takes one to know one, as the saying went.

Richard then dismissed the idea from his mind.

It was fruitless speculating on such things, and the unfortunate side effect of working with people like Mike was that, despite their efficiency, they didn't have any concept of legal boundaries and were quite capable of getting everybody around them into a lot of trouble.

Eilidh had already told him how Mike had attempted to enlist her help in breaking into Fiona Mitchell's house.

Richard had thanked his lucky stars she hadn't been tempted to do it. A police officer breaking into another police officer's house would create the kind of ruckus which would see both of them losing their jobs. As a further consequence, their notoriety would have then spread far and wide across the UK police force and his professional reputation, carefully cultivated over many years, would be in tatters.

He focused on the speedboat once more.

The three men, wearing sunglasses, were chatting casually among themselves. Acting as though they were on a relaxed day trip in the Bahamas no less, thought Richard, instead of attempting to poach a priceless treasure by brute force.

Who could tell, maybe they were intending to flee in that direction once they had the treasure safely in their hands.

The danger inherent in the Viking hoard, or any treasure, was the way in which it fed people's dreams.

Findley, bless him, was already living his dream and therefore seemed to be immune to the treasure's temptations.

For Richard, the journey back to Harris lasted an eternity.

Every choppy wave, and the jolt the boat gave in response, alarmed him. Each time the boat rocked, he was smitten with a vision of the bag slipping out of his hands and disappearing into the water, lost for evermore.

And with every mile, the speedboat continued motoring behind them, waiting eagerly for its prize.

"I'm going to head into the marina at Tarbert, as directed by the harbour master," said Findley, a frown on his face.

"What's he planning on doing about this situation?" asked Richard in a tense voice, his eyes never leaving the speedboat behind them.

From his position at the back of the boat, he hadn't caught a word of the muffled exchange between Findley and the harbour master. In their current dire situation, ignorance wasn't bliss.

"He's hoping to get the police to come down to the harbour and a number of boats will come out and meet us before we enter the harbour. There's too little time to get armed police here. Hopefully, it'll be enough to scare the bastards off."

Richard nodded.

He was feeling sea sick again, but he suspected it was his nerves playing tricks on his stomach.

He knew Mike, who dealt with thugs of every kind, had found himself in circumstances like theirs before, but Richard was struggling to comprehend how Mike had managed to retain his cherubic, baby-faced appearance. Richard felt he'd aged at least ten years in the last hour.

They began to make their way down the inlet leading to Tarbert harbour.

Riven with anxiety, Richard turned his head around to see the way ahead.

He spotted a small flotilla of boats making their way towards them.

Then he heard the roar of an engine behind him and he looked back quickly, just in time to catch the motorboat speeding away in the opposite direction.

Findley cheered and Richard heaved a big sigh of relief.

The adrenaline drained out of him, leaving him feeling as floppy as an empty balloon.

He rested his forehead on the bag.

The treasure was safe.

21

Mike

"So, what's going to happen to your job and this place?" asked Mike, leaning on the bar at the Time or Tide, a tankard of beer in his hand.

Oliver Rust shrugged as he polished a whisky glass.

"Don't know. I've been told David's family are putting it up for sale. I guess I'll be here for as long as it takes for all that to get sorted out."

He looked around the pub, a regretful expression on his face.

"I reckon the new owners will remove the bones and do up the place. I hope it won't become too posh. Would be a shame, that."

Mike nodded, not trusting himself to be able to say anything positive about the gruesome décor.

"What about you, Mike? You heading back to the big smoke, now?"

Mike nodded. "Yes. Very shortly. I've to sort out a few things first and then I'll be heading down south. There's a lot of business piling up in my office and it needs to be seen to."

He smiled. "Hopefully things up here will be a little calmer, now the treasure's been found."

"Yes. It's been wild. This place has been packed, because everybody wants to talk about it," agreed Oliver. "Couldn't believe my ears when I heard about the treasure. Poor Simon never got to see the benefits of it. And I'm telling you, I think it's a crying shame the treasure's now getting sent to Edinburgh. After all, it's part of our island heritage. We could do with a world-class Viking museum right here in Tarbert."

"You never know, you might get it."

"Nah," said Oliver, shaking his head despondently. "The Scottish government's going bust subsidising the ferry services to the islands. They'll not invest in a world-class museum up here."

"Well, to me, a Viking museum in Tarbert sounds perfect. I mean, for nearly four hundred years the Vikings settled in the Hebrides, the Irish Sea, and the Northern Isles. The Isle of Lewis and Harris was Norse. Who knows how many other Viking hoards might be buried and hidden on these islands?"

Oliver smiled, a hint of mischief in his eyes.

"Exactly! Tell me about it. I've invested in a metal detector. That's the way to go I've heard. It's these metal detectorists who are finding all the treasure in Britain nowadays."

"Be careful if you do find anything. Look what happened to Findley and Richard Langley."

Their exciting sea trip back to Tarbert had been covered extensively by the local and national news.

"Mental, right?" agreed Oliver, setting down the glass. "Bet the Vikings didn't realise their stuff was going to cause such excitement hundreds of years later."

"I don't know. It's an interesting point you've raised there, Oliver," said Mike, scratching his chin. "The Vikings were into historical sagas, which they passed down to each other, over generations. You know the stuff I mean, don't you? Long poems telling stories about their warriors and gods and suchlike. I'm absolutely sure that somewhere in their psyche they believed their culture would be making waves in the future."

Before Oliver could reply to this, the door to the pub opened with a clang.

It was far too early for punters.

Mike turned around, knowing Mariella was at the door. He'd been waiting for her.

"Hi, Mariella," said Mike affably as she walked across to the bar.

She was wearing a pair of blue dungarees, a checked shirt, and platform trainers. She was, in fact, looking adorably youthful.

"Morning," said Mariella, climbing onto a bar stool.

"What are you wanting?" asked Mike.

"An orange juice, please."

Oliver made a disappointed face.

"We're not going to be able to keep this place going on orange juices," he grumbled.

He poured the juice and set it in front of Mariella.

"Why don't we take a proper seat," suggested Mike.

"Good idea," agreed Mariella, giving Oliver one of her dirty looks.

They found a table at the far side of the room.

"What's up with him?" asked Mariella.

"Who, Oliver?"

"Yes, the barman," said Mariella impatiently. She looked at him. "Are you being deliberately obtuse?"

"No, I'm not. I've got things on my mind, that's all. Oliver's worried about his job. David's family are planning on putting the pub up for sale."

"Ah, I see."

"How's Nico doing?"

"Fine. He's back in Birmingham, holding the fort as usual."

"Good man."

"Yes, he's extremely reliable. No doubt he'll be asking for another pay rise in the near future," said Mariella with a sigh.

She took a sip of her orange juice.

Mike cleared his throat, wondering if he'd drunk enough alcohol to give him the balls needed for his conversation with Mariella.

"Listen, Mariella, I have to thank you and Nico for what you both did. I'd be as dead as a dodo right now if it hadn't been for your intervention."

"It's fine, Mike. I realised I wasn't ready to see you disappearing off the face of the earth just yet."

"And there I was thinking you'd be delighted with that."

Mariella giggled. "I admit there've been many moments when I thought it might be a good thing if you vanished, but times change, don't they? I must have a soft spot for you, somewhere deep down."

Mike nodded solemnly.

Mariella elbowed him.

"What's up with you? You're very serious today."

"Yes, that's true," agreed Mike. "It's because I've been making some big decisions recently."

"Really? In what respect?"

Mike looked at her.

"I've a business proposition to put to you."

"Oh, yes?" asked Mariella, her eyes curious. "A business proposition between you and me? That's kind of funny. You want us to work together, even after we managed to make a complete mess of recovering the treasure?"

"Yes, it's true we failed in our quest. We lost out on the big one. However, our stay here hasn't been totally futile. I did find quite a few other valuable items in Fiona's house. I'll show them to you later, and see what you think. I've no idea where she got them from. It's going to take me a lot of researching to figure out where they belong to."

"You never told me that," said Mariella sharply. "You keep far too many things hidden from me. You really don't trust me at all, do you?"

Mike pursed his lips.

"It depends," he said at last. "I think if you decided to work on the side of the angels, you'd be a real asset. But I don't think you want to."

Mariella pondered his words.

Mike finished his beer and decided to end his stint on Harris with a last whisky. He was due to catch a flight back to London that evening.

He stood up.

"Do you want another drink, Mariella?"

She shook her head.

Mike went over to the bar, where Oliver was seated, looking at his phone.

"You'll not be kept on if you do that on duty," pointed out Mike with an amused smile.

"What duty? There's no one in this early."

Oliver got off his bar stool.

"What are you wanting this time?"

"A whisky, please. Make it a twenty-five-year-old one, if you have it. It'll be my last for a while."

Oliver nodded.

"We've got a Loch Lomond Grain."

He went and poured the drink.

"That'll be forty quid," he said, placing it in front of Mike.

Mike tapped his card on the card machine.

"You leaving soon?" asked Oliver, pulling the receipt off.

"Yes, I'm afraid so. If you ever come down to London, the Blue Moon's my pub. Based in Hackney. Pop your head in. It's a good one."

"Thanks for the tip, but I think I'd rather head over to Belfast if I've to move from here. But you never know, the accounts have been good in this place. They might well decide to keep me on."

He shrugged and smiled.

"Nobody has a job for life anymore."

"That's so true," agreed Mike. "Life can take you in many unexpected directions. The best way to deal with it is to seize opportunities as they come along so you never have any regrets."

Oliver looked him over suspiciously.

"Sounds like therapy-speak to me. You turning into one of those counselling therapists?"

Mike chuckled at the thought.

"Me? No. I'm just getting old, and getting older means you reflect back on your life. You'll do it, too, when it's your time."

"I hope not," said Oliver, looking terrified at the thought.

"Well, here's to a long life for you, Oliver," said Mike, lifting his glass. "Cheers."

He took a sip and nodded.

"Sublime," he said.

He walked over to where Mariella was seated, arms crossed.

"You developing a man-crush?" she asked, sarcastic.

Mike smiled.

"No. He's a great character, though."

"Takes one to know one, I suppose."

Mike nodded.

"Have you thought about my suggestion?" he asked.

"I've thought about it. I'm trying to figure out what exactly you are proposing. Are you recommending we go into business together? And by that, I presume you mean your private detective business?"

"Yes."

Mariella shook her head.

"Your returns don't compare to mine. I make a fortune. You couldn't compete."

"Does it always have to be about the money?" asked Mike plaintively.

Mariella grinned.

"Most of the time, it is. What planet are you living on, Mike?"

"I was wondering where love comes into it."

"Love?" asked Mariella, her eyebrows reaching high up into her fringe.

"Yes, love. We could make a good team."

She stared at him.

"You're getting old, Mike."

"True," he admitted.

Mariella's head went to one side.

"Why don't you come and join my business?"

"Because we both know my work's more interesting for a start. And I also know you're getting tired of what you do. You could keep ownership of the business, but pass it on to new management."

"It's going to take time to find a good enough jeweller to do what I do," warned Mariella, not denying his points.

"I can help. I've a lot of contacts," said Mike helpfully.

"I thought you couldn't trust me. You went to Fiona's house without a word to me. How's that kind of trust going to work in a business environment?"

"Because I believe implicitly in your good nature. Our situation on the cliff top has shown me your heart's in the right place. I'm only asking you to put your heart into my business and join me in London. I know we can make it work."

"But the chippies aren't as good as Birmingham's," protested Mariella, smiling.

"London has everything in it. If we have to travel to Ruislip or Elephant and Castle to find the right chips, we'll do it."

Mariella's eyes misted up.

"I never thought we'd get to this point," she said, wiping her eyes.

"Neither did I, to be honest with you," said Mike, patting her on the back. "I think I've decided to accept what fate intends for me with good grace. There's no one else in my life but you, and I'm nearing retirement age. We're both not getting any younger. We can have a few years of fun before we sail off into the horizon."

"Sail? No way, José. I'm not going to get on no boat," she vowed with a shiver. "I've my feet firmly planted on *la terraferma*."

"Let's just see how it goes," temporised Mike. "We can't let ourselves get bogged down on discussions about sailing at this stage. One step at a time."

"OK. I agree in principle. As long as I can find an adequate replacement to manage the business."

Mike grinned and clinked his glass on hers.

He drank a mouthful of whisky.

"How are we going to seal the deal?" asked Mariella. She raised her hand, showing Mike's signet ring on it. "Do I get to keep this ring?"

Mike shook his head.

"No, I'm afraid not. I'd like that one back. But I've another one to replace it."

He rummaged in his pocket and took out the ring he'd found in Fiona's house.

He placed it on the table in front of Mariella.

The gold engraving on it glinted in the light and the garnet glowed with a deep fire.

She picked it up and studied it.

"Mike," she said, shaking her head. "Where did you get this from?"

"Fiona's house."

She looked at him.

"What's with the 'working on the side of the angels' pep talk? This is guaranteed to be stolen."

"Actually, Mariella, I've been digging into the ring's background. It was sold by a relative of the Duke of Montrose to an established second-hand jeweller in

Glasgow. The shop was broken into in 2008 and the ring was stolen, along with a number of other items."

Mike scratched his head.

"I lost the trail after that and have no idea how it ended up in Fiona's bedroom. But the shop closed down eleven years ago. The gentleman who owned it is now deceased. It's highly unlikely the police will have an active, open case on this ring. Tragically, jewellery thefts of all kinds are very common, as you know. You can wear this ring, secure in the knowledge that so much time has elapsed it isn't going to be missed by anyone."

Mariella took off Mike's signet ring and gave it to him.

She then picked up the medieval ring and tried it on her ring finger.

It was a little loose.

She tried it on her middle finger and it fitted perfectly.

Mike took her hand and gallantly kissed it.

"It looks beautiful. I hope you're not wanting to resize it. It would be a shame to, given its antiquity."

Mariella nodded, looking down at it.

"It's very pretty. I love it. Thank you, Mike."

She giggled.

"Even if it's stolen property, thank you so very much."

22

Richard

The taxi cab finally came to a halt outside the National Museum of Scotland on Chambers Street, after waiting in a slow-moving queue of cars for a good ten minutes.

Richard paid the fare and got out.

He then went over to the opposite cab door and helped Eilidh to step down from the taxi.

Eilidh was feeling increasingly uncomfortable as her pregnancy progressed, but after their efforts to track down the treasure in Harris she'd been determined to attend the opening night of *The Harris Hoard* in Edinburgh.

A couple of weeks ago, an exclusive invitation to attend the exhibition's opening had landed on Richard's desk at the Art and Antiquities Unit in London. Their invitation had come directly from Professor Neil Purnell, the curator of the museum.

As the opening night was on a Friday, they'd taken the day off work and caught a train from King's Cross to Waverly train station in Edinburgh.

After dumping their bags at the Waverly Premier

Inn on Rose Street, they'd taken a taxi to a small Thai restaurant in the Corstorphine area of Edinburgh.

Eilidh, as a die-hard foodie, had done her research on the Sugar Lily restaurant and the food turned out to be divine. For the last five years, the restaurant had been awarded a "Bib Gourmand" in the Michelin Guide, and both Richard and Eilidh felt it was well-deserved.

Replete with good food, they'd hailed another cab after their meal, to take them to the exhibition.

On route to the museum, the cab had driven them past several picturesque examples of Georgian architecture in the city; the handsome sandstone buildings tinted a dark grey colour by the passage of time.

Once the cab reached the west end of the city centre, it decided to take a road leading southward.

In the distance, for a few moments, they caught a tantalising glimpse of Edinburgh Castle.

First built during the twelfth-century by the Scottish King David I, Edinburgh Castle was perched on Castle Rock, above Princes Street Gardens, and its ancient stonework created a dramatic skyline over the entire city.

Richard had read Edinburgh Castle had been the most besieged place in Britain and one of the most attacked in the world. Given the destruction of so many castles in Scotland by English troops and Scottish clan rivalries, it was amazing Edinburgh Castle had survived history intact.

Gazing up at the solid walls of the castle, Richard felt sorry they didn't have the time to explore it.

However, their visit to the National Museum of Scotland was going to be special, because seeing items such as the Viking hoard on public display was the ultimate goal of any government agency involved in protecting historical artefacts.

Having bid the cheery cab driver a goodnight, Eilidh and Richard turned and looked up at the museum.

A series of arched windows designed in the Venetian Renaissance style towered above them and, right at the top of the building, were sculptures representing Science, Natural History, and Applied Art.

The six heads above the shut wooden doorways were those of Queen Victoria and Prince Albert, James Watt, Charles Darwin, Michelangelo, and Sir Isaac Newton.

Like many of Edinburgh's older buildings, the exterior of the museum was made of sandstone, but what made the National Museum of Scotland unique was the fact it was made with Clashach sandstone from Morayshire, a district situated in the far north of Scotland.

According to Dr. Fraser, keeper of Natural Sciences at the museum, the Clashach sandstone used in the museum's construction was 230 to 265 million years old and had traces of reptiles which had lived when the first dinosaurs roamed the earth. For Richard, this was the perfect type of stone to house collections based on natural history.

Showing their tickets to the uniformed attendant at the door, they entered a subterranean area beneath the main part of the museum.

The low, arched ceiling at the entrance made Richard feel a little claustrophobic, but it was, as Richard and Eilidh discovered after climbing up the steps to the next level, in sharp contrast to the bright and airy building situated above it.

The museum had an impressive façade, but it was the interior, on the floor above the entrance, which took Richard and Eilidh by surprise.

Once they climbed the stairs, they walked straight into the Grand Gallery, which was the central hall of the museum. Made of cast iron construction, the pillars rose over several floors to the full height of the building and the atmosphere reminded Richard of Victorian greenhouses such as the one in Kew Gardens, London.

Wrapped around each floor of the gallery was a balcony and, high above them, was a ceiling consisting of glass panels.

The light, voluminous space resounded with the echoes of the other guests.

Having arrived late, they were guided by a member of staff to the escalator leading up to the exhibition room.

As they rode the escalator they looked across at The Millennium Clock tower, a quirky feature within the museum.

Standing at over ten metres high, it was designed with a variety of materials, including wood, metal and glass.

The clock was no antiquity, having been built in 1999 by five craftspeople, and it was supposed to be a modern amalgamation of a medieval cathedral and an ancient tree. To Richard, it was a product of over-thinking. It had complicated internal mechanics on show and every part of it had an individual story to tell.

Richard smiled to himself.

Time was still haunting him, even at the conclusion of their efforts to secure the Viking treasure.

Richard looked at his watch, wondering if the clock was going to go off soon.

It was ten past eight, so he doubted he'd get a chance to hear it play

The Millennium Clock didn't chime like an ordinary grandfather clock. Instead it played music by Bach. As it did so, the different parts of the apparatus came to life in time to the music. Like a cuckoo clock on speed, basically.

He questioned if the noise of the clock's music and bells ever drove the staff in the museum insane. Possibly, they were used to it, and zoned out when it went off.

They left the escalator and made their way into the exhibition hall.

The curator had gone for the wow factor at the start of the exhibition and had placed the Byzantine chalice and the serpent box in two glass displays near the entrance.

Richard was studying the serpent box, which was shining under the bright light of its display case, when he heard Eilidh exclaim beside him.

He looked up, only to see Eilidh waving at Janey, who was across the room from them.

Janey was smartly dressed in a red silk dress and heels.

She came over to them, with Mark grinning beside her.

"Hello," Janey said, smiling happily at them. "I'm glad you could make it."

Her hair had been curled for the occasion and was

floating down her back in soft waves.

"How are you doing?" asked Eilidh, giving her a hug. "Are you back in Harris, or have you decided to stay near your sister?"

"I'm doing great, thanks," said Janey, waving a hand at the exhibition. "Thanks to the treasure you rescued, I'm set for life. The National Museum of Scotland managed to raise the money for its purchase and as Simon's wife a large share came to me. I don't have to worry about the future now."

She was indeed glowing, thought Richard. What a transformation compared to the frazzled woman they'd met in London.

"I'm so pleased for you," said Eilidh sincerely. "After all you went through, you deserved a happy ending."

Janey nodded.

"I'm not going back to Harris. I need a fresh start."

She reached across and tucked her arm into Mark's.

"Mark's agreed to move down south with me, so I've everything I could wish for."

Mark made a horrified, comical face.

"It's going to be like moving to a foreign country, but I guess I'll get used to it," he said.

Richard and Eilidh laughed.

"England's not so bad," said Eilidh, grinning.

"What about Findley?" asked Richard, looking around. "He's the real hero of the hour. He should be here, too."

Mark shook his head.

"You won't get Findley to come to anything like this. Not his kind of thing. He knows where he belongs and there he'll stay for as long as he's able to."

"He's a wise man," said Janey, nodding in agreement. "He's the only person I've met who's truly content with his life and at peace with it. He refused to accept any money from the treasure, too. He doesn't want it."

"What about you two?" asked Mark, curious. "What are you going to be working on next?"

Richard frowned a little.

"Where to start? We've several ongoing cases, but my main focus in the near future will be to find ways to fundraise for the department. Or we could soon be as extinct as some of the exhibits in this museum."

"I'd be very happy to contribute," said Janey, earnestly.

Richard shook his head.

"That's extremely kind of you, Janey, but I think it'll be but a drop in the ocean. I need to tap into the bigtime corporations and businesses. I'm going to be brainstorming some ideas with a very efficient acquaintance of mine next week, and we'll take it from there."

"Well, good luck to you, mate," said Mark, nodding.

"I'm planning a housewarming do when I get back," Janey informed them. "I'd love it if you could make it. I'll send an invite to your work."

"That would be lovely," said Eilidh with a smile. "If I haven't given birth by then."

And in that moment, the cold reality of having a child in the near future hit Richard like a lightning strike. It was as though the penny had dropped, and he realised his life was never, ever, going to be the same again.

As he stood stock-still, stunned and speechless,

Mark and Janey went to greet some other acquaintances.

Eilidh looked up at him.

"Cat got your tongue?"

Richard cleared his throat.

"Yes, something like that."

"And who's this 'efficient acquaintance' who's going to be giving you some fundraising ideas? It wouldn't be Mike Telford, would it?"

Richard nodded.

Eilidh laughed out loud.

"He's got a nerve. I suspect he's bolshie enough to make people dig into their pockets."

She took Richard's hand and they moved onto the next exhibit.

The panic Richard had felt at becoming a father began to subside as he lost himself in the wonders of the Viking treasure all over again.

They were engrossed with the coin exhibit when Professor Neil Purnell came up to them. Tall and lean, Neil was surprisingly young for a professor. He looked to Richard to be in his early twenties.

He was wearing a grey, anonymous suit, and his appearance was given some gravitas by his goatee and glasses. Behind the glasses, his dark eyes were intelligent and amicable.

"Chief Inspector Langley, I was wondering if you'd like to come with me to look at something we discovered inside the dragon box, wrapped up in pieces of leather. I think they're potentially the single most important find yet. We've not exhibited them, because we're still in the process of assessing them, but I'd be delighted to show you. I'm sure you'll find it absolutely fascinating."

"Of course," said Richard enthusiastically. "Can my partner join us?"

"Yes, absolutely," agreed Neil, nodding his head.

He led them to a door at the back of the exhibition marked "Private" and opened it for them.

They walked down a long corridor and into a room which looked like a laboratory.

Neil switched on the lights.

Richard and Eilidh blinked in the brightness as Neil put on a pair of white gloves. He motioned for them to come across to one of the tables.

Behind them, among the babble of voices, they heard a door open and shut.

Intrigued, they came forward to the table.

Lying on top of a panel of black felt were two small, cream-coloured tablets.

Richard bent down to take a closer look.

There were small runes scratched on the surface of the tablets.

"Runes!" he gasped.

He scrutinised the tablets for a minute.

"Walrus tusk?" asked Richard, when he finally straightened up.

"Yes," said Neil, a pleased look on his face.

"Have you translated them?" asked Eilidh, fascinated.

"Some. We're still working on them."

Neil lifted one of the tablets and showed them the other side, which was also covered in runes.

"It's very exciting," he said. "It appears to be a series of proverbs. The Vikings had many wise sayings, as you'll know, Richard. It isn't the first time runes have been found on walrus tusks, of course, but the runes themselves might be completely new to history."

"Can you tell us what you've read?" asked Eilidh, intrigued.

Neil smiled.

"One of them says: '*A hasty thinker will rue their actions.*'"

Richard nodded.

"Fair enough," he said. "Not very original, though."

"Any others?" asked Eilidh, with a smile.

"This one at the top here," said Neil, pointing at it with this finger, "says '*If the arriving is not a pleasure, the leaving will be.*' I presume it's referring to guests arriving."

Richard and Eilidh chuckled.

Neil placed the tablets on the felt again.

"When will these be on display?" asked Richard.

"Soon, we hope."

Before they fully grasped what was happening, a white hand snaked across the felt and grabbed the tablets.

"I'll take those, thank you very much," said a familiar, smug voice.

Richard turned and stared.

The man had a mask on his face, but Richard recognised the Mancunian accent and the blond hair.

In a flash, the man was gone.

Before he had time to think properly, Richard raced after him, dashing out into the corridor and back into the exhibition hall.

He saw a figure running at the far end of the hall and he chased after him, darting in and out of the guests looking at the Viking exhibits.

Richard charged out of the exhibition hall entrance and into the shop area.

He looked around desperately and caught a quick glimpse of a man with blond hair, before he disappeared onto the balcony at the other side of the room.

It had to be Kev. He was sure of it.

Crossing the room, Richard ran full pelt along the balcony, following the black figure in front of him.

Kev was easy to identify by now because he'd ripped off his mask in order to blend in with the crowd.

Having reached the end of the balcony, Kev started racing down the stairs leading to the lower levels.

By the time Richard reached the top of the stairs, Kev was already halfway down them.

"Stop him!" yelled Richard to one of the staff members, who was looking up at them in bemusement.

Seeing the girl frozen in surprise, Richard did the craziest thing he'd ever done. He launched himself off the step he was on, hitting Kev with a thud as he fell. The pair of them landed head first to the ground, with Kev knocking himself out on the hard limestone floor of the Grand Gallery.

A trickle of blood escaped from Kev's nose and gradually spread across the floor, leaving a crimson stain.

Richard, having landed on top of him, felt he'd survived relatively unscathed until he moved his leg and realised, with a sharp jolt of pain, that he'd broken it in the fall.

He lay back on the hard floor and stared up at the vaulted ceiling. Before long, a sea of faces clouded his view. Out of the many voices, he heard Eilidh's.

"Richard, what the hell were you doing? Are you alright?"

"No, I'm not," he said calmly, looking up at her. "I think I've broken my leg. Have they got the tablets off him?"

"Yes, we've got the tablets safe. Stay where you are, they've called up an ambulance."

"Is he alright?" he asked, gesturing to Kev.

"Yes, he's alive and coming to. Thankfully."

Richard sighed and shut his eyes. It was going to be a very long night.

"*A hasty thinker will rue their actions,*" remarked a humorous voice.

Richard opened his eyes again and glared at Professor Neil Purnell. "I don't regret my actions for a minute," he said sternly. "That bastard put me through the sea trip from hell back in Harris. He wasn't going to get away with the tablets as well."

As he lay there, on the cold limestone floor, he considered the many ruthless individuals he'd come across, who'd managed to rob priceless and unique arte-facts from a number of museums in the UK.

Despite having mixed success in recovering those artefacts, he still felt art detectives had an important role to play in society. After all, art and artefacts were a measure of civilisation, and in protecting them they were acting as the guardians of a country's heritage.

But feeling the pain throbbing up and down his leg, he felt he might have over-extended himself, for once, in his missionary zeal to preserve art for the general public.

There had to be limits placed on an art detective's job description.

If you like this, you may also enjoy: By Force or Fear
Meredith Ryan Mystery One by Thonie Hevron

The shocking end to a hostage situation brings Meredith Ryan, a courageous Sheriff's Deputy, to the attention of a powerful young judge.

As the magistrate's obsession grows, he continues exercising his considerable influence, and Meredith is stuck juggling the inner workings of her career—all the while tracking down a violent killer in the Sonoma wine country.

After losing almost everyone close to her, Meredith realizes that she must take a stand. Even if it costs her. But as Meredith is finally closing in on the Sonoma murderer, she gets snared in a trap that she may not walk out of alive.

By Force or Fear is a police procedural thriller about a brave, young deputy who identifies and faces her enemies—both within herself and the real world.

AVAILABLE APRIL 2023

About the Author

Bea Green grew up as the daughter of a British diplomat and a Spanish mother. She spent every summer at her grandfather's olive tree farm in Andalusia. She graduated from the University of St Andrews in Scotland with an MA in English literature and currently lives in Edinburgh with her husband and two daughters.

Printed in Great Britain
by Amazon

13485112R00202